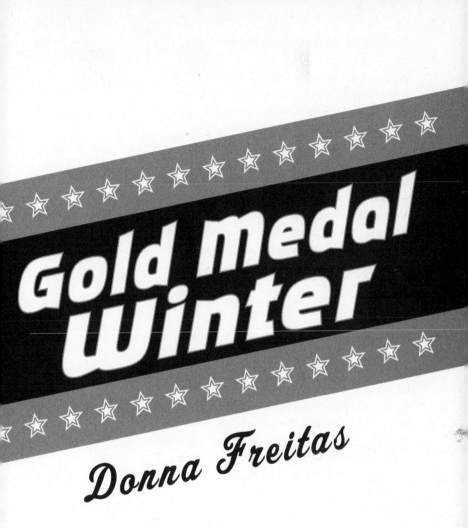

Gold Medal Winter

Donna Freitas

ARTHUR A. LEVINE BOOKS/AN IMPRINT OF SCHOLASTIC INC.

Library of Congress Cataloging-in-Publication Data

Freitas, Donna.
   Gold medal winter / Donna Freitas. — First edition.
      pages cm
   Summary: Esperanza Flores's place on the United States Olympic figure skating
team has come at the expense of an injured skater, so in addition to the pressure of
sudden fame and outsized expectations Espi has to deal with the resentment of her
teammates — and their efforts to sabotage her routine.
   ISBN-13: 978-0-545-64377-1 (hardcover : alk. paper)
   ISBN-10: 0-545-64377-5 (hardcover : alk. paper)
   ISBN-13: 978-0-545-64378-8 (pbk. : alk. paper)
   ISBN-10: 0-545-64378-3 (pbk. : alk. paper)
   [etc.]
   1. Women figure skaters — Juvenile fiction. 2. Winter Olympics — Juvenile fiction.
3. Competition (Psychology) — Juvenile fiction. 4. Figure skating stories. [1. Ice
skating — Fiction. 2. Winter Olympics — Fiction. 3. Competition (Psychology) —
Fiction. 4. Dominican Americans — Fiction.] I. Title.
   PZ7.F8844Gp 2014
   813.6 — dc23

                                                                      2013029144

10 9 8 7 6 5 4 3 2 1   14 15 16 17 18
Printed in the U.S.A.   23
First edition, January 2014

*To anyone who's ever had Olympic dreams,
or who's taken a moment to imagine
what it would be like.*

PART ONE
Olympic Hopeful

"I didn't lose the gold. I won the silver."

— MICHELLE KWAN,

Olympic silver medalist 1998, bronze medalist 2002

CHAPTER ONE

America's Hope for Gold!

Nothing compares to speeding across the ice. The wind rushing against your face and your hair flying up behind you, body angled forward, held up by sheer momentum. You forget about the cold because all you are is a bundle of energy, pushing yourself faster and higher in ways that are not only beautiful to watch but just beautiful to be. Sometimes I want to throw my hands and head back, chin to the sky, eyes closed, and let go, telling the world around me, the chilly air, the wintry trees burdened with snow, the little birds that sing my music, "I'm all yours."

This is exactly what I'd do if I was at home, skating on the pond in our backyard.

But I'm definitely not at home.

"ESPI! ESPI! ESPI!"

That, believe it or not, is a sold-out crowd of almost twenty thousand people chanting my name while I stand at the center of the ice, still in my program's final pose, trying to catch my breath at the US Ladies' Figure Skating Championships.

"Thank you to Esperanza Flores, the last free skate of the evening."

And *that*, believe it or not, is the announcer booming my name over the speakers.

I smile for all I'm worth, even though my lungs are heaving. The cheering from the audience gets even louder.

"Once the judges release Miss Flores's scores," the announcer goes on, "the medal ceremony will begin."

I straighten out of my pose, my hands in the air, waving. Stuffed animals dot the ice all around me. Brightly colored teddy bears. Penguins. Fat lions and fluffy puppies. Little girls of eight and nine are skating around, collecting them in their arms. They're called "sweepers." I remember dreaming of getting to be a sweeper when I was small, clearing away gifts from adoring fans for Olympic hopefuls at this very same championship.

Is this really happening?

"Congratulations, Esperanza," says one of the girls, a shy smile on her face as she hands me a big pink teddy bear. She's tiny, but her legs are cut with long, lean muscles, the legs of a skater. Her eyes shine bright against her dark skin, and she looks up at me like I'm some sort of magical creature come to life.

I bend down and give her a hug. "Thank you. You can call me Espi."

"Espi," she says. Her smile grows wider before she skates off.

Tears push at the back of my eyes. Then I hear a familiar voice shouting, *"¡Mija! ¡Mija!"*

I turn to its source. My mother is down in the front of the stands, jumping up and down like a crazy lady, her chaperone credentials bouncing around her neck with all the movement. My best friends Libby and Joya are with her. All of them are beaming. "Mamá!" I call back. She wipes her eyes. Tears shine on her cheeks in the bright lights. "Libby! Joya!" I shout, waving at them.

Then I see Lucy Chen, my coach, nodding her head at me with barely a trace of a smile showing, but from her, that's all the approval I need.

She's pleased.

No, the way she's rising up and down on her toes means she's *excited*.

My heart pounds. I never imagined I'd compete at Nationals, never mind have a shot at medaling.

Seriously. A shot at medaling!

With one final wave at the crowd, I skate off the ice, stepping through the door the official holds open at the edge of the rink. Someone takes the stuffed animals from my arms, though I can't see who. It's chaotic with so many people milling around and camera flashes from the audience going off like lightning. Sunbursts dot my eyes, but when they start to clear, Coach Chen is standing there.

"You nailed that triple axel," she says, and I can see the pride shining in her eyes. She hands me my skate guards and I put them on. "You've come such a long way, Esperanza. You have a real shot at the Olympic team." She leans in. "I knew you would. I knew it from the first moment I saw you on the ice so long ago." She gives me a hug. "Your scores should be up any minute." She grabs my hand and steers me toward the Kiss and Cry, where a skater and her coach wait for the judges' verdict while the television cameras film the whole, angst-ridden experience. It's called the Kiss and Cry for just this reason — it's the place where you potentially experience the greatest moment of your figure skating career, or where tragedy can befall you and you react accordingly. The thrill of victory and the agony of defeat, all caught on camera for the world to see.

We sit down on a low bench. Coach is tapping her nails against the top of the boards, her eyes trained on the monitor in front of us, where those all-important numbers will either make me or break me tonight. I glance back to where my mother, Libby, and Joya are waiting at the edge of the stands, all of them silent, facing the judges' panel.

"Espi, here they come," Coach says.

Suddenly, the numbers for my free skate start flashing above us on the giant scoreboard high above the center of the rink. I cover my eyes. Then I uncover them but turn away from the monitor. "I can't watch, I can't." My heart pounds so hard I might faint. My fists close so tight my knuckles turn white.

Coach Chen is murmuring, trying to do the math. Then she gasps. "120.67. Combined with your short program, that's" — she pauses, adding up the numbers again — "187.22! You're taking home silver, my darling Esperanza." She swivels me around to face her. "You knocked Meredith into third with your free skate."

"Ohmigosh, ohmigosh," I hear, then realize that it's me saying it.

Coach Chen wraps her arms around me in a big hug. "Go see your mother quickly before you have to go to the Mixed Zone. She looks like she can't wait until afterward."

"Thanks, Coach," I say. When she releases me, I step out of the Kiss and Cry and run to where my mother and my friends are standing with the rest of the crowd. I lean over the wall to better reach them. Soon the arms of everyone I love are around me. The tears that have been pushing at the back of my eyes ever since the end of my program start streaming down my face. The scoreboard flashes the new standings, and it's true: I've moved up from fourth place to second.

"*Mija, mi cielo, mi vida,*" my mother is saying over and over. *My daughter, my sky, my life,* just three of her many terms of endearment for me. "*Mi Esperanza,*" she throws in — a double meaning, since my name means "hope" in Spanish.

"I love you, Mamá," I whisper in her ear, inhaling the familiar scent of her lavender shampoo.

When she pulls away, Coach Chen's husband, John Baxter, is standing there, smiling at me. "Congratulations, Espi. It was wonderful to watch you out there. It reminded me of watching my wife when she was the star."

This is such a sweet thing to say. "Thanks, Mr. Chen."

He laughs at my old nickname for him.

Libby and Joya have been hanging back, waiting as patiently as they are capable, but suddenly they are jumping up and down and squealing. "You're going to the Olympics, Espi! The Oh-*lym*-pics!"

"Thanks for being here," I say to them, grabbing their hands over the railing. "But nothing's certain, so I can't let myself celebrate yet."

"Oh, come on," Joya says, the dozens of twists in her hair

swinging and swaying as she bounces. "That chick supposedly holding spot number three isn't going to make it with that injury she got today. What's her name again?"

"Jennifer Madison," I supply.

"Yeah, well. Her unfortunate exit means you're up, *chica*," Libby says, clapping her purple mittens together, her blue eyes as big and wide as ever.

I look around to make sure no one else has overheard these comments. "Shhhh," I tell them. "It's awful what happened to Jennifer. It's probably going to cost her the Olympics. No one knows yet whether her injury is serious, so the committee is going to wait to make the final decision until after the doctors see her. We probably won't know anything until tomorrow."

The announcer's voice booms over the speakers again. "The final standings are as follows: In first place, we have three-time US champion Stacie Grant, with 188.03," and cheers go up across the stadium. "In second place, we have Esperanza Flores, with 187.22," he goes on, my name naked of any titles, because I simply don't have any. But the crowd is even louder now. "And coming in third, we have two-time US silver medalist and now two-time bronze medalist Meredith Park with 186.95."

Coach Chen comes up behind me and greets everyone with a wave and a big smile.

My mother clasps her hands. "Do you really think this will be enough to qualify Espi for a spot on the Olympic team?"

"We'll see," Coach says. "It will be close, but I think she has a real shot. It was supposed to be Stacie, Jennifer, and Meredith, but ever since Espi came in fourth at Worlds, US Figure Skating has had their eye on her. And with Jennifer likely out of the picture now, I think this silver might seal it for them. And for her," she adds, glancing at me.

"I feel like my heart is going to fly out of my body," I tell Joya and Libby. "I can't believe this."

"Silver," Joya says. "Do you think it's real or just silver-plated?"

This makes me laugh. I'm about to respond when my friends' eyes shift from me to whatever is behind me.

I turn around. Correction: *whoever* is behind me.

Hunter Wills is standing there — the Young God of US men's figure skating, according to the press, who also call him "the Quad King" and "the Ice Prince." He's tall even without his skates, and between his wavy hair and the way his white team jacket makes his eyes seem bluer than the ocean, I can understand why girls are fawning over him all the time.

For some reason, he seems to be waiting to talk to me.

"You were amazing tonight, Esperanza," he says, flashing that winning smile, the one I see every time I open up the *People* magazines my mother leaves lying around the house. "You totally nailed that last jump combo. You got *serious* height. Height like a *guy*. Impressive."

"Hi, Hunter," I say, wishing I could erase the flush from my cheeks. "Thanks. I think," I add, a little offended by his *height like a guy* comment. But still flattered.

"Sure thing. See you at the Olympics," he adds, just before walking away.

Just hearing that steals my breath. The *Olympics*. And hearing it from someone like Hunter, who holds the number one spot on the men's team, practically stops my lungs altogether.

"Did you hear what he said?" Joya gushes once he's out of earshot.

"Yes. The *Olympics*," I say, almost in a whisper, afraid to jinx myself.

Libby rolls her eyes. "Yeah, but he called you *amazing*. Maybe he likes you."

I pull my jacket over my shoulders. I don't know if it's nerves or the chilly rink air that's making me shiver. "What, are you dreaming?" I say to Libby. "That's the first time Hunter Wills has ever said more than a polite hello to me in my entire skating career. And besides, there's all sorts of rumors about him and Jennifer Madison. They're a couple, I think."

Joya taps her knuckles along the low wall that separates us. "Well, now that she's probably out as far as the Games go, I bet they're headed straight to *Splitsville*," she sings, her voice full of the bravado that makes her our school's standout singer in all the musicals.

Now both Libby and I shush her. Paranoid, I look all around, hoping no one overheard. As I turn I stumble right into none other than Stacie Grant, "America's Darling," who — I've learned recently — is less than darling in person.

I smile at her while inside I'm cringing. "Um, hi, Stacie. Congratulations on winning the gold."

Stacie doesn't smile back, but her blond curls are as pert as ever. "Yes, well, it's not as though it was unexpected." She tilts her head, looking at me. Then she runs a finger just underneath the neckline of her Vera Wang skating costume, pulling the tiny rhinestones away from her skin. "I was always going to take first. But what a surprise to have to stand there next to you today."

I swallow. "I'm happy about the silver."

"Enjoy it, since I doubt it will ever happen again. Meredith just had an off day and Jen's already doing physical therapy, so don't count yourself part of the Olympic team yet," she adds before moving on without saying good-bye.

"And don't let Stacie psych you out, Espi," Coach Chen says out of the side of her mouth, even as she smiles at Stacie's coach, Angela East, who just gave her a wave.

I take a deep breath, in and out. Try not to care about Stacie's mean remarks — but it's difficult not to. "She's right. The only reason I'm medaling is because of Jennifer's injury."

Coach Chen grabs my shoulders and turns me toward her. "You and I both know that isn't true. You were born with a natural gift for this sport, plus you've got grace, speed, and height. On top of all this, you're gorgeous. And you're ten times nicer than all those other girls combined."

My mother puts her arm around me from the other side. "That's because I raised Esperanza to be a good girl and to never take anything for granted."

"Yes, Mamá," I say, and roll my eyes a little, but both of their comments help me feel a lot better.

"Hey, Espi," Libby says behind me, her voice a warning. "Um, get ready and wipe those tears away."

As I turn to her, I immediately see what she is talking about. A USFS official stands ready to take me to the Mixed Zone, where the press will be waiting.

That's the thing about being a skater. Reporters and paparazzi pretty much tail you everywhere once you show you're a real contender for a national title.

"You don't have to answer anything you don't want to," Coach Chen says. "But make sure to smile." We wave good-bye for now to my mother, Libby, Joya, and Mr. Chen, and follow the official backstage. On our way there I see Rachael Flatt and tug on the sleeve of Coach's jacket.

"There's Rachael Flatt," I whisper excitedly. Rachael Flatt is one of my heroes. She was the national champion in 2010 and was part of the Olympic team that same year. "She's so amazing."

Coach Chen smiles at me. "Soon there will be young skaters saying that about you, Espi."

Rachael looks up just as I pass. Her face lights up when she sees me. "Nice job today, Espi!"

My jaw drops. Then I remember to respond. "Thank you so much. It's an honor to have your support."

"Of course," she says with a laugh, as though I can always count on her.

Contemplating the magnitude of this encounter any further will have to wait, since the second we arrive in the Mixed Zone, the reporters and photographers swarm all around us. Cameras flash and flicker.

"Esperanza! Do you think you'll make the Olympic team?"

"Espi, are the rumors true that you and Stacie Grant don't get along?"

Microphones form a bouquet in front of me. I look at Coach Chen, who nods. I open my mouth to try and answer one or two of the reporters' questions, but more keep on coming and I can't get a word in.

"How does it feel to be the first Dominican to medal here?"

That's one I'd like to take. Most people don't think of Latinas as figure skaters. When they think of Dominicans, they think of famous baseball players like Manny Ramirez and Pedro Martinez, or they think of salsa dancing. I'm determined to prove the world wrong on this one. Dominican girls may be good dancers, sure, but we can skate too when we put our minds to it. I look around at all the faces waiting for me to speak.

"Fantástico," I say, and smile wide, hoping my one word was the right one.

They burst out laughing, which makes me laugh with them. It calms my nerves a little too.

"I'm just lucky to be here, competing," I go on. "It's an honor to medal and stand up on the podium with such accomplished figure skaters. And if the Olympic committee wants me, of course I'm ready for the challenge."

The announcer cuts through the next question by coming on over the loudspeaker, letting everyone know that the medal ceremony is about to start.

"Gotta go," I say with another smile, and the press starts

moving away, heading toward the best place to film the podium, I suppose.

"Good luck, Esperanza," a few of them say as they leave.

"Great job, you made them laugh," Coach Chen says. "Now give me that jacket."

I shrug it off into her hands. "I'm so nervous."

"Just enjoy this," she says. "It's the best part!"

I nod. Then I run over to where my mom, my friends, and Mr. Chen are still waiting at the edge of the stands. "Thank you for being here. I love you guys."

"You can pay us back later at the party," Joya says with a smirk.

"Does payback include stuffing your stomachs with Luca's cooking?"

"That'll do," she says.

I turn to my mother. "I love you, Mamá." She doesn't respond, because she can't. She's crying too hard. "Oh, Mamá," I say, and lean over the rail to give her a kiss on the cheek.

Coach Chen crosses her arms. "Espi . . ." she warns me.

Stacie Grant and Meredith Park are already waiting by the gate to go out on the ice. I'm the only one missing, so I head off toward the door that the USFS handler is holding open for us, removing my skate guards one by one as I go. Just before I reach Stacie and Meredith at the edge of the rink, I stop, take a deep breath, and look all around the stadium, savoring this moment.

I am always aware that this may not happen again. This medal could be my last. Judges can love you one day and not the next. There are injuries, like with Jennifer Madison, and then there is the simple reality that bodies change and grow in unpredictable ways, sometimes in ones that can end a career almost overnight. The Olympics may stay only a dream.

But nothing is standing in the way of me and that podium right now.

Nothing but a little ice.

The moment I join Stacie and Meredith, the lights in the arena dim. The medal ceremony is starting. The announcer calls out Stacie's name as this year's national champion, and when she steps through the gate, the audience is cheering wildly. I turn to Meredith. I almost want to grab her hand, give her a hug, do something to mark this momentous occasion we are sharing, but she won't look back at me.

Oh well. If we end up going to the Olympics together, there will be time for us to become friends — I hope.

Then, suddenly, the announcer is talking about me and it's my turn to get out there. As I'm skating toward the podium at the center of the ice, where I'm about to become the silver medalist at the US Championships, I hear someone in the crowd yell my name: "Esperanza Flores!" But it's what they add afterward that makes me smile and wave.

"America's hope for gold at the Olympics!"

CHAPTER TWO

Serendipity

Congratulations ESPERANZA says the banner hanging across the entrance of Luciano's, the Italian restaurant where my mother has worked as long as I can remember. She's been doing double shifts ever since figure skating went from a dream to a reality, complete with Coach Chen, championship competitions, and sparkly custom costumes.

"Luca must have had the banner made special," my mother says, shaking her head and smiling as we get out of her tiny powder-blue Honda, which didn't take the hour drive south home from the TD Garden too well. One final clack and clank comes from underneath the car, followed by a shudder. "He didn't tell me a thing. Violet letters, no less. That man loves you like his own daughter."

"And he loves you too," I say, but not loud enough that my mother hears.

Luca — short for Luciano — is the owner of the restaurant, and he is as Italian-American as it gets in Rhode Island, which is very. If Luca didn't have to be in the kitchen for the Sunday lunch shift, which is one of their busiest, he would have come to Boston. And if the rest of his longtime wait staff wasn't covering for my mother, they would have been there too.

His face appears in the window. "They're here," he shouts to everyone else inside, loud enough that we can hear him through the glass.

Luca *is* like a father to me, and the other waiters and waitresses are the family of aunts and uncles I would have if my mom had stayed in the Dominican Republic. She met my real father and they fell in love and married while he was on an academic fellowship in Santo Domingo. They moved to the United States because of his teaching position at Brown University in Providence. He died just after my first birthday, but my mother decided to stay. The American Dream bug bit her pretty hard.

So here we are today.

My mother grabs my gloved hand. "Are you ready to celebrate?"

The air is so cold my breath puffs white clouds. I nod, tighten my thick wool coat around me, and huddle down into my lilac scarf.

"Don't be nervous, *mi cielo*. The competition is over."

The reminder not to be nervous makes my heart thump. "I know, but we haven't heard —"

She puts a finger to my lips. "None of that tonight. I want you to enjoy *this* accomplishment, at least for a little while. And what an accomplishment it is! A silver medal!"

Another car pulls up with Libby and Joya inside, and Joya's dad, Mr. Jackson, in the driver's seat. As my friends get out, Mr. Jackson rolls down the window, despite the freezing temperature outside. "Nice job today," he calls out to me. "Go, Espi!" he adds, pumping his fist.

I laugh. "Thanks, Mr. J."

"I'll be back to get you girls in a couple of hours," he says to his daughter and Libby.

"Bye, Daddy." Joya waves as he backs out.

Libby's pale skin is red with the cold. "Um, is the party outside or is there another reason why we're waiting in the parking lot?"

I shrug and look around at the snow-covered shrubs and the icicles dripping from the one spindly tree by the door. The parking lot is empty except for the staff cars in the corner and the giant patch of ice in the center that won't melt until spring. "It's kind of like being at the rink, don't you think?"

She grabs my arm. "No, it's not," she says, and pulls me toward the entrance. Joya and my mother follow behind us.

"Esperanza!" Luca cries out when I walk inside. Everyone else is clapping and cheering our arrival.

My cheeks flush from all the attention. "Thanks, guys!" The restaurant looks the same as it has all my life — the same dark wood paneling everywhere, white linen tablecloths, the walls lined with fine Italian wines. But violet-colored balloons are tied to all the chairs, and off to the side I see a huge cake, which I'm sure Marcela, the pastry chef, spent all day making. I bet it's red velvet, my favorite. There is a giant television too, which Luca must have had brought in just for today so they could watch me skate. "I can't believe all this. You didn't have to —"

But I can't finish my sentence, since Luca swoops me up into a hug and twirls me around. "Little Espi," he says, setting me back onto the floor. His big brown eyes are glassy with tears. "You made us so proud today."

Even though I'm trying hard not to cry, I wipe tears from my own cheeks. I'm a regular water fountain today. "I can't believe the banner. My favorite color and everything. But all that trouble and I could have lost and then —"

"Nonsense, sweetheart. Just getting to that fancy competition deserves a celebration. Never mind winning a medal!"

My mother puts a hand on his arm. "Luca, this is wonderful. Thank you."

"Of course, of course!" He smiles at her before turning to Libby and Joya. "Welcome, ladies. You must be hungry."

"Definitely," Joya says, already on her way to the back of the restaurant, where the banquet table is laden with food. She pulls Libby along behind her. I bet they're headed straight for the chicken parm. Which is probably right next to the eggplant parm. Which is probably next to the meatballs. Just thinking about it makes my mouth water.

Meanwhile, the rest of the staff crowd around me. "Hi, Betty," I say, hugging the tall waitress with curler-set blond hair that's like a frothy bowl on her head. She and my mom like to have coffee in the morning together before their shifts start.

"Hi, baby girl," she says in that Georgia drawl of hers.

Then comes Marco, who can clear and reset a table with utter perfection in under two minutes. "Espi, those jumps! I held my breath. Luca had to take away my glass of wine because I was drinking it too fast. Nerves," he adds with a dramatic sigh.

This makes me laugh. "I'm glad you survived," I tell him. "I only did barely."

Next is Angela, Marco's wife of thirty years; Anthony, the head waiter since before I was born, I think; Anthony's wife, Maggie; then Gino, the only other cook aside from Luca; and Connie, the hostess. When Marcela leans in for a hug, she says, "The frosting is cream cheese, just how you like it."

"You're the best, Marcie," I say, glancing back at the food table again. Libby and Joya are hovering next to it, picking at the various bowls filled with salads and antipasti, despite the fact that they already have heaping plates in their hands.

I go to my mother, who's standing next to Luca. "Mamá, this is too much. They didn't have to do all of this."

"Espi, they've known you since you were *this* big," she says, cradling her arms like she's holding a baby. "And you know how they love to celebrate. They're happy to do it. They're ecstatic, really." She points toward the big-screen TV where some of the staff are replaying my free skate and oohing and aahing. Marco's got a glass of wine in his hand again and he keeps taking big gulps.

"It's so nice of them," I say, "I just —"

But Luca leans down, cutting me off. "Nonsense, Espi. Go get yourself some chicken parm. You must be starving."

Before I can take his advice, a rush of cold air swooshes by as the door opens. Coach Chen walks in, followed by her husband. Another cheer goes up around Luciano's for her, then a second round of hugs from the staff begins. Coach Chen is popular here at the restaurant, mostly because of how she single-handedly out of nowhere made the dream of competitive figure skating a reality in my life. Even if my mother was pulling quadruple shifts at Luciano's instead of doubles and I bussed tables all night, we never could have afforded the kind of skating career that gets a girl to the Olympics.

My obsession with figure skating goes all the way back to my fifth birthday. Ice-skating parties were a big thing for kids in our town. Elsewhere, people celebrated at Chuck E. Cheese, but for us, there was nothing better than skating in circles to the latest pop music over the crackly sound system. My mother gave me my first pair of ice skates so I could go to the rink with everyone else in my class.

By the time I turned eight I was going every single day, hitting the free ice time every afternoon before the high school hockey practice started. At night when I got home, in between doing homework and helping my mother around the house, I would watch videos online of all my favorite skaters — Sarah Hughes when I was really little, Sasha Cohen after the 2006 Olympics. I was a big fan of Irina Slutskaya from Russia too, despite her unfortunate last name, and Rachael Flatt, who won the 2010 US Championships with one of the highest scores ever. Sometimes I liked to study the programs of Katarina Witt, the East German gold medalist from the 1984 and 1988 Olympics. Even though she competed way before I was born, she was a maven of style like no other skater before or afterward, in my opinion. Well, except for Michelle Kwan maybe. And, of course, I watched Lucy Chen. She was a legend, so how could I not? Twenty years ago she won gold for the US at the Winter Olympics.

I would learn their programs as best I could from seeing them online, and then — with the help of some good instructional videos on YouTube — I would try to repeat them during my time on the ice. The jumps, the choreography, everything. Sometimes I'd mix things up, taking my favorite parts from one program and putting them together with my favorite parts of another. It got to the point where the people who worked at the rink would let me have the ice all to myself for a full thirty minutes after the free ice time ended each day so I could practice. And they would cheer me on. Clap. The whole thing.

My ten-year-old self loved it.

Then one day, the mother of a big-deal high school hockey player had this crazy idea that I should have a real audience for my programs. She pulled some strings, and the very next Friday night, I was the between-periods entertainment for the sold-out crowd at the hockey game. I wore a home-sewn violet skating costume my mother and I had spent the previous four evenings conjuring from a basic body suit and a trip to the fabric store for some cheap chiffon and sequins.

None other than Lucy Chen happened to be there.

She'd just moved to town that fall. Her husband had gotten a job as a math teacher at the local high school, and they'd come to the hockey game to cheer on his students. Even more serendipitously — if that is even possible — I happened to be skating one of her old programs that night.

It was like all the stars aligned in the sky.

As I was coming off the ice, smiling giddily from all the applause around the rink and the thrill of performing in front of a crowd, Lucy Chen was standing there, waiting for me.

"You have talent," she said before I even had a chance to realize who she was.

"Thank you," I said, still in a dreamy haze.

"What's your name?" she fired off next.

"Esperanza Flores."

Now I took her in for the first time — I mean, *really* took her in. All five feet nothing, dark eyes and long black hair, impeccably dressed. It was the long hair that made it difficult to immediately recognize her. I'd always seen her performing with it up in a tight bun. But when I looked beyond this difference, her face was as young and beautiful and as obviously *Lucy Chen, Olympic Gold Medalist* as ever.

"Ohmigosh. You're Lucy Chen! I love you!" My eyes widened. "I mean, um, you know what I mean? Right?"

She smiled in that subtle but friendly way I've grown used to over the years. "I do," she said. Then she laughed.

"Can I have your autograph?" I asked, without thinking about the fact that I didn't have a pen or paper. It's not like there are ample pockets in skating costumes, or any pockets.

"Sure," she said as she beckoned me to a spot against the wall, away from the passing throngs heading to the snack bar. "But only if you tell me who your coach is. I didn't know anyone in this town was serious about figure skating. We're new here."

My cheeks flushed. I don't know why it made me embarrassed

to admit that I had no formal training, but it did. "Um," I said — not an auspicious start to an answer. I stared down at the frayed white laces on my skates, noticing how dirty they were. "I don't have a coach."

When I finally looked up, Lucy Chen was nodding her head, taking this in. Then that hint of a smile paid a visit again. "Yes, you do."

I shook my head. "No, really, I don't. I've just been teaching my —"

But she was scribbling something on a piece of paper, so I stopped trying to speak. She handed it to me. "This is my address. Be there tomorrow morning, nine a.m. sharp. Bring your parents."

"It's just me and my mom."

"Bring your mom, then."

My eyes got wide. "You want me to come to your house with my mother?"

"Yes," she said. A tall blond man walked up then and handed her a hot dog. "Bax," she said, looking up at him, "this is Esperanza Flores, my new student. Esperanza, meet my husband, John Baxter."

He held out his hand, and I shook it. "Hello, Esperanza," he said to me.

"Hello, Mr. Chen," I said without thinking. "I mean, Mr. Baxter." I was red-faced, but his eyes were dancing.

So were Coach Chen's. "You should definitely always refer to Bax as Mr. Chen from here on out. I like that."

"Um. Okay."

He turned to his wife, eyebrows raised. "I thought you were retired."

She swallowed a big bite of hot dog. "I thought I was too," she said. "But I seem to have found a reason to come out of retirement."

"That was quick," he said with a laugh.

With her free hand, she wove her fingers through her husband's. "I'll see you tomorrow, Esperanza. Don't be late."

"Okay," I said, still in a daze about what this encounter meant. Then I came to my senses. "I, um, I mean we — my mom and I — don't have any money for lessons."

For a second, I thought she might cry. She blinked quickly and wiped the back of her hand across her eyes. Then she smiled her big, impossible-to-miss smile. The one she used to wear on the ice that charmed all the judges. The rest of the United States too. And maybe the world on top of it. "You don't need to worry about money. I'll take care of things," she said.

I watched, my jaw hanging open, as she and John Baxter walked away.

Just before she was out of earshot, though, she turned back and said, "Get a good night's sleep, Esperanza. Tomorrow, we start on the road to Olympic gold."

That was six years ago.

Now a Southern drawl behind me says, "Hey, hon."

I turn around to see Betty standing there with two heaping plates of food in her hands. She holds one out to me. "You need to eat, sugar pie. You probably burned a million calories with all that leaping and spinning. I got all your favorites on here."

A big piece of chicken parmesan sits like a crown on top of a pile of pasta, the rest of the plate a mountain of salad. Coach Chen lets me eat pretty much whatever I want, since she agrees with Betty that I do actually burn about a million calories from skating. My stomach growls on cue. "That looks so good. Thanks, Betty."

"You bet, Little Miss Silver Medalist."

For at least a minute, she and I eat happily in silence. Then Libby comes up to us. She's already moved on to dessert, and is scooping up a big hunk of tiramisu. "So when do you find out?" she says with her mouth full. She swallows and goes on. "You know, about the *big* one."

"What — the Olympics?" Betty asks.

Libby rests her fork on her plate and puts her finger to her lips. "Apparently, we need to stop using the O-word because Esperanza doesn't want to jinx anything." She looks at me. "You know, it's really too bad you have to do the homeschooling thing until the O's are over, because it might be nice to have the distraction."

"Maybe," I say, but it's difficult to imagine sitting through Trig right now, even if it was Mr. Chen who was teaching.

Betty's eyelashes flutter at me. "Honey, jinxes aren't going to keep you from going to the O-place. There's no question you are as good or better than all those other girls we watched today. The only question is whether the people who make these decisions are going to see that."

"But Jennifer Madison —" I start, but don't finish, since Coach Chen is crossing the restaurant in our direction, looking like she can't get here fast enough.

"Speaking of Jennifer Madison," Coach Chen says, "she's definitely out. She's going to need knee surgery ASAP."

"Oh, that's horrible," I say out loud.

Libby looks up from her tiramisu. "No, it's not. Not for you, at least!"

"Libby," I try to scold, but a smile is pushing onto my face even as I say this. I can't quite squash it. Am I a terrible person to celebrate Jennifer's pain?

She smiles triumphantly, eyes gleaming. "You feel the exact same way as me. You're just trying to hide it."

"Am not," I protest, but by now I'm grinning.

"We'll know within the next couple of days," Coach Chen says, her eyes intent on me.

"About Jennifer Madison's condition?"

She shakes her head. "About whether you're going to the Winter Games, Esperanza. The call could come any time, but no matter what, it will be soon. Wednesday at the latest."

"Oh," I gulp. For so long, the Olympics have been a dream. Something highly theoretical. A goal to work toward, but never close to a reality. Now, within days, I'll find out if my dream will come true. "Okay," I add, trying to breathe.

Coach Chen smiles, unshaken by my nerves. "I have faith in you, Esperanza," she says. "I always have. From the very first moment I saw you on the ice all those years ago, I knew this time would come. And now it's here." She looks at my half-empty plate. "Now finish that up and get home to bed soon. Olympic athletes need their rest."

CHAPTER THREE

Secret weapon

Music shatters the silence, and I practically fall out of bed onto the floor. The majestic trumpets of the Olympic anthem are blaring from my iPhone, a gift from Coach Chen for my first national competition. Libby and Joya must have changed the ringtone last night. If I were more awake, I'd appreciate the gesture, but those horns could kill a person at this hour.

I grab for it, my eyes still heavy with sleep. Coach Chen's picture looks at me from the screen. When I pick up, for a moment there is blissful silence.

"Good morning, sunshine," she says, her voice almost as familiar as my mother's.

My eyes try to adjust to the darkness. "What time is it?"

There is a pause, then an intake of breath. "Time for all Olympians to get out of bed for their press conference."

"You're not serious." I look at her picture on my phone, as though I can read her expression live.

"Would I kid about this?" The excitement in her voice is plain.

"Ohmigosh."

"You bet. I got the call from John Peterson this morning. Jennifer is officially out."

John Peterson is the head of US Figure Skating and the committee that decides who goes to the Games and who doesn't. I turn on the lamp next to my bed. Try to remember to breathe. "What else did he say?"

"Just the news we've been hoping for ever since you shocked everyone at Worlds — that you've got the third spot."

"I can't believe this."

"Well, you'd better. We're off to the Olympics in two weeks."

I get out of bed and turn on all the lights now. The familiar hues of purple, lilac, and violet on every surface are suddenly bright. "Wow, wow, wow!" I open the door and call down the hall, "Mamá! Ma! Come here quick!"

"Get dressed and make sure you do your hair nicely," Coach Chen is saying, but I can barely hear her. I'm still taking this in. "Leave it down. I'll be there in thirty minutes to pick you up."

My mother's face peeks out of her bedroom. "Esperanza? Is everything okay?"

With my free hand, I beckon for her to come, then I put the phone on speaker. "Tell Mamá," I say to Coach Chen.

"Espi's going to the Olympics, Marta."

My mother's eyes pop wide, losing all signs of sleep. Her mouth opens and closes. Then she throws her arms around me with such force that my phone flies out of my hand and onto the carpet. *"¡Dios mío!"* she shouts again and again.

"We're going to the Olympics!" I yell back at my mother.

"Hello?" Coach Chen calls from the floor. "Espi?"

"Ma," I say, peeling myself out of her grip to retrieve the phone. "Hold the hugs one more sec." When it's in my hand again, I explain to Coach Chen, "Sorry I dropped you. We're a little excited at the Flores house right now."

"You should be. Now get in the shower and I'll be there at six thirty. You've got a press interview for the morning shows at eight, and you need to be in Cranston at the studio all made up and camera-ready by seven thirty. Apparently, Rhode Island's got two Olympians headed to the Winter Games, and you know how this state is about everything."

I can almost see Coach Chen roll her eyes while standing in her gleaming kitchen. She is always talking about how Rhode Island is so "provincial," meaning the whole state is like a giant small town. "Two? Who else?" I ask. There have been years when Rhode Island hasn't had any athletes in the Games, so it's a big deal whenever someone goes. Two people is practically a miracle.

"I don't know yet, but there will be a lot of fawning over the Little Rhody Olympians, so be prepared. And no going online to check that person out! I need you to stay focused."

"Yes, Coach," I say with a little sigh. Coach Chen bans me from the Internet during and around major competitions so I don't psych myself out by reading mean comments about my programs, my costumes, or even my face, and whether people think I'm too fat or too thin or too a million other things. Sometimes the comments are even racist. Of course, I'm only mentioning the negative part. There's generally plenty of love too. But the hate is constant, and I imagine it will get even worse now that I've got Jennifer Madison's spot on the team. I bet Stacie's and Meredith's fansites are already working overtime to say I don't deserve to go to the Games.

But now is not the time to think about that.

Because regardless of what they're saying, I'm still going!

"Promise me you'll stick to our Internet ban," Coach says.

"I promise."

"Good. See you soon," she adds, and her face disappears from the screen.

I look up from the phone. My mother has a goofy grin on her face. "This is a dream come true, *mi vida*."

"I know," I say, but it still hasn't sunk in.

The *Olympics*? Me? Seriously?

"I'm so proud of you." She runs a hand through her thick, short hair. "So proud." She looks me up and down. "Now, start getting ready. As Betty would say, we've got to get you all gussied up."

I laugh. "All right. I'll be out of the bathroom in ten."

"Five, Espi. Your hair is long and thick and takes forever to dry."

"Five, then, Mamá."

"I love you," she says, still with the goofy grin.

"Love you too." I give her a peck on the cheek before racing into the bathroom and getting into the shower before the water is even lukewarm.

Big mistake.

It's winter after all.

The winter of the Olympics, to be precise.

★ ★ ★

Coach Chen pulls up in front of our little house in her sleek black Mercedes at 6:29 a.m. With the motor still running, all five feet of her comes flying out of the car for a congratulatory hug.

"Good morning, Marta and Espi," she cries. She's wearing a long winter-white wool coat and a gorgeous matching suit underneath. She rocks the winter white like very few people can. She looks me up and down in the pool of light spilling from the front of the house. "Nice job with the hair," she says to my mother with an approving nod. "It's too bad she can't wear it down on the ice."

"I know," my mother says. "But it would get in her face, her eyes. Her mouth."

"I'm right here," I remind them. I'm numb and tingly at once, and not from the cold. I look at Coach Chen. "If it wasn't six thirty a.m., I think I might have to start screaming. For joy," I add.

"Glad you reminded me," she says, suddenly all business. "All Olympians to the car," she adds with one of the biggest smiles I've ever seen on her pretty face.

"That includes you," I remind her.

She laughs. "I suppose you're right." To my mother she says, "Make sure you turn to NBC at eight a.m."

"Wouldn't miss it." Mamá looks at me one last time with that proud mother expression on her face, the one where tears are obviously on the way, and then gives me a big kiss on the cheek. "Go, go, go," she sniffs. "I don't want you to be late for your big moment."

"Bye, Mamá," I say, and run around to the passenger side. The first thing I do after getting in is push the button next to my seat that heats it up. Heated seats are the best thing ever, and my mother and I don't get perks like these in our run-down little Honda. Coach Chen's car purrs so quietly I forget we're in it sometimes.

As I look around at the buttercream leather interior, I fantasize about being able to buy my mother one of these some day. Figure skating made Coach Chen rich. She gold medaled into endorsement deals, then invested the money so well it set her up for the future. She actually coaches me for free at the private rink she had built on the gazillion acres of land behind her secluded house. She says that it's "her way of giving back" to the sport of figure skating, which gave her so much. But to me, it was — well, it is — a total dream.

To make sure this is *not* a dream, I pull up the sleeve of my coat and pinch the skin on my arm.

"Espi," Coach Chen says as she pulls out of the driveway, "what are you doing?"

"Pinching myself so I know this is really happening."

"Oh, it's happening," she says, leaning all the way forward to look right so we can cross into traffic. She turns on the classical station low as she maneuvers the streets. The sound of violins calms her nerves, she always says. Driving is not Coach Chen's favorite activity.

"What questions do you think I should prepare for?" I ask as we pull onto Interstate 95.

Coach Chen glances over. "They just want to hear you say

that you're excited, that you're proud to be representing the United States. That aside from Worlds, you've never traveled overseas or so far from home, so this whole experience is new for you. That sort of thing."

My butt is starting to burn, so I turn the seat warmer down to low. "I have definitely never been to the Olympics, that's for sure."

"Espi, this will be easy. Probably the easiest thing you do for a long, long time. The hard part is ahead."

"Which part? The Olympic part?"

"That, yes. But everything that comes with being a part of Team USA pre-Olympics too."

"Team USA?" I whisper.

"You *are* Team USA now, Espi. You and Stacie Grant and Meredith Park. Along with the ice dancers, the pairs, and all the male skaters."

The image of Hunter Wills flashes in my mind. "I'm going to get that jacket, aren't I?" I say in awe. I've always fantasized about walking around in the official Team USA warm-ups and training jacket.

Coach Chen smiles as she cuts over into the right lane so we can exit. "You're going to get that and so much more." We pull off the highway and make a left. "Everyone will be in Boston before we leave for the meet-up and to make the final decision about who will be the alternate for the Team Event. It's great for us, since you'll be so close to home."

I look at Coach. "You mean it's not automatically Meredith?"

But she's distracted, unsure whether to keep going or turn around. "I think I should have made a right when we got off the exit. The studio is off of Pontiac Avenue. I still can't find my way around this state sometimes! You'd think it would be easy, it's so small," she adds.

Figure skating is a very individual sport where usually it's everyone for her or himself — aside from the pairs and ice dancers. But with the Team Event, each country can medal as a group, though not everyone gets to skate for the event. One out of the three men will compete, one out of the three women, and one each of the two pairs and ice-dancing teams. Stacie, of course, will skate for it, but the coaches elect alternates in case there is an injury or some other unforeseen circumstance. I wait to press Coach further about my chances until she's figured out where we are.

"The Team alternates haven't been decided yet?" I say as we pull into the station's parking lot. "I mean, I thought it would automatically be Meredith."

She turns the car off. "Of course you have a shot! Don't forget — you beat Meredith at Nationals."

"I bet Stacie and Meredith are angry this isn't decided yet. I'm sure they feel like Meredith deserves the honor more than I do."

Coach cocks her head. "You can't worry too much about them, Espi. And this isn't a contest of who's been around the longest. This is about who gives the US the best chance at Olympic gold, and ultimately, that is going to be *you*."

"You sound so sure of that. Why?"

She smiles like she's up to something. "Because we're going to unleash our secret weapon."

"What secret weapon?"

"Your quad sal," she says, like this is obvious.

My jaw drops open. "But I only land it, like, maybe a third of the time."

"No, you land it half the time. And you've been landing it half the time for over a year now."

"You want me to up those odds in two weeks?"

"This is the Olympics, Espi. It's not the time to be conservative. You're going to give this every ounce you've got."

"I'm not Miki Ando, though," I remind her. Miki Ando is a former World Champion and the only ladies figure skater to ever land a quad in competition. She first did it in 2002 at the Junior Grand Prix Final. Men like Hunter Wills land quads all the time, but in the ladies' competitions, virtually never. "And no American has ever landed one outside of practice and no woman has ever gone for one at the Olympics —"

"No more *no's*," Coach Chen interrupts, stopping me from my protest that *I can't* and *I shouldn't* and *I could never.* "I have faith in you, Espi. Remember? So we'll take a leap together this time." She smiles and gives my shoulder a squeeze. "Now let's go get you ready for your big television appearance," she adds, and we get out of the car into the cold quiet of the early morning.

CHAPTER FOUR

Cinderella story

"*I* wonder who the other Rhode Island Olympian is," I say to Coach Chen in an effort to stop thinking about the quad sal. She's too busy micromanaging Sandra, the makeup lady, to answer, though. I never wear makeup unless I'm on the ice, so I'm enjoying this Monday-morning exception.

"Maybe it's a skier," Coach Chen says finally, after shaking her head *no* to violet eye shadow and redirecting Sandra to a hue that is basically the same color as my skin.

"Um, I like violet," I say, but my protest is to no avail.

"I doubt it's a skier," Sandra says.

"I bet it's someone who does one of those weird sports," I say. "Like curling."

"I kind of like curling," Sandra says as she touches up my lips with gloss. "Whenever it comes on the television, I can't seem to stop watching it."

Coach Chen checks her phone for the time. "We need to get you upstairs. It's almost time."

"You look great," Sandra says. Then she sends me off after brushing my cheeks one last time with blush.

"Thank you." I glance in the mirror quickly. It's always

startling to see how makeup makes my dark eyes seem bright against my olive skin.

The studio is set up talk-show style: A two-person couch with a separate, matching comfortable chair is arranged behind a coffee table. The lights are dim. Giant cameras are poised all around the set, and big microphones dangle from above.

"Hi I'm Jenny the producer thanks for coming down here so early why don't you sit there on the couch right there yes exactly thanks," she says all in one breath while leading me to the spot where she wants me for the interview and sitting me down. Apparently, punctuation is not included in her speech patterns.

Also, apparently, I am the first one here. Both the To-Be-Determined Other Olympian who will sit on my right and the talk-show host who will be on my left are missing. Coach Chen watches me from where she stands between two cameramen and shrugs.

Then Joanie McNulty walks in, all smile and perfectly coiffed blond hair. She wears a bright pink sleeveless dress that reaches her knees and shows off her toned muscles. I've seen her forever on the Rhode Island NBC morning show, but she's even prettier in person.

"Esperanza," she cries as she comes over, both hands out to grasp mine. Everything about her is sparkly. Her eyes, her lipstick, her jewelry. "Congratulations! You must be so excited, and we're all so excited for you."

"Hi, I am. Thank you, Ms. McNulty."

"Oh, call me Joanie. Please."

Jenny the producer approaches again. She looks me up and

down, then turns to the rest of the technical staff. "We need her miked right away is there someone here to mike her we're going to have to run it through the back of that dress anyone anyone? Hello hello?"

"Hi, I'm Mike," says the man who comes over with the mike. I want to giggle, maybe because of the funny coincidence in his name, or maybe because the way that he's trying to string wires in through the side of my dress and out through the neckline without being awkward makes me nervous. But soon he says, "All done" and heads away, so I sit down again and remember to breathe.

"Where is Danny Morrison has anyone seen Danny Morrison?" Jenny rattles to whoever cares to listen.

Joanie takes her seat next to me, fluffs her hair, and crosses her legs. Her heels have five-inch spikes that could definitely be used as weapons if she ever gets mugged. "Danny Morrison is our other Rhode Island Olympian. Do you two know each other?"

I shake my head no, trying to place the name.

"I thought you might," she goes on. "You're both in high school and you're both ice skaters."

Both her reveals surprise me. Winter Olympic athletes are often on the other side of twenty in terms of age. "I'm confused. He's a skater?"

This makes her laugh. "Oh, no. He's a hockey player. The first high school hockey player to ever make the US Olympic team," she adds with pride.

"Hockey?" I say, my heart sinking like a stone.

I know all about hockey players from growing up in my hockey-crazed town in this hockey-crazed state. Hockey players are arrogant, bullish meatheads who can't get enough of themselves and who walk around like they are God's gift to girls on this earth. They're treated like kings, so they learn to act like kings too.

Libby and Joya both love them. Obviously.

And if I know anything about how the television networks cover the Olympics, especially here in Rhode Island, then this Danny Morrison and I are going to be seeing a lot of each other in the next few weeks. We'll get paired up for press again and again. The small-state connection plus the fact that we're both in high school seals it.

Dios mío.

"You should see him play," Joanie McNulty is gushing.

Just then the door to the studio opens and a ripple of *oohs* and *congratulations* erupts across the room. Apparently, Danny Morrison has arrived, though I can't see him because of the crowd. Even the cameramen turn away to greet him.

Producer Jenny is immediately ready to pounce. "Danny so glad you're here no time for makeup you look fine just head right over there next to your fellow Olympian Esperanza Flores have you two met?"

I wait for the famous Danny to emerge from the throng, expecting to see a big, broad-shouldered guy, your typical high school athlete with crew-cut hair and a thick neck. But what my imagination expects and what my eyes actually see in front of me are two different things entirely.

Danny Morrison doesn't look like the hockey players I know from my town. He's smaller than I expect. No, *small* isn't the right word. He looks more like he'd be a runner for track than one of the meaty hockey guys. His hair is dark, almost black, and instead of having the standard short cut of guy athletes, it's long enough that he has to keep brushing it out of his eyes. Which are blue. Like, *really* blue. And instead of looking arrogant as he gets miked up, he seems more on edge than anything else.

Like he might be as nervous as I am.

"Ten nine Danny sit down right away eight seven," Jenny is counting.

"We're starting already?" I croak as he takes the spot next to me.

"Don't worry, this will be fun," Joanie says.

I have to move a little so Danny and I aren't sitting on top of one another. The couch is not exactly big. As I wiggle to my left, I wonder if the network planned this: *Squish the Rhode Island Olympians together like they're a couple!*

The thought makes my cheeks flare red.

"Three two," Jenny is whispering.

There literally isn't even a second left for introductions. I look over at Danny, who's watching the cameras, a blank expression on his face.

One, Jenny mouths, her finger in the air.

Suddenly, we're on.

Joanie's face lights up immediately. "Good morning, Rhode Island," she begins, launching into the introduction to the show, what's in store for the morning and what guests will be on later. It isn't long before she gets around to us. "Today we're with two special young people, both of whom are off to the Winter Olympics in just a couple of weeks! Esperanza Flores will represent the US in ladies' figure skating, and Danny Morrison is about to become the youngest hockey player to ever make Team USA." She turns to us. "Welcome, Esperanza and Danny."

"Good morning, Rhode Island," I say nervously and with a little wave. This makes Joanie's smile brighten, so I guess I did all right.

Danny just nods his head. It's possible he means to smile too, but the look on his face is more one of pain.

"So, Esperanza, this morning it was confirmed that Jennifer Madison will not be going to the Olympics because of an injury, and *you* were chosen for the coveted third spot for ladies' figure skating. How does it feel?"

Well. If I answer that I'm excited, it will sound like I'm happy that Jennifer Madison got hurt. But I don't want people to think I'm not over the moon about the Olympics either. As my brain sorts this out, I remember I'm on live television and I need to say something soon. "Jennifer Madison is a great skater," I begin, hoping that whatever *should* come next will magically find its way into my mouth. "And I am sure she is dealing with a lot of disappointment right now. I only hope that I can do her spot justice at the Games."

Joanie is nodding, her expression very serious, like we are negotiating world peace and not on a frothy morning talk show. "So you want to honor Jennifer when you skate for gold."

I see Coach Chen frantically shaking her head no. She stops short of running a finger across her neck or making a big X with her arms, but just barely. I'd better backtrack. "Well, it's more that we will *all* be honoring Jennifer, and a whole host of other people too. We're representing the United States, but also the people who've spent years helping us get where we are today. For me, that would be my mother and the staff at Luciano's Restaurant, who have supported me and my skating since I was little, and, of course, my amazing coach, Lucy Chen." My heart is pounding. This is almost as bad as being out on the ice at a major national competition. I hope Luca is happy with the free advertising.

"I'm glad you mentioned Lucy Chen," Joanie says. "She brought back gold for the US two decades ago, and I understand that she literally found you by accident and took you under her wing. Does that make you feel like Cinderella?"

Oh geez. A Dominican Cinderella? Seriously? Coach Chen is rolling her eyes. I hope no one else notices.

"I'm not sure I'm really the Cinderella type," I say, realizing that Danny Morrison to my right is trying not to laugh. If we weren't on live television, I might make an annoyed comment. It's not like *he* has to worry about anyone calling him "Cinderella" before the Olympics. That sort of thing only happens to girls.

Joanie is undaunted. "A *Spiñorita* is more like it, then?"

"I've never heard that one before," I say, and laugh — I can't help it. For the first time since the cameras started rolling, I start to relax. "I bet my mother will like it."

"So *Spiñorita* it is!" Joanie sounds delighted.

I shrug and try to keep smiling. "Sure." Before Joanie can change the subject to something else, I decide to say something I actually want to say — something real. "Most important of all, I'm really grateful to Coach Chen," I go on. "It does feel a bit unbelievable that I'm going to the Olympics. I actually pinched myself on the way here this morning to make sure it was real."

Joanie McNulty likes this, I can tell. She looks thrilled, like she just won the lottery, or someone bequeathed her a nice house in Newport on the ocean. "Well, to all of us here in Rhode Island, you're certainly our Cinderella story of this Winter Olympic Games." Her eyes shift to Danny. Finally, I can breathe. "Now, Danny, you also got bumped up to the team because of another player's injury," Joanie is saying.

Huh. So he and I are in the same boat. This makes me a little less annoyed at how much he enjoyed my being asked the Cinderella question. I hear Joanie and Danny talking to each other, but in my relief at having the spotlight off of me, I can't tell you what they are discussing. My brain settles into a happy fog.

That is, until I hear Joanie say the following, complete with a *Danny and Esperanza, sitting in a tree* underlying tone to her voice: "You two Rhode Island Olympians are going to be seeing a lot of each other in the next few weeks! What do you think about being thrown together in such a high-excitement situation?"

Dios mío. Good thing olive skin makes blushes less noticeable. I'm searching my head for a response when Danny answers. "The Olympics don't offer much time for getting to know someone who isn't also on your team." He glances over at me, and my brown eyes meet his blue ones. "So while I'm happy to meet another member of Team USA, I'm sure we'll both be more focused on training to win than on each other."

"Exactly," I agree.

Then the interview is over as suddenly as it started, and Danny Morrison and I are separated by the various people who want to ask us additional questions. By the time the crowd around me dissipates, he's gone.

He left without us officially meeting off-camera, and I have to admit, I'm slightly disappointed about this. But only slightly. He was right about one thing. Focus is the name of the game if either of us wants to win, so I'd better get my game on.

The rest of the day is all press all the time, including taping one of those background stories the networks love to show about American athletes to try to reel in viewers. When I finally have some peace, it's already way past dinner, and I'm ready to fall into bed. I suddenly long for some normalcy, to go back to the days when I was just Esperanza Flores and not Esperanza Flores, America's Hope for Gold.

Which basically was the day before yesterday.

Even now, in the privacy of my lilac-hued bedroom, the cheesy connection the press has made between my name and "hope" makes my eyes roll. I don't know which is worse, though — that one or *Spiñorita*.

"Mija," my mother says, appearing in the doorway. Her hair is pulled back in a headband, and her fluffy pink slippers peek out from under her robe. She comes over and sits down on the edge of the bed, looking tired from running around all day at the restaurant. "The next few weeks are going to be so exciting. Everything is going to happen very fast, *cariño*. And I want you to try not to lose yourself in all the fame and the competition. It's very easy, you know?"

"Fame?" I ask with a laugh.

She nods. "You will always be my little girl, Esperanza. No matter what happens next."

"I know," I say. "I'm glad I'll have you there to remind me."

Her eyes cloud over.

"What?" I ask.

"Oh, nothing, really." She smiles. "Now get some rest."

"Good night," I tell her. As she shuffles off, a protective pang jabs at my insides. I wish life was easier for my mother and she didn't have to work so much and so hard to keep us afloat. Mamá *has* to go to the Olympics. Going to the Games will give her something like a vacation, and she needs that for herself just as much as I need her to be there for me. Maybe soon I'll be able to get some endorsement deals and contribute more to our life.

Then again, that won't happen without gold.

I push this thought away. For now.

Just before I'm about to fall asleep, my phone rings with the horns to the Olympic anthem for the gazillionth time today. Apparently getting picked for Team USA makes a girl popular. I look at the screen, but I don't recognize the number, so I send the caller to voice mail. Just as I'm about to turn out the light, the phone rings again with the same number. This time, I answer.

"Hello?"

"Hi, teammate," says a boy on the other end.

"Teammate?" I ask.

"Esperanza, it's Hunter Wills. Remember me?"

That he actually asks this is pretty hilarious. What girl under eighteen doesn't know Hunter Wills? What girl over eighteen doesn't, for that matter? "Of course I remember you."

"Well, good. I found your number on your Facebook profile. You should probably fix that before long, or you're going to start getting a lot of random phone calls from fans."

"Oh," I say, unsure what's more startling: that Hunter Wills went looking for my phone number and called me out of the blue, or the possibility that I'm going to have to start hiding my identity from "fans." Fans? Ha! What a crazy thought. "Thanks for the tip."

"I don't want to keep you. I just wanted to say congratulations, and that if there's anything you need — anything at all — I'm here for you."

"Okay. Me too," I say, then cover my face with my free hand, my cheeks burning. Like Hunter Wills needs *me* looking out for him, not to mention the part where he has an entire staff of managers and publicists already doing just that.

Why is it that I can land triple jumps one after the other on the ice, but when I talk to boys, I land on my butt?

"Thanks," he says, and I can almost hear him smiling on the other end. "I'll keep that in mind. And I guess I'll see you really soon? Our practice in Boston is barely over a week away."

"So I've heard. And I guess you will see me," I say. Then I

cover myself completely with my quilt. Perhaps hiding and total darkness will help better responses to emerge from my mouth.

He laughs. "Have a good night, Espi."

"You too. Bye," I say.

I take in the events of this day one last time before going to sleep.

I woke up to find out I made the Olympic team.

I was on television and did press all day, because I, Esperanza Flores, am going to the Olympics.

I got a phone call from *People* magazine's Hottest Winter Olympian to offer his friendship and support as we both head to the Olympics as part of Team USA.

Notice how the Olympics keep coming up on that list?

I pinch myself again on the arm to make sure this isn't all a dream.

"Ouch," I say, letting go. I reach out and turn off the light on the bedside table, then snuggle down into my blankets and pillows, a smile on my face, Hunter Wills floating in and out of my brain. But for some reason Danny Morrison skates in out of nowhere and edges Hunter out as sleep comes and takes me away.

CHAPTER FIVE

Boys on ice

"*Arms* as far back as you can get them! That's it. . . ." Coach Chen is saying as I spin on the ice. "Careful not to bend too far forward . . . now *shift!*"

I do what I'm told . . . and I land on my butt.

At least it wasn't my head.

I pop up quickly, brush the ice from the edges of my skating skirt, and wait for Coach Chen to make her way toward me. Today she's wearing red, with a headband holding her long hair away from her face.

"Okay, Espi," she says. "Make like a table so I can show you the technique one more time."

With my left leg straight out behind me, I bend forward so that my body is parallel to the ice. It's called a spiral position. I've been practicing a camel spin, but not just any camel spin. During this one, if I can master it, midspin my body will morph so that by the time I come out of it, my back will be arched toward the ice and my outstretched leg will be bent toward my head.

It's really beautiful, but it's also *really* difficult. You practically have to be a contortionist to do it.

Which is the point, of course.

Coach Chen places a hand on my side. "All right, *Spiñorita*," she says, showing me how to roll onto my back, as well as how the slight curve in my outstretched arm and the bend in my knee will ease me into the right position. The tug along my muscles is very distinct, and I wonder if I can re-create it while moving. "You may be turning fast, but the shift is gradual," she says. "That's what makes it so pretty to watch."

I got the nickname Princess of Spin after Worlds last year. I've loved doing spins right from when I first started to ice skate. They make all the blood in your body rush out toward your fingertips. There are sit spins and upright spins. It helps when you're as flexible as a noodle like me.

Coach Chen steps away, and I straighten up. "Got it?" she asks.

I go over it one more time in my mind and nod. "I think so."

"Good. Now try it again." Coach Chen crosses her arms.

I push off the ice and skate into the curve of the rink, gaining momentum until I am ready for the leap that begins the spin. Fans of ice skating always want to know if the spins make you dizzy. They certainly look like they would when you're watching them from afar, and when I was first teaching myself to do them, half the time I would end up sitting on the ice, the world turning as fast as I was. But then my brain got used to spinning and things just clicked. I pick up speed and start my spin, gathering momentum, faster and faster until I am feeling my way into the arch Coach Chen was showing me. I roll onto my back midspin, and almost lose my balance in the process, but I make the transition and manage my way out of the spin without toppling over.

Coach Chen lets out a whistle. "It wasn't pretty, but you did it! Now do it again. We need to get to the point where it's pretty too."

I gear up to go again. I'll probably do this element five hundred more times today, but I don't mind. It's nice to return to some semblance of normalcy, like practice. When I'm here at Coach's rink, the place where I've spent half the waking hours of the last six years of my life, it feels like home. There aren't any reporters watching or curious onlookers anxious to decide whether I have what it takes to medal at the Winter Games. It's just me and Coach Chen and the ice.

The way I like it.

"Why don't we break for lunch, Espi?" Coach Chen says several hours later after I nailed the spin ten times in a row. Prior to this, I spent a good deal of time getting up off my butt. "Are you going home, or do you want to have lunch with me?"

"My mom said there were leftovers in the fridge."

Coach Chen eyes me. "Salad and healthy grilled chicken, I presume?"

"Of course," I say with a laugh as the two of us skate toward the exit. Coach Chen knows that I live on a diet of Luciano's and my mother's delicious Dominican cooking.

"Do you need Bax's help with your math lesson tonight?"

I mull this over. It would be nice to have Mr. Chen's help, but I think I'm too fidgety for trig today. "Maybe tomorrow?"

She nods. "I'll see if he's free. Be back here at two p.m. okay? We've got a lot of work to do. Dance class to start. And your programs are great, but we've got to up your level of difficulty if you're going to be competitive for gold, and we've got to do it quickly. Mai Ling can do a triple axel in her sleep — she's like a machine — and Irina Mitslaya's footwork is killer. Plus there's Stacie to consider. They're what that quad sal is for, and these two weeks of practice are going to fly."

"Don't I know it," I say, and step off the ice, thoughts of *quad sals* and *competitive for gold* dancing in my head, along with the intimidating images of Mai and Irina and Stacie. I need to not let this happen. *Confidence and focus, Espi*, I tell myself while I unlace my skates and slip them off. Coach Chen is already out the door and on her way up to the house.

After pulling on my sweats and bundling up under my coat, I leave the rink and take the path Mr. Chen keeps shoveled between our two houses. About a year after Coach's offer of private lessons, when it was obvious my training was becoming serious, the little cottage next door to the Chens came up for rent, and my mother and I moved in. This meant I could get to practice easily without anyone driving me — a pretty essential convenience, since my mother works so much at the restaurant and I'm not old enough for my license here in Rhode Island.

When I arrive at the house, the midday sun peeks out from the clouds and hits the pond in a way that sets the ice shimmering. With the rays of light coming through the trees and the hush of the snow, and despite the fact that I've been at practice all morning, my mother's homemade rink calls out to me. Instead of going inside for lunch, I find myself heading across the yard toward the frozen pond.

My mother first froze a pond over for me when I was eight and we were living at our old house a couple miles down the road. That way I didn't have to go to the public skate all the time and I could feel like I had my very own rink. It was maybe the sweetest thing anyone has ever done for me. But my mom is like that. I get to do whatever I want on my rink, and no one competes with or judges me when I'm here. Plus our backyard is really beautiful, so it makes skating feel magical. It might be my favorite place on earth.

As the sun emerges into this gray winter day, the ice shines. I sit down on a tree stump and quickly lace up a pair of my old skates, the ones I always keep in my bag for when I'm out on this pond. Before I know it, I'm back on the ice, flying across a pool of golden light.

And this time I'm skating for no one but me.

Libby shows up after school. I'm in the kitchen, just back from my afternoon practice. (Dance class, check. Circuit training, check. Quad sal, no check. But tomorrow.)

Libby's hair is pulled back in a ponytail that makes her blue eyes look huge. "So," she says, going into our fridge to see what's on offer. "Dish."

"Dish what?" I ask, deciding to play dumb.

"You know. The latest scoop."

"Scoop? Um, the ice cream is in the freezer and the bowls are in the cabinet."

Libby turns and gives me an eye roll. "I want the full update on the post-announcement press frenzy."

"No, you don't," I say, because I know exactly what Libby is digging for, and I'm going to make her work for it. This makes me feel slightly evil, but she does the same thing to me all the time. I pick at my leftover pesto pasta, but pasta really needs to be eaten right after it's cooked, so I don't make much headway.

Libby retrieves a bowl of pinto beans from one of the shelves, then the Tupperware container of rice and another of stewed Dominican chicken. She goes to work putting it all onto a plate. "I'm waiting," she says, while spooning the beans into a careful pool that won't touch her rice. *It's okay for them to touch once they're in my mouth, but not before they get there*, she always says.

"Be careful or the sauce from that chicken thigh might contaminate those beans," I warn, watching as a stream slides in the poor unsuspecting pintos' direction.

Libby blocks the potential pollutant with a cleverly poised knife. "Spill."

First *dish*, then *scoop*, now *spill*. "Can't you just ask me a direct question about what, exactly, you want me to spill?"

"Someone is stubborn today," she observes.

I look down at my green-flecked pasta. "I'm not *trying* to be stubborn. I just get nervous about boy-related topics, and I don't have any to speak about anyway. You know that."

"I didn't ask you about boy-related topics."

I cock my head, giving her a *come on* look. She's *always* interested in boy-related topics.

"I didn't!" But then her focus is diverted to the endangered rice on her plate, which she must valiantly save from the onset of beans with a spoon. Crisis averted, she goes on, "Okay, fine. I *am* curious about your assessment of Danny Morrison." Before I can open my mouth, she adds, "In comparison with Hunter Wills, if you were asked to make one. Or pick which one you like better. Which I am. Asking, I mean."

"One of your best friends just found out she's going to the Olympics and you want to discuss boys?"

She puts a hand to her chest, her blue-manicured nails the same color as her eyes. "How long have we been friends?"

This makes me laugh. "I *have* noticed that you can be boy-crazy."

"Boy-crazy? *Moi?*" Libby asks, batting her eyelashes in such an exaggerated way that we both are laughing now. Libby's precious rice goes unprotected for a good long giggle session, and I almost forget the Olympics are barely two weeks away.

I love how my friends do that to me.

Most career skaters seem to have friends mainly within the sport. Stacie, Meredith, and Jennifer, for example, have famously become best friends over the years. The three of them are always walking around together backstage at competitions, doing press together, and whispering to one another in this way that must be nice if you're on the inside of their little clique. But to an outsider, like me, it feels kind of exclusive. Even though their friendship is rumored to be rocky because of the jealousies and hurt feelings that come up when one beats the others — "one" almost always being Stacie — for the most part they seem inseparable.

Except for now, when an injury has broken Jennifer Madison out of their pack. I wonder how Stacie and Meredith are handling it. It must be disappointing for them. Which also means they must be disappointed to be going to the Olympics with me.

I've never had a good friend who is also a skater. My friends and I are more your average high school girls first and the activities we each do second (singing for Joya, cheerleading for Libby, skating for me). Maybe it's because of the way I came to elite competition — no formal training before Coach Chen entered my life, and zero affiliation with one of the bigger, more famous skating clubs. Or maybe it's simply the way my mother and I live that has landed me a relatively normal middle and high school existence. I only started homeschooling at the beginning of this school year. One thing is sure: What I think of as "normal" in terms of my life and friends is totally abnormal for your average Olympic-level skater.

And I can now apparently count myself one of those.

"I can't believe you're, like, an Olympian now," Libby says as though she's read my mind, while extracting her beans from the advance of a nearby onion. "I'm friends with an Olympian! Maybe that will get me some dates."

"I'm not an Olympian yet," I say.

"But you *practically* are."

"I think that technically I become an Olympian during the Opening Ceremonies. Or maybe I become one the first time I skate to compete."

"Wow. That will be both a historic and also horribly nerve-wracking moment."

"Um, thanks for that."

Libby pops a forkful of chicken into her mouth and swallows. "It's true, isn't it?"

"Maybe. Probably." I sigh. "Let's go back to the boy topic."

Her face lights up with a smile. "That's fine by me."

The kitchen door at the back of the house swings open to let a rush of cold air inside, along with Joya. She's bundled up in a hat, gloves, and big red wool winter coat. If my color is lilac and Libby's is blue, Joya's is definitely red.

"Hey, J," Libby says. "You're just in time for boy-related conversation."

Joya's eyebrows go up as she unspools the long scarf around her neck. Then she pulls off her gloves, shrugs off her coat, and places them in the living room, which is divided from the kitchen by an ugly old green coach. She joins us at the table. "And Espi is into the boy talk?" she asks Libby, before turning to me. "Are you?"

I shove my barely-eaten pasta away. "Now that you're here, we could talk about play practice instead. How was it?"

"Oh, you know," she sighs, snatching one of the forks off Libby's plate to dig into the Tupperware container with the chicken. "Drama, drama, drama. Jake Manzo, the guy playing Tony?" Libby and I both nod. "He's like maybe a head shorter than me. I think we look sort of dumb together onstage."

"I'm sure you look great," Libby says, snatching her fork back and restaging her food barrier.

Joya's eyebrows go up again. "Yeah, right. A black girl playing Maria and an *I*-talian playing Tony in *West Side Story*? I've seen the movie. Who's ever heard of a black Maria?" She goes for one of the spoons now and digs it straight into the container of rice.

Libby watches it go a bit wistfully. "I'm sure you at least *sound* great."

"So what if you're black?" I ask. "There's no rule saying black girls can't play leads in musicals."

Joya swallows her last bite. "*You* should be playing Maria," she says. "At least you're Latina."

"First of all, if we are going to get technical, Maria and her fellow Sharks are Puerto Rican. I'm Dominican-American. *Nada que ver*," I say, pulling out the Spanish for effect. In this context, *nada que ver* is just a dramatic-sounding way of saying that one thing doesn't have to do with the other. "And while we're being technical about race and ethnicity and people's assumptions about who can do what based on such things" — I look at Joya specifically — "who's ever heard of a Dominican skater? Much less one who's going off to the Olympics on Team USA?"

"But that's different," Joya says, eyeing me.

Libby takes her spoon back and wipes it off with a napkin. Thoroughly. "No, it's not," she says. "Black Marias, Dominican Olympic figure skaters — who cares? All that matters is you're good enough for the job, right? Joya, you are by far the best singer and actress at our school, and Espi happens to be one of the top three ladies' figure skaters in the United States. End of story."

"Okay, okay. I agree with you." A grin appears on Joya's face. "I definitely am the best singer and actress around. And Espi's probably the greatest Dominican ice skater in all of history." She places both hands on the table in front of her. Slowly and dramatically, she turns toward me. I *did* say she was an actress. "Speaking of, let's get back to bugging Espi about boys on ice," she says.

"Boys on ice! I love it," Libby agrees.

I swallow. "There are no boys in ladies' figure skating."

"But there are boys in *men's* figure skating," Joya says. "Like Hunter Wills. As *one* example."

"And there are definitely boys in men's hockey," Libby says. "Like Danny Morrison. As *one* example."

Joya is tapping her fingers across her chin. "And you, Esperanza dearest, are on both of their radars."

"I am not on anyone's radars," I protest. "I didn't even meet Danny Morrison. Not really, I mean. We sat next to each other on a sofa for an interview. He was out of the studio before we could even be introduced. I'll probably never see him again. The Olympics are huge. Team USA is huge. Tons of athletes milling everywhere . . ." I trail off.

"Aha," Libby says. "So you've been thinking about this Danny Morrison situation in great detail."

"There isn't any Danny Morrison situation." I feel like I've been caught in the act, but I'm not quite sure what act exactly. I look at Joya. "And there isn't any Hunter Wills situation either. No radar. Nothing to see here."

Joya produces my iPhone from I don't know where, since I thought it was in the other room in my bag, and places it on the table. Klepto. She has the calls list up on the screen and she's pointing to Hunter Wills's name. "Then *what* is this about?"

Okay, time-out again. It's possible I saved Hunter's number with his name and photo after he called the other night. So sue me.

"I am not on trial here," I protest. "But you should be. What were you doing going into my bag?"

"I didn't go into your bag. You left it on the coffee table in front of the couch, and when I went to set my coat and things on it, I noticed it was flashing that you'd gotten a message." I'm about to continue my protest when Joya holds up a finger. "A message with *Hunter Wills's* face on it!"

This catches me off guard. "He called?"

Joya shows me the screen so I can see the list of outgoing, incoming, and missed calls. Then she shows it to Libby.

"Correction," Libby says. "He called *again*."

"It's nothing. He's just being nice. He said I could come to him with questions if I had them, and that he could be, you know, a resource for me at the Olympics, if I needed one."

Joya laughs. "I bet he said he'd be a resource."

My cheeks flare again. I am *so* not good at boy talk. I'm usually too busy on the ice to get any better at it. That there is any talk of boys in relation to me right now is pretty much an Olympic miracle.

"Now let's turn to the subject of Danny Morrison," Libby says, pushing her plate toward my abandoned pasta. Her food is a lost cause to her since the edges have all run together. "Who I thought was exceedingly cute on that morning show interview."

"I don't know," Joya says. "He's not really my type."

Libby looks at her. "Your type seems to be six-foot-five, star of the basketball team, and named after a former president," she says, in reference to Andrew Jackson, the forward on our high school team, whom Joya's had a crush on for two years. "Or else Hunter Wills."

"I have broad taste," Joya defends herself. "Danny Morrison was a little aloof-seeming."

"You mean *mysterious* and *intriguing*," Libby corrects her, getting up to retrieve some ice cream from the freezer.

I've been looking from one to the other as though I'm at a tennis match. Now I make my way into the conversation. "Danny Morrison *laughed* when the announcer asked me if I felt like Cinderella, and not in a nice way, which was annoying if you ask me. But more important, can you believe she asked me if I felt like Cinderella? Hello, feminism? I'm not some little princess in a pink poufy dress. I had to work hard to get where I am."

Joya pulls the container of ice cream closer to her so she can dig in. "I don't know," she says. "Seems to me ice skating is a very princessy sport. You wear sparkly, bedazzled costumes with dainty little skirts made of chiffon or satin, sometimes embellished with other theatrical ornaments like feathers. Occasionally these costumes have matching glittering crowns. And when you finish your programs, people shower gifts at your feet like you're royalty."

I take a deep breath and open my mouth to protest, but I've got nothing, so I have to let it out in defeat. "I suppose that does sound a little princessy."

"There is nothing wrong with princessy," Libby says.

"Nobody's doubting you had to work hard to get to the Olympics, Espi," Joya says. "People like a good story, and your *come-from-nowhere, immigrant-mom, not-your-average-figure-skater* underdog tale sounds pretty Cinderella to a lot of people — not only in the princess sense, but in the Classic Sports Story sense." She pauses to take a bite of ice cream. "You know, like *Hoosiers*. Or that Olympic gymnast who nailed her vault with a sprained ankle to win gold. You're this Winter Games' Cinderella story."

Listening to her words, I start feeling all tingly. You know, getting chills. The good kind. "The press has been saying that about *me*?"

Joya nods. "They have. So get ready to own it."

"Maybe they'll give you a nice dress to wear to the ball after you win, Spinderella," Libby says.

"Or even better, a gold medal," Joya says.

I smile at both of them. "A girl can dream. Thanks for your support, guys."

"It's not just a dream anymore, Espi. It's, like, *happening*," Joya says.

Eventually the conversation moves on to other topics, and after we clean up the kitchen, we say good-bye, since I have practice all day tomorrow and they have school. But when I stand in front of the mirror before bed, I look at myself, trying to imagine the Ice Princess everyone is hoping I'll be. I can't quite see it.

Not right now, at least.

Maybe she's there and I just haven't found her yet.

CHAPTER SIX

Espi and Danny sitting in a tree

The next morning, when I get up and go to the kitchen, Betty is drinking coffee at the table, waiting for my mother. Her hair is under a plastic shower cap, which she uses to cover the curlers all over her head. This is actually a totally normal occurrence in my house.

"Hi, sugar," she says with that amazing Georgia accent.

"Good morning," I say as I set my place at the breakfast table.

She slides the orange ceramic teapot toward my spot. "It's probably ready by now, hon."

"Thanks." I've been trying to drink this lavender herbal tea stuff with no caffeine, since added jitters are no good for a skater. We have enough to worry about without our hearts and heads racing extra fast.

Inside our kitchen cabinet is an assortment of skating mugs I've collected and that people have given me over the years. A number of them have prettily drawn ice skates surrounded by various embellishments — snowflakes or a few stars or pink and red hearts. There are a few with little cartoon ice skaters with their legs in impossible positions, doing spins or simply with their arms outstretched. Then there are the ones with sayings on them, like your basic I LOVE SKATING!, but also:

PEACE! LOVE! SKATE!
FIGURE SKATING TRIPLE THREAT
I ONLY SPEAK ICE SKATING
I DO MY OWN STUNTS

One in particular catches my eye this morning and my hand goes for it automatically.

IF FIGURE SKATING WAS EASY,
IT WOULD BE CALLED HOCKEY.

"Mamá should be down any minute," I tell Betty, grabbing my plain yogurt and fruit from the fridge. "She's still getting ready in the bathroom."

When I turn around, Betty is eyeing my mug choice, a slight grin on her face. "Thinking about hockey players this morning?"

I slide into my chair a bit uneasily. "What do you mean?"

Before she can answer, my mother enters the kitchen, beaming. "We need to talk about your skating dress today!" she sings. She has on her Luciano's waitstaff uniform, which consists of a white pressed oxford shirt, knee-length black skirt, black stockings, and comfortable black flats. "For the *Oh-lym-picos!*"

I want to hug her for many reasons right now, skating dress enthusiasm being only one of them. "I already have my skating costume," I point out.

My skating dress for the short program is black with a matching skirt and a halter neck, plus a swirl of sparkly beading all up the front. For my free skate, I have this hot red number with gold rhinestones that decorate the neck and all the other edges. They are both simple and classic — classic in the sense that Coach Chen once wore them, actually.

I've always worn Coach's old dresses after they've been altered to fit me. Even with her generosity, it's not like my mother and I have the money for fancy tailor-made costumes like the ones Stacie and Meredith wear. Besides, my mother can sew like the best seamstress around. We started altering Coach's dresses out of necessity, but now it's more of a tradition.

A good-luck charm.

At least in my head. And we know how superstitious athletes can get about such things.

My mother does a quick little salsa dance, which elicits applause from Betty. "Espi, you are getting new and *improved* skating costumes for the Olympics!"

"We can't change my skating costumes now!" I cry out. "It could cost me the gold! Or the silver! The bronze even!"

All applause and dancing halts. "What if I told you they were specially designed skating costumes?" my mother asks. "Like the kind you used to dream about."

"I like having Coach Chen's."

"These new ones will be Vera Wang."

I almost knock over the jam jar on the breakfast table. "Vera Wang?"

"The one and only, *mija*."

"But she designs for Stacie Grant."

My mother puts a hand on her hip and gives me a *why are*

you being so difficult look. "She called last night. She wants to design for you too. I thought you'd be happy."

"I am. I think. I'm more startled than happy."

"I always wanted a Vera Wang wedding gown," Betty comments. She's been quietly sipping her coffee while my mother and I go back and forth. "Maybe she'll make you a beautiful white strapless one."

"Um, strapless would fall down," I point out. "I can't be flashing anyone during a program."

"It won't be white either," my mother says, and joins us at the table, coffee in hand. "She wants to make a red one to highlight your Spanish origins."

"But we're Dominican."

"I know, honey. I think she meant your music."

"Are you sure?"

"Pretty sure."

"Technically, my music selections are French and Cuban," I say. My short program, where I wear the black costume, is set to music from *Carmen*, which is a French opera with Spanish characters. Katarina Witt used it when she skated in the 1988 Olympics, and Coach Chen always says she sees a lot of Katarina Witt in me. My free skate music is salsa and it's kind of awesome, which is why the hot red dress I usually wear is perfect. My mother helped me pick the music out, which is also why her seamstress efforts seem important to preserve for the Olympics.

Mamá takes another long gulp of her coffee. "I'm not sure it matters, *mi cielo*. And you'll look beautiful in a red Vera Wang on the ice. Just think about it!"

"Vera Wang did an entire line of red wedding dresses recently," Betty says. "They were very pretty."

Both Mamá and I turn to Betty. "So you're that big of a fan?" I ask.

Betty nods. "When a famous designer picks you for something special, sweet pea, you should go for it. It's like those Hollywood actresses who have designers give them dresses for the Oscars. How often does a chance like that come along?"

I look from Betty to my mother, both of whom have stars in their eyes at the thought of Vera Wang dressing me for the Olympics. Superstition is just that: superstition, isn't it? I should get over my irrational fears and simply be grateful that someone like her would notice me. So even though it doesn't quite sit right, I decide to go along with it.

"Okay, you've convinced me," I say. "And you're right, Mamá. It *is* what I've always dreamed about. I'm sure it will be beautiful. Amazing."

"Good," she says, draining the rest of her coffee. "I'll send in your measurements." She and Betty get up. "We're headed to Luciano's."

"See you later, Mamá. Bye, Betty."

"Skate well today, *mi vida*," my mother says, and off they go.

Today must be the coldest day of winter, I decide, shivering and picking up the pace on my way to the rink. I should have worn a hat, but I hate how hats always press my ponytail down into my head, giving me a headache. I suppose I could wait until I get to the rink to put my hair up for practice, but I always tell myself it's not a long walk and I'll survive.

That is, until I am literally shaking in my boots. Like right now.

I practically sprint the rest of the way, leaving a trail of tiny white puffs behind me from my warm breath in the icy air. When I arrive, I fling myself at the heavy door of the rink. The temperature inside seems balmy compared to outside, which should tell you how truly freezing it is today, since the rink is a pretty cold place in general.

The clock on the wall says 7:45 a.m., which means I am fifteen minutes early.

This makes me smile. I love having the rink all to myself, even for only a little while.

I strip off my winter gear, piling everything on the nearest bleacher. Then I pull off my boots, my warm-ups, and the sweater I have wrapped over one of my favorite old costumes. It's lilac and silver, with delicate chiffon capped sleeves. When I'm gearing up for a big competition, wearing something I've actually competed in helps get me in the mood. After lacing up my skates, I run right out onto the rink, relishing the welcome sound of my blades scraping against the ice and the feel of my skirt flying against my legs and up behind me. I actually say "Good morning!" to the rink, in greeting. I've been talking to the ice since I was little, but I only do it if I'm totally alone, so it minimizes the embarrassment factor.

Except now I hear someone laughing.

Which means I'm so totally not alone.

"Good morning to you too," Danny Morrison calls back, the laughter still plain in his voice. He's in full hockey gear, except for the helmet and big fat gloves, in skates at the other end of the rink. "Or were you not talking to me?" He skates toward me like a hockey player, all brutish and unpretty and fast. When he comes to a stop, I'm lucky not to get covered in all the ice his blades throw up into the air.

"I wasn't talking to you," I say out of stupidity, and because my brain has apparently fled the building.

"Oh?" He looks around. "But I'm the only one here."

"Why *are* you are here, exactly? Did you pick the lock?"

"Your coach let me in. She's up at the house."

"My coach knows you're here? She didn't tell me you would be."

"It is *her* place. Maybe she didn't have time. I got the call this morning. And I'm not some delinquent who breaks into private hockey rinks."

"Figure skating rink."

"Right."

We stand there, blinking at each other. I'm starting to feel underdressed. My skating costume seems awfully skimpy next to all that neck-to-shin hockey padding. Also, I'm kind of chilly since I haven't warmed up, and we *are* standing on a block of ice. My wrap sweater is on the bleachers, but I can't seem to move to go get it.

He sticks out his hand, like to shake. "We never formally met the other day. I'm Danny Morrison."

I look at his hand. "That's because you showed up late, then left without bothering to say hello."

This actually makes him grin. "So you were disappointed?"

"I didn't say that."

"Not directly. But you implied it."

"I implied nothing."

"I think you did."

"Did not." *Dios mío.* What am I? Six years old?

Danny's grin only gets wider. Meanwhile, his arm is still stuck out toward me. So I sigh, relent, and shake his hand.

"I'm Esperanza Flores," I say.

"Nice to finally meet you."

"Um, why are you here again?"

"The press is coming to film us this morning."

If eyes can bug out of one's head, that is definitely what mine are doing right now, and I'm certain it isn't pretty. "What? The press? But Coach Chen and I have a lot of work to do. We don't have time to be entertaining reporters."

He cocks his head. "You think I'm any different?"

"But hockey isn't choreographed like figure skating."

"So you're saying your sport is more difficult than mine?"

"I did *not* say that."

"No. But you *implied* it."

Here we go again.

Danny turns and skates off toward the place he left the rest of his gear. I follow after him, feeling awfully dainty and small. We reach the other side of the rink, and he puts on his gloves. When he looks at me again, hockey stick in both hands, eyes narrowed, I skate backward a few feet. "At least I'm not a Cinderella," he says.

My eyes narrow now. "Aren't you, though?"

He whacks his hockey stick a couple of times against the ice. "You think I look like a Cinderella?"

I roll my eyes. "I meant in the classic sports underdog way, given that *both* of us have replaced injured team members."

This silences him.

"Ha," I actually say out loud triumphantly. I meant to gloat silently. Oops.

"Whatever," he says.

I decide to change the subject before this gets any worse. "You never said why the press is coming to film us."

He shrugs under all that shoulder padding. "You know how they are."

"Not really. I'm new at this."

"Me too. But I've watched enough Olympic coverage to know that they're trying to turn the two Rhode Island underdog teens who are off to the Olympics into some romantic story."

He said that with such a straight face and this *who cares* tone, like it doesn't even bother him that the press would do this. "Seriously?"

"Probably."

"You and I, um, we're not going to be, like, *The Cutting Edge* or something. You know that, right?"

"What's *The Cutting Edge*?"

I roll my eyes. "Of course you've never heard of them."

"Them?"

"They're movies. The original one is classic as far as figure skating goes. Right up there with *Ice Castles*. Then there are three remakes," I explain to him, while a part of my brain is shouting: *Quit now, Esperanza! Quit while you're ahead! He doesn't need to know this!* "*The Cutting Edge: Going for the Gold* — that's the second one. *The Cutting Edge 3* — that's *Chasing the Dream*. And *The Cutting Edge: Fire and Ice*, which is number four. They're all the exact same story. An Olympic-level skater for pairs loses her partner and needs a new one. A down-and-out injured hockey player reluctantly agrees to try being her partner. At first they hate each other. They fight. Sparks fly. *'Toe pick!'* and all that. Eventually they start getting really good together. They fight again. Then they win gold and fall in love . . . um . . ." I trail off.

Have I mentioned Danny Morrison has started to look at me with fear in his eyes? My cheeks are hotter than my mother's Chimichurri sauce.

"Esperanza! Danny!" Coach Chen's voice rings out loud across the rink.

"You and I *aren't* like *The Cutting Edge* was all I was trying to explain," I say before skating as fast as I can toward Coach Chen.

When I reach her, she takes one look at my face and her eyebrows go up. "Oh, Esperanza, what did you say to him?"

"Nothing. Nothing at all. Did you forget to tell me something this morning?"

"I sent you a message!"

"You did?"

"I did."

"Oh," I say as I realize my phone is still probably on the coffee table where I left it last night. I spent fifteen minutes debating whether I should call Hunter Wills back, but ultimately chickened out. "I guess I didn't get it."

"I guess you didn't." Coach's eyes are on the boy in hockey gear I can hear skating up behind me. "Hi, Danny. Welcome."

"Hi, Ms. Chen," he says. "It's nice to meet you."

"You can call me Lucy."

"He can?" I ask her, surprised.

"Of course." She gives me a *calm down* look, then glances at the clock. "Channel Ten will be here any minute. I'm sure it won't take long," she says to Danny, then turns back to me. "It had better not. You and I have a ton of work to do." She notices what I'm wearing. "Nice costume," she adds with a smile. The lilac dress was one of her favorites too back in the day.

Coach's iPhone lights up with a message. "They're here," she says.

Within about six seconds, the rink is swarming with cameras and tech people and Joanie McNulty. "Hello again, you two!" she sings, all smiles.

Then for the second time this week, she is peppering me with questions, but this time while holding a large microphone in her hand with the number 10 and the NBC peacock symbol stamped at the base. She's all bundled up in a coat with a fur-lined hood, and I have to admit, she wears it well.

Happily, with all the chaos, Danny and I don't have many more moments alone for conversation. We just do what we're told, which is basically him skating really fast and hockey-player-like around the ice, while I do figure-skater-like activities in the center.

Then they actually have us race each other. We tie. *Ha!*

This time I remember to say that to myself only inside my brain.

As we are catching our breath at the far end of the rink, Danny turns to me. "You're fast," he says with something that sounds a lot like admiration.

"You are too," I say, holding my tongue back from alternative commentary like, *What? You thought skaters weren't as good as hockey players?* or *What? Just because I'm a girl, I can't beat you?*

"If you let yourself take just a couple more power strokes into those jumps, you'd get more height," Danny says, and he sounds totally serious.

I look at him funny. "How do you know that?"

"I'm a hockey player."

"Yeah, but you don't need to worry about jumps."

"Hockey players know how to jump," he says. "When another guy goes down in your path on the ice, you'd better be ready to fly over him, or you're going down too."

"Oh," I say, because my tongue is tied again. "Thanks for the tip."

Danny looks toward the other end of the rink. The television crew is packing up. "Guess we're done. Gotta go. I have practice too. Nice to finally meet you, Esperanza."

"Espi," I say. "You can call me Espi."

"See you, Espi," he says, and I watch him skate off.

During practice, I make little adjustments here and there to try out what Danny suggested.

And wouldn't you know, he was totally right?

CHAPTER SEVEN

Quadruple threat

"*Guess* what came in the mail for you?"

Coach Chen is holding a big brown box with US Postal Service tape all over it. She's just walked back into the rink from the house, where she was supposed to be getting drinks and a snack for break during our second practice of the day, which has been blissfully without press reporters and television cameras. Just work, work, work, the way we both like it. She tilts the package so I can see that it's addressed to me, care of Lucy Chen, and it's from US Figure Skating.

"What do *you* think it is?" I ask, rather suavely and calmly if I do say so myself, even though I feel like doing a little salsa dance. I have a feeling I know what's inside.

"Let's open it and see." Coach Chen and I sit down on the bleachers, the box between us. She hands me a pair of scissors. "You do the honors and I'll watch." She takes out her iPhone and readies it for a picture.

I cut and rip and cut some more, finally freeing the flaps so I can open up the top. Inside there is a lot of paper, which I toss onto the floor. I have to admit, the sight that meets my eyes causes me to let loose a rather girly squeal, coupled with some foot stomping for joy on the bleachers.

Coach Chen is capturing this for all posterity on her phone. Hopefully not as video. I wouldn't want to scare posterity with all the noise I'm making.

Gently, I lift up my Team USA jacket. Underneath it are my Team USA warm-ups.

"I can't believe these are really for me."

"Try on the jacket," Coach says, still in unofficial photographer mode. "Go, go, go," she urges, waving me on with her free hand.

I slip one arm and then the other into the sleeves and shrug it up over the white costume I have on today, glad I didn't wear something that would clash.

It fits perfectly. I can't stop smiling.

"Beautiful," Coach Chen sings, and walks behind me to get a shot of the back. "My Olympian!"

"Our Olympian too," Joya calls out on her way into the rink. "You can't have her all to yourself."

Libby is close behind her. "Nice costume," she says.

My friends sometimes come to watch me at skating practice after school gets out. Today will be one of our last opportunities before the Games. My mother should be arriving soon too, since she's not working tonight at Luciano's.

"I'm so excited," I say.

Joya runs a finger across the fabric. "You should be."

Coach Chen puts her phone away. "Has Espi told you about the Vera Wang costume?"

Both my friends gasp.

"What color?" Libby asks.

"Red," I say with a shrug of my shoulders. I'm still a bit nervous about the wardrobe change.

Coach Chen gives my arm a gentle, reassuring squeeze. "Our Esperanza is superstitious about not wearing one of my old skating costumes."

Libby shakes her head. "But it's Vera Wang!"

"You sound like Betty," I say.

She clamps her mouth shut.

"Okay, ladies," Coach Chen cuts in. "Time for us to get back to work."

My friends heads over to the spot on the bleachers where they always sit, drinking from their thermal mugs — coffee for Libby, tea for Joya — and eating whatever snacks they managed to steal out of Libby's kitchen cabinets. Libby's house is always full of cookies and other things my mother and Joya's parents are not inclined to stock. We love going over there for sleepovers.

Alas, sleepovers are a thing of the past these days. Maybe post-Olympics they will become a regular occurrence again.

Coach Chen puts her hand on her hip and eyes me. "Today we're going to work on your quad sal."

I laugh a little maniacally. "Sure, why not?"

"Come on, *chica*!" Joya yells.

Libby's clapping. "Woo!"

"Espi, don't forget that you've done these before. I wouldn't be asking you to go for it if I didn't think you were ready."

"Uh-huh. Sure."

You have to understand: Even doing a triple axel is kind of insane for a girl, so a quadruple salchow is close to unheard of. While male skaters like Hunter Wills have been doing quad jumps for ages as easy as eating a nice sandwich, we ladies have struggled with this particular move, mostly because it's hard for us to get up the power and momentum to do four full turns in the air.

The quad jump in competition is the Holy Grail of US ladies' figure skating.

When I started going for quads, Coach and I used what's called a pole harness for help. Imagine a giant fishing pole — but with a person at the bottom of the line. Coach acted as the fisherman, holding the pole up in the air, while I wore the harness that dangles down from the end. Coach and I skated around the ice together, and she could help support me during the jump so I had more height and therefore more time to rotate once I was in the air. It also helped protect me from a couple of bad falls.

I've been off the harness for ages now. In fact, I've been landing quad sals on my own and in the privacy of this rink for well over a year. I would just never dare one in a competition. I'm too inconsistent. When I say I've been landing them, I mean that about 30 percent of the time I come out on my feet. Which means that the other 70 percent of the time I am skidding on my butt across the ice. Why risk a fall at a championship? At the Olympics, for that matter! Especially when you can do all the triple jump combinations that I can.

I am the Princess of Spin. The *Spiñorita*, even. Not the Quad Queen!

"Espi?"

"Yes, Coach."

"I'm waiting."

"Yes, Coach."

"It's not like you've never done them before."

"Yes, Coach."

Then she says, "Picture yourself quad sal-ing past Stacie Grant and Mai Ling toward gold."

"You said the magic words," I respond this time.

Here goes everything. As I get going across the ice, picking up speed in that way that I love, going as fast as I can as gracefully as possible, my legs pump and the bleachers on either side become a blur in my peripheral vision. The image of me in my Team USA jacket appears in my mind, with my new Vera Wang skating costume underneath it, the red fabric and accompanying sparkles peeking out at the neck. But most exciting of all is the gold medal dangling from my neck, completing the ensemble. The gold medal I've just won at the Olympics because I landed a quad sal.

Maybe even two!

This is what's going through my brain the very second I head into my jump, my body shooting up, up, up, my arms pulled tight, spinning once, twice, three times — three and a half — until gravity starts pulling me back to the earth. And I . . . and I . . .

. . . crash in a total girl heap on the ice.

Huh. Well, that little fantasy didn't help at all.

"Ouch," Libby calls out from the bleachers, her voice carrying high into the cavernous rafters of the rink.

"Yeah, thanks, Lib," I call back as I pick myself up.

Then I hear clapping. "Let's go, *mija!*" my mother is shouting. "You can do it, *mi cielo!* Land that quad, *mi vida!*"

Cheers rarely heard at skating competitions in the past, I'm certain. She must have walked in just before my jump.

Coach Chen smiles as she pulls her long black hair up into a new ponytail. "Listen to your mother," she says. "Now go again."

Attempt number two gets me double *ouch*es — from both Joya and Libby this time — and some loud *Vamos, Esperanza*s from my mother. Try number three is more of the same.

But try number four . . . a quad for a quad?

This time, I pump my legs even faster, whizzing by Libby, Joya, and my mother so fast that my eyes start to tear, and suddenly I'm heading into the jump with more height that I've ever had, spinning so fast I almost can't see. One, two, three, three and a half . . .

. . . and I land it perfectly.

This gets me whistling and shouting from my cheering section and a big throaty *Yeah, mija!* from Mamá.

I can tell Coach Chen is pleased too.

But all she says is, "Again."

This pretty much sums up today's afternoon practice. Quad after quad after quad until I've gone for six. They're exhausting to do. A couple of them I land, but the rest land me on my butt.

"I don't know about this," I tell Coach as the two of us skate toward the other end of the rink, where everyone is waiting for us. "If I risk even one quad in my free skate, it could be all over in an instant."

"Exactly. You could have the gold just like that," she says

with a snap of her fingers. "I told you, you have to have faith in yourself, Esperanza."

"It's more that I have faith in gravity," I quip, "and gravity does not want us ladies doing quad jumps. Gravity tends to say a big, fat *no sorry* when we try them."

Coach eyes me as we wait for my mother, Libby and Joya to join us. "We're not giving up. Not just yet," she says. Then the four of us make our way up to her house where we'll be having dinner tonight.

After we finish eating, my mother starts talking. "So Luca offered to throw viewing parties at the restaurant during your programs at the Games. Isn't that wonderful?" she says while picking at her tiramisu. I notice she's not looking at me. "He's going to have big drink and dinner specials. It will be the kind of event Rhode Islanders love. You know how people here are about the home team." She spoons some tiramisu into her mouth quickly before going on. Nothing to see here. "Everyone will be so excited. And I'll get to watch you with all the people who love you, Espi."

Her spoon gets placed upside down at the edge of her plate. She is still refusing to look at me. Her eyes are boring a hole into Coach Chen's enormous handcrafted rustic knotty kitchen table. "It will be really nice."

No one moves. Joya and Libby have frozen still, Libby's spoon in midair and Joya's in the process of scooping. Coach Chen is staring at my mother while she picks at the top button of her blouse, something she does when she's worried or nervous.

I blink a few times. "Mamá," I say in a small voice. "You're not coming to see me skate at the Olympics?"

Chairs scrape against the shiny white tiled kitchen floor as Joya and Libby murmur something about having to go home and study. They give me quick, awkward one-armed hugs — awkward because I am still sitting in my chair, not moving or speaking, tears welling in my eyes.

"Talk later, 'kay?" Libby says before they slip away for the night.

Which leaves my mother, Coach Chen, and me alone to discuss my mother apparently staying behind while I go off to fulfill my dreams at the Winter Olympics. Except here's the thing:

In my dreams, my mother is watching me compete.

In my dreams, my mother is waiting with a hug, regardless of what happens.

In my dreams, if there is celebrating to do, my mother is part of the celebration.

How could she not come?

This answer is, *she has to.*

"Is it the money?" I ask, sniffling again. "Because you can take everything in my bank account." I glance sideways at Coach Chen through my blurred vision. I can't help it. Coach Chen has given us so much already, but I know if she wanted to bring my mother to see me at the Olympics, she could do that too. Guilt bubbles up inside me for even having this thought.

My mother reaches across the table and takes my hand. "*Querida mía,* this isn't about the money. I wouldn't miss you at the Olympics for all the money in the world."

"Then what is it?" I cry.

Coach Chen takes my other hand. "Espi, there seems to be a problem with your mother's visa. Since she's not a citizen, there are . . . complications. USFS is trying, but so far it hasn't come through."

"I wish I'd been less stubborn and jumped through all those hoops for citizenship years ago," Mamá says. "Then this wouldn't even be an issue."

I say through tears, "But this is once in a lifetime! Can't the government make a stupid exception?"

"I wish they could, *mija*. It doesn't work that way, though."

I try to blink away some of the tears. "I don't understand. How can I skate on behalf of the United States if they won't even let my mother watch me do it?" I turn to Coach Chen. "Isn't there anything that can be done?"

She sighs. "I'm doing my best, Espi. I'm pulling every string I have to pull. So is USFS."

"What if I can't skate well unless she's there? What if I don't medal because I don't have her support?"

"Esperanza!" my mother says. "Don't talk like that."

"You've done it before," Coach reminds me. "At Worlds."

My voice is so tiny, it almost doesn't exist. "But I didn't medal at Worlds. I just showed up on people's radar. The Olympics are different. They mean *everything*."

"There's over a week left," my mother is saying, but I can barely hear her. "You never know. The visa could still come through. And you are going to be fine no matter what, *mi cielo*. I will be with you in spirit. I promise."

"I don't want you there in spirit," I whisper. "I want you *there*." Not only am I not being courageous or brave, I am making the two people who love me most in the whole world feel terrible, which is more bratty than anything else. I can't seem to help it, though.

"And I want to be there too, Esperanza. We're doing the best we can to make it happen. You just need to be prepared that it might not."

I take my hands back from my mother and Coach Chen and get up from the table, leaving behind my half-eaten dessert. I stare out the floor-to-ceiling wall of windows in Coach's kitchen, which looks onto the woods behind her house. The glass reflects my mother and Coach behind me, lit up by the bright chandelier at the center of the room. I can only see Coach's profile, but I see my mother's face straight on, which means I can also see that she's trying hard not to cry. Her nose has that shrunken-up look to it, and she's blinking really quickly, like I was just a few moments ago. By now I've stopped trying not to cry and tears are streaming down my face.

I wipe them away.

Time to stop weeping and whining.

So I turn around. "Mamá," I say, going to her. I bend down and give her a big hug, and now the tears really start to flow down her face. "Please don't cry. I'm sorry I'm being difficult. You are always there for me however you can be, and you've spent your whole life working to provide for us and to support my skating however you can, and I am so grateful for that. I know you and Coach Chen are doing everything you can to make this right. If the visa doesn't come through, I'll miss you at the

Games, but I'll carry you in my heart. It will be okay. And that's so nice that Luca is going to throw those parties! He cares about you very much."

"He loves you, *mija*," she sniffles.

This actually makes me chuckle just a little. Mamá is in total denial about Luca's affection for her. "Yes, but he loves you too."

"I'm sorry, Esperanza," she says. "I wish things were different for us."

"You don't need to be sorry, since you've done nothing wrong. And regardless of what happens, I love the way things are with us, Mamá, because it's always you and me, which means I get you all to myself. Just how I like it."

This gets a little smile from my mother.

I stand up. Then I notice that Coach's cheeks are tear-stained too, and she never cries. That's when I know she must be really trying to fix this situation and pull every string she has. Coach Chen is like that.

So I go over to her and give her a big hug too.

"Thank you for doing your best," I whisper into her ear.

Then my mother and I go home.

That night, when I get into bed and I'm trying to sleep, all I can think about is how terrible it will be if my mother misses the Olympics. How it will be so much harder to focus. How I'll feel lost without her rocklike presence.

But both Coach and Mamá are right: I have to try not to let any of this get to me. It would break my mother's heart if my Olympic dreams were crushed because I fell apart without her.

In some ways, her absence makes winning gold even more important — so I can show her she has nothing to worry about. That she has raised a young woman she can be proud of and who can stand up and stand out all on her own.

I need to make my mother proud no matter where she is. I owe her that. Winning gold would honor how hard she's worked and how much she's sacrificed to give me my dream.

I pull the covers tighter around me and adjust my pillow. When that doesn't bring sleep my way, I roll over onto my other side.

Coach Chen is right. To win gold, I need to nail those quads. It's a gamble, but if I do it, I'll really have a shot at beating all that competition. Mai Ling. Irina Mitslaya. Stupid Stacie Grant.

Just thinking of Stacie's smug little smile makes me want to win.

I've got to do whatever it takes.

Be creative.

Be daring.

Be bold about it.

No more being afraid and resistant.

That's it, I decide right then, as the clock ticks toward midnight and I am still too awake for my own good. The quad sal is going into my program *si o si.* It will change *everything.* It will make the competition shake in their skates, and not because of the cold. Nailing even just one quad will let me waltz straight on in to Medal Central.

Okay. Maybe I'm getting carried away.

But one thing is for sure: Once I've made this decision, blissful sleep finally pays me a visit, and I drop off into dreamland.

CHAPTER EIGHT

If there's a (Hunter) Will(s)

But then I wake up the next day and in the glaring light of the winter morning I think to myself, *Really, Esperanza? Being the first lady figure skater ever to land a quad sal at the* Olympics? *Who are you kidding?* And all that courage and confidence I mustered up last night goes *poof!*

Dios mío.

I get out of bed and start getting ready for the day like it's any other, because what else can I do? The big January-February poster calendar my mother made so I can count the days to the Games seems a little intimidating. I've been X-ing off each one since the US Championships, and already we're at January 17. Coach and I leave for the Olympics on January 27. Exactly ten days from now.

Ten days left for my mother to get her visa.

Ten days left to make myself gold-medal-worthy.

Actually, even less, since beginning the 23rd, the rest of the figure skating team arrives in Boston for our pre-Olympic practice. That's less than a week away, and I can't count on getting much serious training done during those days. There will probably be drama and a lot of acting up and showing off on the ice, petty jealousies and all sorts of other unpleasant things, just because that's the way skaters roll.

At least Hunter Wills will be there.

I am calling him back today. No more chickening out. I don't know what my problem is. He's been so nice to me.

"Good morning, *mi cielo*," my mother says when I enter the kitchen. She's waiting for me, house keys in hand, all dressed and ready to go to Luciano's.

I give her a kiss on the cheek. "Hi, Mamá. I'm coming with you this morning." When she gives me a skeptical look, I remind her: "Coach and I only practice in the afternoon on Fridays, remember?"

"You don't have to chaperone me," she says, draining some coffee.

Tears push at the back of my eyes. "Mamá, we have only ten days left until the Games. I need to spend time with you. Especially if . . . you know . . ." I can't seem to bring myself to say what we're both thinking: *Especially if you can't come with me to the Games.*

"While I'm chopping vegetables and grating tubs full of mozzarella?"

"I can help." I love being in the kitchen at Luciano's helping with prep. Though it's possible I eat more than I prep.

"But you have other things to do."

"Like what?"

"Studying, *mija*. You're supposed to be in a self-guided program?"

"You think I'm really going to get anything done before the Olympics?"

"Espi —"

"Everyone at Luciano's is like family and I need to see my family before going away and if I don't it will be really hard on me!" I say all this in one big breath. My voice turns up high and thin at the end of my sentence, showing all my stress and anxiety.

A big sigh from my mother. "Fine. Go get your coat. Betty's outside in the car."

I give her another peck on the cheek. "Give me one minute and I'll be out," I tell her, then put on my coat, hat, scarf, and mittens. At the last second, just before I go out the door, I run to my room for my Team USA jacket, carefully folding it into my bag. I can't resist doing show-and-tell at the restaurant.

"Good morning, Betty," I say when I get into her big boat of an old Chevrolet.

"Good morning, sugarplum," she drawls. "How's the training going?"

"Oh, you know. Intense. But okay, I think."

She backs down the driveway, then we squeal away down the street.

Inside Luciano's, Marco is setting up the tables for lunch. Half the place is still bare of silverware and glasses since it's early. Anthony, the head waiter, is nowhere in sight, and neither is Luca, but a lot of clanging and activity comes through the door of the kitchen, which is propped open to the main dining room. Gino and Marcela must be hard at work already. They sometimes arrive as early as 5:00 a.m.

Marco makes his way over. "Hello, *bella*. How's our little Olympian?" He gives me the typical Italian two kisses, one on each cheek.

"You know," I say. "Nervous."

He runs a hand across his bald head. "Me too, me too. It's a nerve-wracking thing, this Olympics, isn't it?"

Marco's worry is so sweet. It makes me love him even more. "It will all be okay no matter what, Marco," I say, and wish that I could so easily console myself.

He nods and grabs the dish towel hanging from his pocket to wipe his face. "Marta gives us daily updates on your progress. Your new spins. Your Vera Wang dress for the ice skating." He holds up a short, thick finger for each thing he names. "That cute ice skater that keeps calling you."

Seriously? I put my hand over my eyes, like this might help me hide from the embarrassment I feel. "Mamá," I yell in the direction of the kitchen, where there are many chopping-against-a-cutting-board sounds. The chopping comes to a halt.

"What did I say?" Marco asks.

"It's not your fault," I tell him.

My mother peeks her head through the doorway. "Yes, *mija*?"

I have a feeling she knows what's coming from the extra-innocent tone of her voice. She must have been listening to my chat with Marco. "Have you been spying on my cell phone?"

"No," she says quickly, then runs back to her vegetables. Chopping ensues again.

"Uh-oh," Marco says. "I *did* say something I wasn't supposed to."

"It's okay," I call back over my shoulder since I am already marching into the kitchen. The lights are bright, the walls white, and all the fixtures other than the cutting board countertops are silver metal. Gino is behind the line where they plate and put up food. Marcela is in her pastry corner rolling out dough.

But my mother is nowhere to be found.

"Where is she?" I ask.

Gino jerks his head in the direction of the giant fridge.

"The walk-in?"

He shrugs. Then gives in and nods.

I open the tall door to find my mother standing there, red pepper clutched in one hand, between a big bucket of sliced onions, some tubs of butter, and an entire shelf of fresh broccoli. "You realize the fact that you're hiding makes it seem like you are guilty of something," I tell her.

"Oh, Espi, *mi amor, mi vida, mi cielo, mi niñita —*"

"Ma," I interrupt. "Terms of endearment aren't going to help. You told the entire staff that Hunter Wills has been calling me — a fact that I have not shared with you previously — which means that the only way you know this is because you have been spying on my phone!" I wrap my arms around me for warmth. It's worse than an ice rink in here. "Can we go back into the kitchen?"

My mother's eyebrows go up. "I thought you might like to talk about this with some privacy?"

"Privacy? Why would we need to have this conversation in private? Everyone already knows everything anyway."

"I'm just proud of you, *mija*. I can't help myself."

This softens me a bit. But not completely. "You're proud that Hunter Wills is calling me? Why is that any of your business?"

"Because it's exciting! He's very cute. I think you'd look good together."

"Mamá!" My cheeks would turn red if it wasn't so cold in here. "That's not the issue. The issue is that you were looking into places that are *private*."

"But you left your phone on the table and it lit up with a call and I saw his face on the screen. It was an accident. Then the missed calls list came up and I noticed he's called more than once. He's a nice skater, Espi."

I take a deep breath, inhaling the freezing air, which is not terribly helpful. "Okay, Mamá. But try not to tell everyone else about *that* particular stuff next time? I know you're proud of me. The Hunter Wills thing is private, though."

"Okay. I'm sorry. I understand." She zips her lips with her fingers.

Then we walk back into the kitchen, where warmth happily greets us. I shut the fridge door behind us and clamp it tight.

"All better?" Marcela asks.

My mother looks at me.

"Yes," I sigh.

Gino is still filleting chicken. "You should call him back."

I open my mouth to protest, but Marcela gets there before I can.

"You really should," she says. "We've been eager for more updates."

I seal my lips into a straight line. Then I grab my bag, head back out into the dining room, and pull up a chair in the farthest, most private corner of the place. I take out my phone and stare at the dark screen like it might talk at any moment.

I look both ways and behind me, then find Hunter's info and send him a text.

Hey. Sorry I hvn't calld.

Then I set my phone on the table.

It immediately lights up with a message.

Call now then is all it says.

So I do.

He picks up on the second ring. "Hi, Espi."

"Hi, Hunter."

"How's things?"

"Oh, you know. Training. And more training."

"I do know."

Then there is a pause. The silence makes me a little panicky. What does one say to the famous Hunter Wills, male skater phenomenon? But suddenly I think of something relevant. "I got my team jacket yesterday," I say, all eager and excited because I can't help sounding that way when I talk about it.

"Isn't it the best?" he says, which is the perfect response.

"It is," I respond enthusiastically, and somehow with just this little tidbit, we fall into a real conversation. I tell him about my mother probably not going to the Games and how bummed I am and he commiserates. He tells me about a disagreement he had with his coach and I sympathize, even though Coach Chen and I never fight, so it's hard for me to imagine. We talk about life pre-fame and post-fame, and he reminds me that I'd better get ready to be famous myself. Then we talk about dumb stuff like our favorite bands and television shows and apps and what our non-skater friends think of having a friend going off to the Olympics, even though all my friends are non-skater ones, which I have to explain to him.

Hunter Wills talks to me like he's just some regular guy, talking to a regular girl.

It's kind of awesome.

Just before we hang up, I say something to try to impress him. I do it without thinking, because Hunter has eased me into the kind of intimate conversation that makes me feel like we're already close and I can trust him, and it seems like the most natural thing in the world that I would tell him this detail.

"So I'm adding a quad sal to my free skate," I say.

There is a long silence. "You could win gold with that," he says.

"I know. That's the idea. I was hoping you might have some pointers."

"Let me think about it. I'll text you a list."

This makes me smile. "That would be amazing."

Hunter Wills is going to help me with my quads!

When we say good-bye, I think to myself that maybe Hunter's support is just the kind of boost I need to survive the Olympics. Maybe with his advice I could take home gold. And he *is* really cute, just like everyone says.

Suddenly, becoming the Quad Queen doesn't sound half-bad.

In my post-call delirium I don't even get mad when I turn around and see the entire staff eavesdropping on me. Instead, I model my Team USA jacket for them, basking and smiling in all this love.

CHAPTER NINE

Almost famous

"**Go** Ravens," I scream. "Go Libby!"

Libby turns and gives me a look that says *stop shouting my name.*

"Go Libby!" Joya yells anyway. She smiles sweetly and waves.

On Friday and Saturday nights, our whole town turns out for high school hockey games. Coach and my mother thought I should have a night out with my girlfriends as though the Olympics are not just on the horizon — even though they totally are.

So here I am, sitting in the bleachers of Holt Arena with Joya, waiting for the game to start. Joya and I haven't really come for the game, though. We're here to watch Libby cheer for our school's hockey team.

"Let's get started, are you ready?" she is yelling right now, smiling big, those blue eyes wide and her blond ponytail bouncing high up on top of her head. She claps her mitten-covered hands alongside a long line of girls from our school who are also clapping and yelling in the very same way while wearing very short skirts with tights.

"Woo!" Joya yells. "Go Libby!"

I cover her mouth, trying to stop her. Libby gets mad when we cheer for her while she's cheering.

Joya turns to me. "Is it weird being here tonight?"

"No. Why?" I ask.

"Because of what this place means. And, you know, like, where you're headed in a week."

I think about Joya's comments a moment. Holt Arena is where Coach Chen "discovered" me during a hockey game just like this one. It's also the same place where I spent years going to the public skate every single day it was offered before Coach came into my life. Me and Holt Arena go way back, in other words.

I shake my head. "It's not weird. It's kind of nice. In a full-circle sort of way."

"That is some circle you've made," Joya says.

I'm smiling, but then my smile falters. "My mother's visa still hasn't come through yet."

Joya reaches over and squeezes my hand. "There's still time."

I nod like I believe this, but my confidence wavers with every passing day. Then I turn my attention back to Libby. "Look at her chatting up Marty O'Connor."

"She could win a gold medal in boy conversation," Joya says.

Libby is the biggest flirt I know. She bats those eyelashes of hers like she was born doing it. I cannot bat my eyelashes at all. Whenever I try, it's like I'm sending a message with Morse code or my allergies are acting up.

And Marty O'Connor is falling for Libby's tricks hook, line, and sinker.

Go Libby, I cheer, but only very quietly inside my head.

The stands are filling up, and pretty soon our entire school plus the rest of our town squeezes onto the bleachers. Joya and I say hi to people I remember from freshman year as they pass and find seats around us. Matt from Lit class. Sarah Ann from Chem. Noel, also from Chem. Jason from American History. Mr. and Mrs. Altman from down the street, whose son is a first-year on the hockey team. They're all acting sort of normal around me, but also sort of weird. I am tempted to go to the bathroom to see if I have a large piece of spinach from that salad I ate with dinner stuck across my two front teeth.

Then Marianna, Hattie, and Norah, an inseparable trio who make up the absolute tip-top of the popular crowd — so popular they generally ignore everyone else who is not as exclusively royal as they are, which is basically everyone else at school — actually make their way over just to say hi to Joya and me.

Once they are out of earshot, Joya turns to me. "What was that all about?"

I shrug. "No idea."

Then something even weirder happens.

Jonathan Mays, a really nice senior who plays on the soccer team, comes over with a paper and pen in his hands. "Hi, Joya, hi, Esperanza," he says, a little awkwardly and a little nervously too. His eyes keep darting around the rink, looking pretty much everywhere but at us. "Congratulations on the Olympics and everything." He holds out the paper and pen to me. "Um, can you sign this for my little sister?"

Joya covers her mouth, maybe with surprise, maybe to stop herself from saying something ridiculous to Jonathan or me, or all of the above.

I take the pen and paper from him. "Sure, Jonathan," I say, though my voice is anything but sure. This happened after Boston, but then I was still at the TD Garden, and the people asking were part of the crowd there to watch the figure skating — not people I've grown up with in town. "What's her name again?"

"Jennifer," he says, his eyes still not meeting mine.

When I look down, getting ready to write, I see that it's not just any paper he's handed me. It's a photograph that his sister must have printed out.

A photograph of me doing one of my spins.

It's all official looking and everything. My name is written across the top in fancy bubble font, and across the bottom it reads, ESPERANZA FLORES, AMERICA'S HOPE FOR GOLD!

"Where did you get this?" I ask, and when Jonathan gets a panicked look on his face, I add quickly, "I mean, where did your sister get this?"

He shifts from one foot to the other. "I think on one of your fansites."

"My fansites?" I ask, eyes wide.

Joya is tugging on my arm. "I'll explain later. Just sign it," she whispers.

So I do: *To Jennifer, Best wishes, from Esperanza Flores* in cursive. I hand it back and he goes running off. "Explain what?" I ask Joya.

But she doesn't have time to answer. A line has formed next to us on the bleachers that curves down the stairs toward the cheerleaders.

"Hi, Mrs. Formicola," I say to one of our neighbors.

"Congratulations, Esperanza," she says, her made-up brown eyes blinking behind the big leopard-print framed glasses she wears. "Would you sign this for me and the mister?"

"Sure," I say, and take a postcard from her that she must have gotten from the rack near the bathrooms. It's for Luciano's and it has a picture of chicken parmesan on the front. When I give it back to her, the next person steps up. Then the next and so on and so forth. Joya helps by asking each person what they'd like written. I sign all sorts of things. Napkins. Lots of postcards. Some notebook paper. Definitely more than a few photos — an exact copy of the one Jonathan had of me spinning, and others too. One of me on the podium in Boston getting my silver medal, and another of me doing one of the triple axels in my program. There is even one of me holding a bouquet of roses and waving at the crowd.

Where did people get these things? I mean, have they been walking around town with pictures in their backpacks and purses in case they ran into me? Tonight marks the first time I've been to a school event in a while, probably since Joya's performance in the fall musical back in November. I wonder if this is just a fluke or if it would happen if I came to another game.

The experience makes me both giddy and weirded out.

The line goes on and on, and I keep signing until the announcer comes over the loudspeaker to ask people to take their seats for the national anthem. There are a few more *Congratulations, Esperanzas* before Joya and I settle down and pretend like that didn't just happen.

But it totally did.

I catch Libby's eye but she quickly looks away. The pep has gone out of her clapping and cheering. Ugh. Libby, Joya, and I have always done a good job of supporting one another's various activities and sharing the spotlight. Tonight was supposed to be all about Libby and *not* everyone in the stands making a fuss over me and asking for autographs.

"Libby's mad," I say to Joya.

"She'll get over it. It's not like you planned what just happened."

"Definitely not." I try to catch Libby's eye again, but she's expertly avoiding looking in our direction. "When you said you'd explain later about the photos people had and all that — what did you mean?"

Joya bites her lip, then releases it. The very bottom of her front tooth is edged with shiny red lip gloss. "I'll explain after the Olympics."

"Why?"

"Um, it has to do with stuff online and Facebook, et cetera. I don't want to be in the doghouse with Coach Chen," Joya adds as we all stand for the national anthem.

"Okay, sure, I understand," I say, trying to stem my curiosity. But it's not easy.

During the entirety of the national anthem, I try to look my patriotic best, but my mind is spinning. This sort of anxiety is exactly why Coach Chen bans me from going online. Normally I just put the thought out of my head and block the temptation. I don't even check email. I'm so busy anyway, it's not like I have time to go tooling around online. But now I'm starting to get really worried.

What if everyone hates me?

What if that's what Joya's afraid to tell me?

Thinking about this makes me feel stifled in my warm rink attire. I take off my scarf and then my gloves, trying to remember to breathe. The national anthem ends and we sit back down.

"Does everybody online hate me?" I ask Joya. "Is that why you won't tell me anything?"

She looks at me like I must be crazy. "What? No. Are you nuts?"

I study her face, getting a good look at each of her hazel eyes.

She leans back. "What are you doing?"

"Performing a lie detector test."

"I didn't know getting an inch from my eye could detect lies."

"It's my personal secret method."

"It's unnecessary."

"Why is that?"

"Because I'm not lying!"

I grab my scarf from the bench and begin wrapping it around my neck again since now I'm starting to get chilled. "You're really not?"

Joya takes a big breath, in and out. Very dramatic, like everything she does. "I promise I'm not. In fact," she goes on, looking both ways, as though Coach Chen might be lurking nearby, "when you go online after all of this is over, I bet you will be psyched. People are excited for you and about you. Really, really, really. There is a lot of love for Esperanza Flores going around."

I put my mittens back on, feeling reassured. "Okay. I believe you. I won't ask any more."

"Good, because I don't want to tell you any more. Coach Chen may be small, but I don't want to cross her."

This makes me laugh. The two hockey teams skate out onto the ice. The game is about to start, and they face each other. "If only Libby didn't feel cross."

"She'll calm down. Again: not your fault what happened. We'll go talk to Libby between periods and get everything cleared up."

I am about to respond when the lights dim and an announcement comes over the loudspeaker that almost makes me fall through the hole between the bleachers.

"Playing tonight for the Jays, in his last game before the Winter Olympics, is Rhode Island's own Danny Morrison!"

The crowd jumps to their feet, cheering. There is actually a spotlight that shines down on the place where Danny Morrison is standing on the ice underneath all his gear and padding. He raises a hand, though it seems somewhat reluctant.

Joya leans in. "Did you know your Olympic buddy was going to be here tonight?"

"Of course not," I say, perhaps a bit too defensively. "I had no idea. And he's not my Olympic buddy!"

"Yes he is."

"Is not."

"Totally is. Just be grateful that no one has connected you with him tonight."

But Joya speaks too soon.

Suddenly, a second spotlight shines on the place where we sit and I'm blinded. It takes a moment for my eyes to adjust. While this is happening, the announcer goes on, "And here to cheer on her fellow Olympian is Rhode Island's own Esperanza Flores, who is off to the Winter Olympics for ladies' figure skating!"

My cheeks burn like they might be trying to cook something. This might be the most embarrassing thing that has ever happened to me. The announcer is making it seem like we are boyfriend-girlfriend! Like I am here to cheer on Danny and not Libby!

The crowd around us is going wild.

Dios mío.

"Smile and wave, smile and wave," Joya is hissing next to me while smiling hugely like the great actress she is and waving herself. She actually lifts up my arm for me, then shakes it a little. It flops around like a dead fish.

I finally remember myself and smile and wave all on my own, which prompts Joya to mutter, "Thank you," next to me.

While I continue to smile and wave, my eyes adjust enough to the spotlight to see Danny Morrison looking my way. And all I can think is: *Oh no! He probably thinks I came here to see him just like the announcer says! He has no idea that I came here to see Libby cheer!*

And then: *Oh no! Libby! What will she think? This night is becoming all about me!*

I seek her out down by the cheerleaders. She is not clapping with the rest of them. Her big blue eyes are narrowed. Her ponytail is suspiciously higher up on her head. She takes it down and puts it back up when she is nervous. Or annoyed.

Then mercifully, the spotlights go off, the lights go back up on the rink, the crowd's attention shifts to the ice, and the ref drops the puck to start the game.

"That was really intense," Joya says.

"Libby is going to doubly hate me."

"Again, not your fault. You didn't plan this."

"I know. But still. Imagine if something like that happened just before one of your plays."

"I would be happy to share the spotlight." She laughs. "Literally."

"No you wouldn't."

"Would too."

I tilt my head and look at her skeptically. "Come on."

"Okay. Maybe I'd be the tiniest bit annoyed."

"Or more than a tiny bit."

"Hey, pay attention to your boyfriend down on the ice. He's pretty good."

"Joya."

"Espi."

We go back and forth like this through most of the first period, while alternately and obediently doing whatever the cheerleaders ask of us. We give them an *R*, an *A*, a *V*, an *E*, an *N*, and an *S*, yelling out *"RAVENS!"* at the top of our lungs when asked what it spells. We show serious spirit when it is requested. And we watch as the cold shoulder Libby was giving us starts to thaw until she seems to be enjoying herself again.

With our attention so focused on the cheerleaders, I mostly forget that Danny Morrison is playing down on the ice. Mostly and not entirely, because during the first period he scores twice, which makes people freak out, even all the people from my high school.

"What was that all about?" Libby wants to know during the break between first and second periods. We are in the ladies' room, and Libby and Joya are touching up their makeup. "The autographing and the spotlight thing. Did you plan that?"

I can tell she's trying to be all, *No big deal, nothing to see here*, but there's an edge to her voice. At least her ponytail hasn't gotten any higher, which I take as a positive sign.

"People just started lining up," Joya says. "It was totally out of Espi's control."

Libby eyes me suspiciously. "Did you come here tonight because you wanted to see Danny Morrison play?"

"No! No way! Absolutely not! Who do you think I am?" She's doing that eye-narrowing thing again, so I continue babbling before she can ask more questions. "I came here to see you and you only. I didn't even know what team we were playing tonight, and I didn't know which team Danny Morrison played for either, because when I was on TV with him that first day, I was so nervous I tuned out all of his answers. And then because of Coach's Internet ban, I didn't have the chance to look him up."

"Protest much?" she says.

"It's true, Lib," Joya says. "Espi was in total shock. And majorly embarrassed by the attention and the association with the hockey hottie."

"Okay," Libby sighs.

"Hockey hottie?" I say to Joya.

"Don't deny that he's cute, Espi," Libby says.

"Fine. But more interestingly," I go on, in an attempt to shift the focus away from Danny, "Hunter Wills and I talked on the phone yesterday for, like an hour."

Libby's eyes widen to their normal state, which is very big. Relief floods through me. The feeling is short-lived, however, since I now need to answer all of Joya's and Libby's questions about my conversation with Hunter.

When I feel I've endured enough inquiries, I turn the tables back on Libby. "Let's talk about you flirting with Marty O'Connor before the game started. I saw it happening with my own two eyes, so don't try and deny it."

Of course she doesn't. She's Libby. We stay inside the ladies' room until the break is over, mostly because I think we are all aware that if we go back outside, we might face the autographing issue again. We do the same thing between periods two and three and manage to make it through the game without further incident.

When the game is over, Danny's team is victorious, and I tell

Joya that I want to wait outside while Libby changes into her street clothes.

"You want to wait in the ten-degree air?" Joya asks.

"I love the cold," I say.

Joya eyes me. "You want to avoid running into Danny Morrison doing his victory lap through the crowd."

"That is a distinct possibility."

"All right, fine," she says.

We explain our plan to Libby, who rolls her eyes.

"It's your funeral," she says.

Aside from a few random autographs as people leave the arena, everything is calm and normal again, as though people forgot everything that happened at the start of the game or that I'm going to the Olympics. While the vast majority of me is relieved, a teensy part is a little disappointed we didn't run into Danny Morrison before the night ended. Or that he didn't run into us.

CHAPTER TEN

Hooray for Title IX

The next few days pass in a blur.

I go to Joya's play rehearsal Monday evening and confirm that she makes a great Maria, no matter what insecurities she has. I eat a lot of leftovers from Luciano's and catch up with the staff while I wait for my mother to finish her shifts. I talk on the phone a couple more times with Hunter, who gives me pointers on my quads. I get absolutely no homework done. I do *not* see Danny Morrison, nor am I forced to do embarrassing press with him — which I have to admit makes me slightly relieved but also slightly disappointed.

I practice twice a day with Coach, like always. I master my new spins like a pro and land those triple axels like always.

But the quad sal still eludes me.

In fact, I seems to be getting worse, not better, with Hunter's advice. I might still be the Princess of Spin, but I am definitely not becoming the Quad Queen to his Quad King. Plus, I feel a twinge of guilt each time I go sprawling across the ice, like somehow I'm being punished for telling Hunter about a move that is supposed to be a secret.

"Esperanza!" Coach Chen calls out to me.

"Hmmm?" I answer absentmindedly. I am in the final pose of my short program, staring up into the wooden rafters of the rink's ceiling. I'm not sure how long I've been standing like this, but my music stopped more than a few seconds ago. I come out of the pose and roll my head left, then right, to stretch the back of my neck.

Coach skates toward me. "You need to focus! Where is your brain today?"

"It left the building, I think."

"Well, go get it and bring it back."

"Easier said than done."

She looks me up and down. "What is eating you? I've never seen you like this. You're usually so unflappable. Is it your new costume? Are you being superstitious again?"

I shrug, looking down at my Vera Wang that arrived yesterday. I give it a little swivel and swirl by twisting my torso back and forth. "Not really," I answer. "It's beautiful. I love it."

This is true. I do love it. The red isn't a bright candy-apple type red. It's a darker, more romantic hue, and it's the softest thing I've ever put on my body. Some of the ruffles down the side and on the skirt are structured, so they always stay the same wavy shape, and there aren't any beads or rhinestones to make it scratchy. Yet the entire thing glitters.

Coach skates around me in a circle. "It *is* beautiful on you."

"Thanks," I say, but only halfheartedly. My love for the dress does not alleviate my superstitions. Perhaps it's Vera Wang's fault I'm not landing my quads more consistently. But then I think about the other thing that's really eating me. "My mother's visa still hasn't come through."

Coach smiles sadly. "I'm working on it, Espi. Don't lose

hope." She sighs. "Let's run through your long program one last time and then we'll call it a day, okay?"

"'Kay." I skate over to the other side of the rink to the place where my program begins, and get into my pose.

Soon salsa music comes on over the speakers and I try to let myself be moved by the rhythm. "Dominican girls are born to dance salsa," my mother always says, and Coach took that belief and transformed it into a program that only someone who can feel the sound in her hips can get away with. It makes me stand out among the other figure skaters with more traditional music. Between the fun upbeat footwork and the experience of gliding across the ice at near-blinding speed, skating this program usually makes me feel like some strange otherworldly creature that can do things — leaps and jumps and spins — that aren't quite human.

But this doesn't happen today. It's like I'm made of lead.

The music cuts off a full minute from the end of my program and I'm left spinning in silence. I haven't even gotten to the quad sal yet.

"Esperanza!"

I open up and the revolutions slow until they come to a stop. Coach's skates scratch across the ice as she approaches. "What is with you? Is it more than superstition? Your mother? Is it plain old nerves?" She shifts since I'm avoiding staring directly at her. "Or is it about our Boston practice weekend? Meredith and Stacie?" She crosses her arms. Takes a deep breath. "Is this about a . . . about a boy?" Coach's voice goes really high and disbelieving on the word *boy*.

I finally look at her. "What if it's all of the above?"

"Then I'd say it's time to call it a day."

"On that bad a program?"

"Tomorrow will be different."

"Can I ask you something?"

Worry wrinkles Coach Chen's brow. "Of course."

"It doesn't matter if someone else knows I'm trying for a quad sal if it's not going to end up in my program because I can't land it, right? I mean, it's not a secret weapon if we're not using it. . . ."

"Espi," Coach says in a warning voice. "Who did you tell?"

"Um."

"Espi. Spill."

"Just Hunter Wills," I say in a small voice.

Coach takes a deep breath and lets it out. "Why Hunter?"

"Because he's the Quad King and I thought he'd have some good advice. It turns out not so much. At least his boy-quad advice doesn't seem to transfer."

"Is that the only reason you told him?"

"Why else would I?"

"Oh, Espi." She sighs again. "Because you were trying to impress a good-looking boy — who also happens to be famous and share your love of figure skating."

My cheeks get hot. Talking to Coach about this is kind of embarrassing. She's not my mother, but she's a little like a second mom. "We were talking on the phone and it just sort of . . . came out."

"Can you trust him not to tell anyone else?"

"I think so."

Coach is searching my face like it holds some clues about Hunter's reliability. "Let's hope you can. We don't want it getting out that a quad is even a possibility, because we don't want someone like Mai Ling going for one on the off chance she can get it in time for the Games. We definitely don't want Stacie trying for one either."

"But . . . I thought . . . shouldn't I be doing one by the time we practice together in Boston? Won't it matter for getting chosen as the alternate for the Team Event? I thought you wanted me to put it in my free skate so I have a shot."

Coach shakes her head. "We're going to add a triple axel where the quad should be — which should seal it for you. Then the quad will be the great surprise of the Olympics for all involved." She leans forward, studying me again. "Well, except for Hunter. I hope he's worthy of you."

"There's nothing going on," I protest. "Really. It's just a few phone calls."

"Hmm." Coach glances at the clock on the back wall of the rink. "Bax is going to be home any minute, and we need to get dinner ready."

This perks me up. "Fancy Chinese?"

She nods and smiles a little. "Yep. Your favorite. Now go on to the house and change. I'll close up here. And don't tell anyone else about our secret weapon!"

"I won't," I say with a laugh. "And thanks, Coach," I add with meaning before skating off the ice, grateful that she knows sometimes skaters have an off day too.

And today was just one of those for me.

I hope it turns out to be only one and not, like, twenty-five.

"Esperanza Flores," Mr. Chen booms when he comes through the front door and sees me sitting on one of the plush white living room couches. He plops down on the sofa across from me, kicks off his shoes, and puts his feet up on the ottoman. "Where's my wife?"

"She went to get the Chinese."

"Ah, excellent. There's nothing like a little Chen's brought to you by a Chen. Chen's is good for the soul. I love a little Chen's," he says with a big laugh, clearly pleased with himself.

I wrinkle my nose. "Please stop now before I lose my appetite."

The best Chinese in Rhode Island comes from this little hole in the wall called Chen's. Coach likes to joke that she makes it herself because the take-out boxes say CHEN's on the side. Mr. Chen likes to talk about it because it's a cheesy way of complimenting his wife.

"I'll stop, Esperanza Flores. . . ." He gives me a grin. "America's Hope for Gold!"

I groan. "Oh, come on!"

"But it's what everyone is talking about." His grin gets bigger. "Esperanza Flores: The Flying Dominican Spiñorita!"

"Stop torturing me."

"You love it."

"I don't."

"Do too. Admit it."

I crack a smile. "Maybe a little."

"I knew it," he says.

"Tough day at school?"

"Not tough. Just a lot of right angles." This is Mr. Chen's way of saying that his day did not go smoothly, like a circle is smooth. He talks in shapes and math, I suppose because he's a math teacher. He crosses his arms over his middle. "You?"

I sigh too. "Mine was also full of right angles."

"Sorry to hear that."

"Tomorrow is another day. Right? That's what your wife said at least."

"It sure is, Espi."

The doorbell chimes. Before Mr. Chen can extract himself from the couch cushions, I jump up. "I got it."

Libby and Joya are standing there when I open the door. Joya walks in before she's invited. "This place is insane."

Libby waits there politely. "She always says that."

"She does. Come on in."

"That's because it is," Joya calls back over her shoulder.

"I know. I'm just used to it." I close the door behind Libby.

The thing about Coach's house is that it's basically made of glass. Floor to ceiling windows on all sides, surrounded by solid forest, especially birch trees that the Chens planted everywhere. Between the snow on the ground and the white peeling bark and the branches naked of their leaves, the view is pretty much classic winter wonderland.

As we head through the living room toward the kitchen, Mr. Chen is still sunk into the same spot on the sofa, but now he's reading the newspaper. He lowers it. "Hi, ladies."

"Hi, Mr. Baxter," Joya says.

Mr. Chen makes his wacky mad mathematician face. "Did you ladies know that your friend Esperanza is America's Hope for Gold?"

I roll my eyes. "I told you to lay off the cheese!"

But Joya giggles. "I think everyone knows Espi's nicknames by now."

I grab her arm and drag her toward the kitchen. Libby follows us, laughing the entire time. Joya hops up onto one of the stools at the countertop and looks around, taking in the various snowy views. "Like I said, totally insane."

"We know," Libby says.

"Where's your mom?" Joya asks me.

"On her way, I guess."

"So where's the Wang?" she asks next. "I want to see it immediately."

This makes me laugh. "Do you mean the Vera Wang dress?"

"What other Wang could there be?"

"I want to see it too," Libby says, climbing up onto the stool next to mine.

"I'll go get it," I say. "Back in a sec." I leave the kitchen and go to the downstairs bathroom, where the costume is hanging on the back of the door. Even though it needs to be cleaned, I couldn't bear to rumple it up with my other laundry. It's too pretty. I take it down, the glittery part sparkling, and bring it to the kitchen, holding it up for Libby and Joya to get a good look.

Libby's eyes widen and Joya's face lights up. "That, my dear Spiñorita, is what you call a winning skating costume," she says.

"It is," Libby seconds.

I run my fingers across the skirt. "It *is* nice."

"So nice, I'm tempted to try it on even though you've been wearing it all day."

"Eww, Joya," Libby says.

"On that note, I'm going to put it away again," I say. When I return to the kitchen, my friends are discussing my hesitation about what they have officially have dubbed "The Wang."

Joya studies me. "The Wang is beautiful, Espi. What's the problem?"

I shrug, like I don't know, when of course I do.

Libby twirls her blond hair around one of her fingers, while studying me. "You're superstitious about not wearing one of your coach's former costumes for the first time, and doing so at the Olympic Games, of all places."

I sigh. "Yes, exactly. You know me well, Lib."

"Don't be so dramatic," Joya says. "Everything will be fine. Better than fine probably."

"Like you should talk," I say to her. "Miss Drama Queen."

The door to the garage opens and in walks Coach Chen, followed by my mother, both of them carrying copious brown bags stamped CHEN'S on the side.

"Hi, Mamá," I say, going over to give her a kiss and taking the bags from her.

"*Hola, mija.*"

Coach Chen passes the rest of the food to Joy and Libby, then the five of us start unpacking it. Before we sit down to eat, the front door bell rings and Mr. Chen goes to answer it, returning with a surprise seventh dinner guest.

"Hello, everyone," Luca says, setting a big bakery box on the kitchen counter.

"Hi, Luca," I say, going over to give him a hug. I peek in the box and it's just like I thought: heaping individual servings of tiramisu. "Hmmm. I'm glad you're here."

My mother is blushing. "It was Luca's night off," she explains.

Coach Chen looks at her. "I told you we can always fit one more."

Everyone starts to claim seats near their favorite Chinese entrée, Libby and I jockeying for the chairs closest to the moo shu vegetables, and Joya challenging my mother for proximity to the pineapple fried rice. It isn't long before we have scarfed down every last bit, and only a few lonely grains of rice stuck to their boxes remain. When everyone is in a food coma, almost too full to talk and trying to digest, Coach Chen starts clearing things for dessert.

But Mr. Chen stops her. "I'll do it. You sit, hon. You've been working all day."

"So have you," she protests.

He smiles proudly at her, while piling my mother's plate on

top of his. "You're training Olympians, though. It's far more glamorous than math."

She sits back down. "Thanks, Bax."

One of the things I love about the Chens' relationship is that even though Coach Chen had a wildly successful and public career, first as a skater and now as an Olympic-level trainer, and it's her money that pays for this huge glittery house, Mr. Chen never seems emasculated by his wife's success and money. In fact, he seems to enjoy its benefits greatly.

As any liberated man (or boy) today should.

Libby, Joya, and I learned about the term *emasculation* in last year's American Lit class, and the mysterious world of boys suddenly made so much more sense. Emasculation is something a boy (or man) feels when he thinks his masculinity is threatened by a girl (or woman). This happens basically any time someone of the female species is perceived as successful in something outside of domestic activities like vacuuming, washing clothes, or raising children, because she steps into territory previously and nearly exclusively occupied by boys (or men) — territory like politics, or like being a doctor or a lawyer or the CEO of a major corporation, or just being smart at math.

Another prime example would be sports. Before 1972, when Title IX was passed by Congress, requiring equal opportunities for girls and boys to play sports during school and college, all sports were pretty exclusively male territory. But ever since, girls have grown up playing sports like it is the most normal and natural thing for a girl to do — because it *is*, obviously.

What doesn't make any sense to the three of us about this whole emasculation drama is *why* some boys (and some men) are still potentially threatened by our awesome selves. Even if we act girly (because we *like* to act girly), whenever we're a little publicly successful, they might run away from us all emasculated and stuff.

Not *all* boys (and men), obviously.

But some.

Which is a really dumb thing, if you ask me.

"Would you like a big piece or a small one, Esperanza?" Luca asks, because he is now serving everyone tiramisu, while Mr. Chen is doing the dishes.

I look around. No emasculation anywhere around here.

"Small," I say, despite the urge to ask for a heaping plate. "I'm already stuffed."

Luca is also a good example of a liberated man. Even though technically he's my mother's boss, my mother could totally beat him in a cooking contest, and he would be happy if she did, I think.

All this reflection makes me wonder something: Would Hunter Wills still be calling me if *he* was the underdog and *I* was the star? If our roles were reversed?

Hmmm. Something to think on.

To my chagrin, the night and our dinner is over all too quickly. Good-byes are said, and soon my mother and I arrive at our house.

My mother gives me a hug good night. "You get some rest tonight, *mi cielo.*"

I notice she has a distinct glow in her cheeks, and I wonder if it's from hanging out with Luca outside the restaurant.

"Things are going to happen fast from now on," I tell her, trying not to think too much about having to say good-bye to her so soon. "We're not going to have any more quiet dinners with the people we care about again. Not until after I come back from the Games, at least."

"Yes, but I bet you are going to make some nice new Olympic friends in the next few days. What about that Hunter Wills?"

"Sure, Mamá," I say, turning red at the mention of his name, and feeling slightly uneasy, though I'm not sure why. "I'm sure that's true. Sleep well."

My mother laughs. "You'll see, *mi amor*. It will turn out okay no matter what."

"Hmmm," I respond noncommittally. Then I head down the hall to get into my pajamas, hoping all the way that my mother is right.

PART TWO
Olympic Teammate

"I can't say, 'It doesn't matter if you win or lose.'

It's not true. You go in to win."

— KATARINA WITT,

Olympic gold medalist 1984 and 1988

"Esperanza?"

Coach Chen enters the rink just as I come out of one of my spins. I skate toward the edge.

"We need to leave for the welcome party ASAP," she calls out.

I look back longingly at the ice. "Do I have to go?"

"Of course you do."

"Just checking."

"I'm going up to the house now."

"Okay."

"You're coming soon, right?"

"Yes."

"See you in five minutes. I'll warm up the car."

Silence.

"Right, Espi?"

"Um." Pause. "I suppose."

Coach narrows her eyes. "See you, Espi, and that's an order."

I take a deep breath. Take one last glance around the blissfully empty rink. Sometimes, when I stand on the ice all alone, it feels like I am meant to be here, like I was born to skate on frozen water even more than walking the earth. I am tiny and big at once — a small person, sure, but strong and skilled enough to know how to make the most of who I am when I'm out here.

On the ice, I'm special.

I've known this to my core since I was a little girl.

If only I can remember it over the next few days as I share a rink with Stacie and Meredith and the rest of Team USA, all of whom are more experienced than I am at this next part — the one where you show what you're made of to a crowd and a panel of judges, and the entire world watches you while holding its breath. The part where you deal with the competition all around you, lobbying to knock you out of contention. Which is also the part where it's no longer just you and your love of skating, but where everything can become one big mind game, and your job is to try to block this out and remember who you really are and what you came to do.

Which is win.

Gold, ideally.

I really hope I can get all these parts right. It's like having to be a one-girl show. Perhaps I need to consult Joya for pointers.

I get off the ice and head up toward the house to meet Coach.

By the time we arrive at the Boston restaurant that is hosting the Team USA welcome party, people are already happily partaking in the beverage options, which mostly consist of healthy smoothies, juices, and other nonalcoholic drinks. There are healthy snacks too, the kind where you can hear the crunch in someone's mouth practically all the way on the other side of the room.

We're not at Luciano's anymore.

There is also a whole slew of skater types everywhere: the pairs and ice dancers, coaches for all possible permutations, and, of course, the men and the ladies. This last group includes Stacie and Meredith, both of whom are off in a corner of the room whispering to each other.

I stand on the perimeter, watching all of this as though I'm at a competition, waiting on the edge of the rink for someone to call my name so I can step onto the ice.

"Esperanza!"

Hunter Wills is standing at the center of everything, beckoning me to cross that line between being on the outside and being in the middle of it all. I take a big breath and join him.

"Hi, Hunter," I say. Even though we've talked on the phone — especially *because* we've talked on the phone — seeing him in person is nerve-wracking. What does it all mean? Does it mean anything? How's a girl with no boy-type experience who spends all her time skating supposed to know these things?

Answer to all of the above: I have absolutely no idea.

Hunter has an icy juicy-looking drink in his hand. "So that's the great Lucy Chen over there. How long have you been working with her?"

"Six years. Since I was ten," I say. "How was the trip here?" Hunter came in from Colorado like most everyone else, since that's where a ton of Olympic skaters train and live.

"Longer than I like. Busy. Cramped."

"I hate flying."

He laughs knowingly. "You're going to enjoy the trip to the Games, then. Get ready to clock a lot of airplane hours."

"I know. My stomach feels queasy just thinking about it."

Hunter gestures at the buffet spread against the wall. "You should eat something."

I hesitate. Is he trying to ditch me? "I guess I should," I say.

"Let's go see what's on the menu," he says, then grabs my hand and drags me along behind him. He doesn't let go until we both have plates and we're piling them with various healthy salads.

So Hunter isn't trying to ditch me. In fact, he spends the better part of the next hour introducing me to everybody in the room, all of whom he's known for years. I meet Janie and Johnny, the top pair on Team USA — and no, that's not a joke. They're brother and sister and they're both blond and blue-eyed, in a Libby sort of way. I meet Jason Mifflin and Oliver Mason, the other two male skaters, and Tawny Jones, the willowy ice dancer, whom I happen to have loved and admired for years now. She's really friendly to me, though her partner, Malcolm Jackson, is painfully shy. I meet the various coaches in the room and people from US Figure Skating and basically anyone who happens by with a smoothie in one hand and an hors d'oeuvre in the other.

I'm definitely the only Dominican at this party, but that's okay. I'm used to being the only Spiñorita around for miles.

The only people Hunter doesn't whisk me over to are Stacie and Meredith. Plus, every time I glance in their direction, they are glaring back. I wonder if they believe I not only stole the Olympic spot of their Jennifer, but I'm stealing her boyfriend too. This makes my heart race and flutter, and not in a good way.

"What?" Hunter is studying me while munching on a cucumber slice piled high with hummus.

"What, what?" I answer. Meredith is watching us, while Stacie leans in and whispers something to her. It's possible they might both breathe fire if I get too close.

"You keep getting this strange, wide-eyed look on your face. Like something's wrong." Hunter turns to see whatever it is that keeps getting my attention. "Oh," he says, as if he suddenly understands all of my behavior during the entire evening. "Don't let those girls bother you."

"But aren't those girls also your friends?"

"We're acquaintances. I don't know that I'd call them friends."

"Huh."

"Huh, what?"

"Huh, I think you know exactly what I'm huh-ing about."

Hunter laughs even though I wasn't trying to be funny. "Enlighten me, please."

"Really? I actually need to?"

"Yup."

I sigh. Then I take a big sip of my strawberry-mango-banana smoothie, after which I worry that I have a big reddish-whitish mustache on my lip. I wipe my mouth and glance over to Stacie and Meredith, who pretty much *are* breathing fire in my direction now.

"Fine," I say to Hunter. "Regarding the two other skaters across the room" — I avoid saying their names, since all I need is for them to overhear us talking — "I thought you *were* friends with them, not only because you go way back in competitions, but also because of Jennifer Madison."

Hunter furrows his brow. "What about Jennifer?"

"Come on, Hunter. You *know*."

"Here we go again. Just come out with it."

"You two are a thing. Or were a thing. Maybe you still have that thing?"

"Me and Jennifer?" he asks, like this is a crazy idea.

"That's what all the gossip magazines say."

"There's a reason why they're called gossip magazines."

My heart does the little flutter again, but this time it's in a good way. "So it isn't true? About you and Jennifer?"

He shrugs. "I would say that they *exaggerate*."

"Oh." The fluttering stops immediately. "So it *is* true."

"I wouldn't say that either."

"Okay. So what is it, then, between you two?"

He shrugs again. "It's complicated. You know."

"Sure. Of course I do," I say, but I totally don't.

I wish I spoke boy.

Alas, I only speak figure skating.

So this is where I steer the conversation next.

"About that quad technique you were telling me about the other night . . ." I say softly. We stick to this subject until everyone at the party is all smoothied and snacked out, and tired from traveling too.

"That wasn't so bad, now, was it?" Coach Chen asks just before we are about to get in her car and head back home. "You and Hunter were awfully cozy," she says out of the side of her mouth as she waves good-bye in Stacie and Meredith's direction.

They roll their eyes the second she looks away.

"We weren't cozy," I say.

"I don't want to have to start worrying about you," she says. "Being thrust into the figure skating spotlight so suddenly can really throw a person — I know from experience. But you need to maintain that excellent Esperanza concentration and focus I know you're capable of."

"I know, Coach," I say, wishing I had as much faith as she does about whether I can get back that blissful confidence I had when no one knew who I was and I wasn't an Olympic hopeful.

Most of the others are heading to a hotel just down the road. Coach suggested that we might like to stay there too so I could bond with the rest of the team, but I told her I didn't want to, because this is the last chance I have to spend time with my mother, whose visa is still MIA.

All that is true. Though it's not the whole truth. This whole Team USA thing is intimidating.

When we get home, just before I get out of the car, Coach stops me. "Espi," she says. "It's all going to be okay."

I nod.

"It is."

I nod again.

"Say something."

"Good night?"

This makes her laugh. "All right. Good night to you too."

I hope it's a good one. I'm going to need all the good nights I can get to survive the next several days of dirty looks from

Meredith and Stacie and the weird boy signals from Hunter. Not to mention nudging either Stacie or Meredith out for the Team Event alternate spot.

Yeah, that too.

No big deal.

Not at all.

CHAPTER TWELVE

Making a public spectacle

"*Luca* would like to throw a going-away party on Sunday afternoon," my mother says when I walk into the kitchen the next morning. "For the whole team," she adds.

"Hi, Betty," I say to Betty, who is sitting at the table, curlers and all. To my mother, I say, "That's nice of him, but not very practical. We're an hour's drive from Boston."

Betty raises her SKATING FOREVER mug like she's toasting me. "Good morning, sugar."

"Yes, but they'll already be here," my mother says. "Coach Chen says she's having the team down to her rink for your final practice before you leave Monday."

"She is? That's news to me. And I still don't know," I say.

My mother looks hurt. "Why not? You're not ashamed of us, are you?"

"No!" I protest loudly, and both Betty and my mother jump. "No way," I add more softly this time. "I'm just not sure eggplant parm is this group's style. You should have seen all the raw vegetables last night at the team get-together." Even though I think most of the Team USA crowd would have fun at Luciano's and find it a nice change of pace, Meredith and Stacie are intimidating. And for some reason, they make me feel embarrassed about the things that make me, well, me. I'm afraid to share my home life and places like Luciano's with two girls who seem so judgey and unfriendly.

"I bet they would like Luciano's," my mother says, the hurt in her voice still clear.

Betty finishes a sip of her tea, eyeing me. "You've got no reason to be ashamed about who you are, hon."

"I know. I'm not! Can we just think about it?" I ask, turning to my mother.

"Don't think too long. Luca and I will need at least twenty-four hours' notice to plan."

"You and Luca are doing a lot of recreational activities lately," I say.

My mother grabs her keys off the counter, suddenly in a rush. "Esperanza, what are you talking about?" she asks, then takes Betty's teacup right out from under her nose and puts it in the sink.

"Nothing really, I guess," I say innocently, and Betty and I share a conspiratorial look.

"Apparently your mother and I are leaving," Betty says. "Even though if we go now, we'll get there with fifteen minutes to spare." She pulls on her coat and gives me a hug. "See you, sweet pea."

"Bye, Betty."

My mother is waiting for me to give her a hug before she leaves. I go to her. "Betty was right, and you have nothing to be ashamed of, *mi amor*. You go knock 'em dead today."

This makes me laugh, even as my throat tightens and tears push at the back of my eyes. "Okay, Mamá, I will," I tell her, and watch as she trudges through the snow and gets in the car to go to work.

The men are already out on the ice warming up when Coach and I arrive at the practice rink in Boston. We're just in time to catch Hunter nailing the highest quad I think I've ever seen. Meredith and Stacie are sitting off to the side on one of the bleachers, watching him. The ice dancers and the pairs are nowhere to be found, but I bet they're at ballet class. Coach Chen immediately huddles together with the two other ladies' figure skating coaches. They whisper conspiratorially and nod my way and toward Stacie and Meredith.

If I was truly courageous, I would go over to Stacie and Meredith, sit down, and say hello, like the three of us having to be on the same team isn't a big deal. Like we're all going to be great friends any minute now.

But I don't do this, of course. Because we're not.

And I'm too chicken. I'm practically made of chicken right now. I'd be better named Esperanza Pollo than Esperanza Flores.

"Espi!" Coach Chen calls to me. She points to a spot on the bench next to Meredith and Stacie, who both roll their eyes at each other as I approach.

I go over and sit down, but leave a good two feet of space between us. "Hello," I say, all formal-sounding and ridiculous, because everything feels so awkward.

"Good morning, Es-*pee*," Stacie says, all extra sweet-sounding, except for the part where she emphasizes the *pee* syllable. What are we, ten-year-old boys? "How's it feel to be *Cind-er-el-la*?" she goes on, pronouncing this title like it's the worst insult someone could possibly bestow on me.

Before anyone can say anything else so stimulating and friendly, our three coaches are on us. Angela East, Stacie's coach, seems truly nice, and the smile she gives me is genuine. Mark Danson, Meredith's coach, stands between Coach Chen and Coach East. He not only towers over his two female colleagues, it's obvious he believes himself the boss among them, even though, technically, nobody is the head coach of the figure skating team at the Olympics.

As I look up at Coach Danson and his unsmiling face, and the way he's got his big muscled arms crossed over his chest, his legs shoulder-width apart, all I can think is: *This is a man who is afraid of being emasculated!*

I have to stifle a giggle.

"The purpose of this time is for you ladies to get used to working alongside one another," Coach Danson begins, as though someone has put him in charge.

Seriously? *You ladies?* Who talks like that?

"And to learn not to get in each other's way," he goes on, staring directly at me.

Coach Chen gives him a sideways glance. "What Coach Danson is trying to say," she cuts in, "is that these practice sessions are an opportunity for the three of you to work *together* and, most of all, to *support* one another. You are each here as individuals, but you are also a team — and this year, a *team* that could bring home gold."

Coach East is nodding. "Here in the US, you are the stars. The cream of the crop. But when we get to the Games, you'll have the Russians to contend with, not to mention China and Japan, and we all know how good those girls are." She sounds genuinely sympathetic about us having to face our world-famous competition. "We can't emphasize enough that the three of you are going to need to lean on each other and psych each other up, not *out*."

Is it me, or is she actually staring directly at Stacie when she says this? Like she knows exactly what kind of girl she coaches and how she acts around other skaters. Or, to be more specific, how she acts around *one particular* skater — *me* — since Stacie and Meredith are obviously besties.

Stacie stares hard right back at her coach. "Good thing at least *two* of us have gone head-to-head with all those skaters before, and at least *one* of us has come out on top on a number of occasions. Right, Meredith?" She turns to her friend for confirmation.

"Stacie," Coach East scolds.

Meredith is nodding, her long red waves swinging and swaying with the movement. She has the prettiest hair, and if she would actually be nice to me at some point, I would tell her this. But then she has the nerve to say, "Stacie and I have the Team Event medal all sewn up, so no worries there. I'm sure I won't have to skate, of course, but I'll be ready as alternate if there needs to be a sub."

Perhaps taking some scissors to that hair would make me feel better.

Coach East says in a very sweet but very firm voice, "No one has decided who will be the sub yet. There's still plenty of time for seeing who is best."

Which causes Coach Danson to turn to Coach East and look at her like she just sprouted antlers.

Which causes Meredith to huff and puff and run away to the bathroom, even though I'm not sure she actually knows where it is.

"I'll go get her," Stacie says with a sigh, and takes off after her.

Coach Chen is visibly shaking her head now, and I wonder if she regrets that we are stuck practicing together for our last days in the US before the Olympics.

I certainly do.

Later, I watch Stacie out on the ice as she does triple jump after triple jump after triple jump. It's kind of insane how consistent she is. I mean, I do triple axels, which are about as good as it gets, but watching Stacie nail triple flips and triple lutzes like they're a walk in the park is pretty intimidating. I've seen her skate a million times in competitions, but to see her this good at *practice*, a time when you're allowed to experiment and try new things and even *fall* — or at the very least stumble a few times — is daunting.

No wonder she's America's Darling.

Meredith stands down by the ice. She actually looks away as Stacie flies through the most difficult elements of her free skate.

I can't decide if this is because Meredith is afraid her friend Stacie might mess up, so it's easier not to watch, or if it makes her feel bad that she doesn't have that level of difficulty in her program. Meredith does a double axel–double toe–double loop combination pretty amazingly — but it's still not the same as having all those triples.

"Stacie!" Coach East is calling out.

But Stacie ignores her and goes right into her combination spin. It's fast and basically flawless — well, until she bobbles and almost falls, having to come out of it too early to even make it a level-two spin.

Out of the corner of my eye, I see Meredith smile. It's a little one, almost a secret smile, but I definitely see it.

Interesting!

It almost makes me like her more. At the very least, it gives me hope that maybe she and I could bond a little.

"Hey," I hear behind me and almost jump.

"Hi, Coach," I say as she joins me. We watch Coach East and Stacie deep in conversation out on the ice.

"Are you feeling better now that we're here?" she asks.

I look at her like she's crazy. "Do you actually think that the way Stacie and Meredith are acting makes me feel *better*?"

"Espi, they're just nervous around you," she says in a low voice. "They know you're a real threat, and they're trying to psych you out."

"A threat? I doubt that's how they see me. And what about that whole speech you coaches gave us earlier today about working together and supporting each other?"

Coach nods in Angela East's direction. "She meant it. She's been trying to rein in Stacie's attitude for ages, but Mark Danson could care less about anyone other than Meredith. If he had his way, we wouldn't all be here together now."

"He seems better suited to coaching Stacie rather than Meredith."

Coach laughs. "Seems like it, doesn't it?"

Meredith skates out onto the ice, her red hair a bright shock against so much white. She starts her short program without the music. At first I wonder why, but then I realize it's so she can hear her coach's insane screaming about everything she's doing wrong.

"Did you wake up stupid this morning? Is that why you're tripping over yourself?" Coach Danson yells at one point.

"You know why you don't have a triple axel like those other girls, don't you? It's because you eat too much to get their speed and height!" he shouts later.

It's *shocking*. And horrible.

Coach Chen's face is red with anger. "That man should not be allowed to even be in the same room as Meredith."

"But before, he was so defensive of her."

Coach scoffs. "More like he's defensive of his ability to coach her."

"Look at that footwork, though," I say, nodding in Meredith's direction on the other end of the ice. "She's the only one among the three of us that gets a level four, so she definitely wins on that front. I bet the judges give her a plus-three on it."

"You're going to get a plus-three on your quad sal," Coach Chen sings in a whisper, a big smile on her face.

"More like a minus-three when I fall on my butt," I respond.

"Don't be negative, Espi! You need this to win."

This time, I don't say anything. I just glue my eyes to Meredith, even though I'm not really paying attention to her program.

In figure skating, judges assign a Grade of Execution (GOE) for each element in a program, ranging from -3, if there's a big mishap like a fall, to +3, which is very rarely awarded because it means the element was done perfectly. Most people will stay between base, which is 0 if they just perform average, and +2 if they do well, like bronze-medal well. Getting assigned a +3 is *very* rare, but it's exactly the kind of grade whatever lady who wins gold at the Olympics will be getting — that's what will put her over the top.

The components score is important too, of course. It basically has to do with how "pretty" you skate. The judges score you in interpretation, performance and execution, skating skills, choreography, and transitions. Mai Ling, who's a powerhouse, suffers in this category because she skates like a machine, while Irina Mitslaya always scores high because she's so graceful. I usually do fairly well here, though not as well as Irina.

"You're up, Espi," Coach says, pulling me out of my thoughts. "Keep your focus. Let's do your free skate first."

"I'm not going for the quad sal, right?"

"Right. We're saving that for the Games."

I nod, relieved.

Much to my surprise and joy, I skate a flawless program. Coach Chen whistles and claps when I'm done.

"Nice job, Espi," Coach East calls out, which makes me like her even more.

But when I come off the ice, Stacie is scowling like she's bitten into something rotten and Coach Danson looks angry. I can't tell what Meredith is thinking. She just has a blank look on her face.

The tension makes me suddenly tired. Figure skating might be pretty to watch, but the drama that goes on behind the scenes is as ugly as ugly gets. When we're finally done for the day, I feel like I've been through a war.

CHAPTER THIRTEEN

Skate for your life!

The frozen pond in my backyard entices me when I get home.

Despite the long day.

Despite the bickering, the snide remarks, the drama.

Despite the fact that I need to start packing to leave for the Games on Monday.

Despite the fact that it is a cold, dark winter's evening.

Despite all of the above, I turn on the floodlight. The trees closest to the house are bright and the ones farthest away are silver and ghostly. Everything is silent. I head down to the pond, drop my bag on a stump, put on my skates, take the ponytail holder from my hair and shake it loose, and then get out on the ice to enjoy the peace and quiet. First I simply skate in circles, enjoying the sound of my blades scratching the ice and the wind rustling the trees above. Then I move into the center for some spins and a few jumps, before resuming my trips around the edge of the pond, as though I'm a little girl again, just out here for the fun of it, and not on my way to the Olympics in a few short days.

It's moments like these when I can remember my figure skating roots, which I really need to do right now. Not to mention have some alone time.

The alone time gets cut short, though.

"Esperanza?"

I know that voice. I didn't before, but oh boy, now I do.

"Hunter?" I call out, turning around.

He is standing at the edge of the pond, watching me, a golden halo shining around him from the light at his back. I am all the way at the other end, in the shadowy part, which is good since he can't see the shock on my face and my inability to wipe a sudden, giant smile away. Every time I saw him today, it was either from a distance or when he was surrounded by other people. To say I'm surprised he's here is not enough to describe my state right now.

"Do you want some company?" he asks, like his presence in my backyard a whole hour away from Boston is a totally normal event.

"What are you doing here?"

He shifts from one foot to the other. "I thought I'd say hello?"

"Hello."

"Hi. So, can I join you? Or do I need to wait for the formal invitation?"

"Oh," I say, feeling like an idiot. "Do you want to join me?"

He grins ear to ear. "Definitely."

I head toward him and watch as he trades his boots for his skates, then steps onto the ice. A part of me wonders whether this is really happening, whether Hunter Wills is actually on the homemade rink at my house, which, I have to say, is a pretty romantic place during the daytime, never mind at night.

"I'm not actually stalking you, I promise," he says when he reaches me on the ice. "It's just that Jason has a friend nearby he wanted to see, and when I realized how close he'd be to your house, I hitched a ride."

"But how —"

"I found a listing for Flores in the phone book. You're the only one in this town."

My eyes get big. "Did you ring our doorbell?"

He nods. "I thought it would be better than breaking in."

"Yeah, I think that's probably true." I laugh.

Hunter skates in a circle around me, but his eyes never leave mine. "When nobody answered, I took the liberty of coming around to the back. I read about your skating pond in one of the profiles of you online, so I had this sneaking suspicion I'd find you here. Even though I thought it was a little weird, since it's like thirty-five degrees out." He looks around. "This place is beautiful."

I look around us too, up at the trees glowing in the dim light and the stars high up in the center of it all. "I know. My mother does this for me every winter — with a little help from her friends, of course. She's done it ever since I was a little kid and fell in love with figure skating."

Hunter's blue eyes are sincere. "That's kind of amazing."

"My mother is a pretty amazing person," I say, trying to ignore the twinge that hurts my heart at the thought of having to say good-bye to her on Monday. We start a big loop around the edges of the pond. "This used to be one of the only places where I could get on the ice, but ever since I started training for real with Coach Chen, it's where I come to skate just for fun, or to remember why I love what I do, or sometimes a little bit of both." I sigh, long and loud, without meaning to. "Not to be melodramatic or anything."

"It's not easy being the youngest person around," Hunter says, taking a pair of gloves from his pocket and putting them on.

"Right. And don't forget I'm also the new person."

"Being new can be fun. You're like the shiny new toy for the press."

"I am *not* a shiny new toy. And I definitely don't need the press on my back. They like to make stuff up. Cinderella stories and fairy tales and all of that."

Hunter looks over at me as we head into the curve at the back of the pond. "So it's just a rumor about you and that hockey guy?"

My eyes widen. "There's a rumor about me and Danny Morrison?"

"Uh, yeah." Hunter laughs. "More than one. You didn't know?"

"My coach won't allow me online until after the Olympics."

"Seriously?"

I nod. The two of us slow until we come to a stop and face each other on the ice. Teeny, tiny snowflakes are actually starting to fall, and I almost want to laugh. "She doesn't want me to get pulled into any drama," I explain, trying to ignore the fact that this setting is only getting more goofily romantic by the minute, like we're two people in a movie and not in real life. "She also doesn't want me to get upset if and when people say mean, awful things."

"Wow. Your coach is strict."

"Or maybe smart?"

"Well, no one is saying anything bad about you. At least not that I've seen. But there is a lot of talk about the 'Rhode Island Romance on Ice.'"

"Oh no! Really? That's so cheesy!"

"The press loves the cheese."

I pull my scarf a little tighter. When we're not moving, I start feeling the cold. "I worried that might happen. People keep shoving Danny and me together." I groan in frustration. "Why do they have to invent stories like that?" I shout into the darkness. "Don't they know it's not real?"

Movement off in the distance catches my attention suddenly. There are people streaming into my backyard.

Swarming, really.

People with cameras.

Real live paparazzi.

"Uh-oh," Hunter says, watching them now too.

They are getting closer. Approaching the pond. It's like I called them to us.

"How do they know we're here?" I ask, perplexed, my heart hammering as they stream around the edge of the pond, like they all got together and came up with an attack plan. It's a little bit like the beginning of a battle scene in those Lord of the Rings movies Mr. Chen is always trying to make me watch.

"ESPI! HUNTER!" they call out as they run toward us.

"Uh, it might be my fault," Hunter says sheepishly. "I've been trying to shake the press all day. They like to follow me around, especially pre-Olympics."

"ARE YOU A COUPLE NOW?" One yell emerges above all the others.

"What are we going to do?" I ask, deciding to ignore that question for the moment. "This has never happened to me before."

"Well, I've got plenty of experience. Just follow me," he says, skating off toward the very back edge of the pond.

I skate after him, my head turning side to side as the press follows us around the edges of the ice, right toward the place we'll end up. With every passing second, they only get closer. "I'm not sure how this is going to help."

"Trust me," he says. "Now wait for it," he adds as they come closer still, cameras poised and at the ready. Then, "Come on!"

Hunter grabs my hand and we fly toward the other side of the pond as fast as our skates can carry us, straight toward the protective safety of my house. I glance back when we are halfway there. The paparazzi are already on their way toward us again, but on foot and with all that gear, they're no match for Hunter and me. We run straight off the ice and put on our guards as quickly as we can manage before grabbing our stuff off of the tree stumps and running up the path toward the door to the kitchen. We might have a good lead, but not enough to change into our street shoes. The press is still coming around the pond, stumbling along in the snow, when we are already up the back steps and tumbling inside.

I slam the door behind us and lock it.

Then I collapse to the floor with Hunter, our backs against one of the cabinets. The two of us catch our breath. In between heaves, I start to laugh and so does he.

"I can honestly say that has never happened to me before."

Hunter looks over and rolls his eyes. "Welcome to my life."

We undo the laces of our skates and set them by the door. Hunter pokes around a bit in the living room and down the hall. "Is anybody home?"

I shake my head. "My mother's at work."

"The bathroom . . . ?"

"Oh! Down the hall, second door on the right," I tell him, hoping the bathroom isn't too much of a mess with girly things like nail polish and curling irons everywhere.

My heart is still pounding from our run.

Or maybe also because of Hunter Wills's presence in my house.

I can hear the press people clamoring just outside the door. I totally forgot he was a gossip magnet. And a paparazzi magnet. That he's basically one giant boy-shaped magnet.

And I am now apparently tangled in his magnetic pull, whether I want to be or not. Which means I may end up being gossiped about too. Even if I already was before, now it will certainly get worse.

Dios mío.

I must have a panicked look on my face right now, because when Hunter returns to the kitchen, he takes one look at me and says, "Esperanza, it will all be okay."

"Will it?"

"Sure," he says, like this happens to him every day. Because it probably does. "This is just a normal part of an elite skater's life. You'll get used to it."

"I don't know if I can. It's definitely not normal for me."

Hunter peeks out from behind one of the curtains, then he checks the time. "I should go soon, and it might as well be now. I don't want to be late to meet Jason, and the press is going to camp here until I come out, regardless of how long I take. We both need our rest before tomorrow anyway."

I scramble to my feet. "Don't they ever get tired?"

He shrugs. "Not really."

"Well, good luck with that," I tell him, glad it isn't me who has to fight my way through all those people with cameras.

Hunter has a strange look on his face. "At least the rumors about you and Danny Morrison will go away after tonight."

When he leans toward me for a second, I think he might be going to kiss me.

And he *does* kiss me, but on the cheek, which, honestly, is just as surprising since I am not expecting any kissing action this evening. I am not in the business of expecting kissing action from boys in general ever, since yes, it's true, I am sixteen and I've never been kissed.

So sue me! This kind of thing happens when you're a really serious athlete. Or so I hear. It's not a big deal. Not at all!

"See you tomorrow, Espi," he says as he pulls away. Then he grabs his bag and his skates, like it's no big deal that he just kissed me on the cheek. Like he's been planning it all night or something.

And maybe he has.

"See you," I croak, all flustered and blushing.

He opens the door and heads out into the cold and mayhem, like this is just another evening in the life of Hunter Wills.

Well, let me tell you: This is *not* just another night in the life of Esperanza Flores, which is why I immediately have to conference Joya and Libby in on a call so I can analyze every single detail of every moment of the evening with their assistance, and also why I absolutely cannot get any sleep, even though I really need it.

What with the Olympics coming up and everything.

CHAPTER FOURTEEN

Scandalous

Apparently, I do get some sleep, because I wake up to a surprise.

Coach Chen is sitting at the foot of my bed. She's all in blue today and her hair is tied back in a neat bun.

"What are you doing here?" I ask. "Am I dreaming?"

She sighs. "I wish."

"Uh-oh. What's wrong?"

"You had an adventure last night," she says.

She states this, really. No question marks in sight.

I sit up. Hug a pillow tightly as I try to stay calm. "Maybe," I say, drawing out each syllable.

"Esperanza, you have to be careful what you do and who you are seen with now. You are going to the Olympics as a *figure skater*, and by definition, people are fascinated with you." Another big sigh. "No one can ever get enough of young, pretty figure skaters."

I raise the pillow until it's level with my eyes, as if hiding might make whatever is about to happen go away. "What aren't you telling me?" I ask, my words half muffled.

She blinks. Then blinks again. "There are rumors about you and Hunter Wills."

I lower the pillow a little so I can talk better. "You didn't tell me about the Danny Morrison rumors, so why are you telling me about the Hunter Wills ones?"

"Because this time it's different."

"Why?"

"Because Hunter Wills is a famous playboy, and now you're linked to him."

"So? It's just another rumor."

"That may be," Coach Chen says, though from her tone it doesn't sound like she totally buys that claim. "But this rumor is going to change your day-to-day existence."

"How? Why?"

"Espi, there are press people camped on your doorstep."

"What? Still? But they were here for Hunter, and he's gone."

Coach Chen gets up and goes over to the window. She peeks out the lilac-flowered curtain. "Well, now they're here for you."

I get up and join her there. She moves aside so I can see.

Dios mío. The reporters are like a swarm of bees who got confused about which season it is.

"Your mother can't even get out of the house for work. And Betty gave up trying to get in."

"Oh no. How are *we* going to get out?"

"You're going to have to go through them so they'll follow you and your poor mother can head to work in peace."

"My poor mother? What about poor me?"

Coach Chen steps away from the window. "This isn't her fault."

"And it's *mine*?"

She crosses her arms. She might be tiny, but it's an intimidating kind of tiny sometimes. "Well, Esperanza, no one else had a romantic skate on a starry night all alone on a pond with Hunter Wills other than you, am I right?"

I swallow. "How do you know that part, exactly?"

"There are pictures all over the place of you online!"

"Maybe you should have an Internet ban too?" I ask sheepishly.

She exhales with a groan. "The moral of the story is the following: You don't need this kind of distraction. I don't want you online for a *reason*, and that reason is because I don't want you getting caught up in *more* drama than the experience of competing at this level provides. This is a dream come true for you *and* for me! I knew you could do this, and here you are."

"I know," I say in a small voice.

"Then I'm sure you also know that spending time with Mr. *Phenom*" — Coach Chen rolls her eyes — "is not going to help you. He eats up the press like they're breakfast. He loves it. But all hanging out with him is going to do for you is hurt your focus."

"But he's helping me with my jumps," I say in a smaller voice, as if this makes up for anything.

"Leave *that* kind of help to me," she says. "I wish you'd never told him about the quad, Espi. Hunter Wills is not out to help you. Trust me."

"How do you know that?"

Coach starts grabbing the things I need for today and shoving them in a bag. "Well, for one, isn't he dating Jennifer Madison?"

I look at her with surprise. "You got that on the gossip sites."

"I read them like everyone else," she says, like this should be obvious. "Just tone it down on the Hunter Wills drama until *after* the Olympics. Okay?"

"I'll try."

"Not try. *Do.*"

"Yes, Yoda."

Coach Chen ignores this remark. "Now come with me. You can shower and get ready at my house, but at the moment, my job is to get you through that storm of press outside so your mother can get to work in peace." She beckons when I hesitate. "Don't forget, Espi, I have a little experience with this from back in the day. I've got the exit down, and I'm going to start teaching you this morning."

"Okay," I say, then take a deep breath and follow her lead.

My first and also most important lesson of the morning:

It's one thing to *do* press, when they invite you somewhere for an interview, or you open up, say, a private ice skating rink to them for a special segment, when there are producers like Run-on-Sentence Jenny, and there is organization and structure and calm, even amid the nervousness-producing parts.

It's a whole other thing when the press just *shows up* uninvited.

Then they are like a pack of animals.

Wolves.

Their existence, their *persistence*, or dare I say, persecution, is overwhelming. It is also unbelievable. They try to lure you in with very transparent methods, but it's obvious that the second you come close, they'll pounce.

"Excuse us — no questions today," Coach says as she expertly pushes through the clamoring swarm of arms and microphones and camera flashes and all the shouting. She has a permanent smile on her face, yet her arm is up and out and making room for us.

"Hello, everyone," I'm saying as we move forward little by little toward Coach's car, where Mr. Chen is in the driver's seat with the engine running. I have a smile on my face, just like Coach said I should. "I'll be happy to answer your questions after I take home the gold," I sing, like I do this every day, just as she instructed.

Be nice, she said.

But be firm, she also said.

And above all else, *keep moving*.

"I counted a total of forty-five press people," Mr. Chen says once we're both in the car.

He takes us back to their house, where he gets in his car to head to school and Coach runs around to the driver's side. Within moments we are off to Boston, mostly without being followed, we think. Yet the press is everywhere when we arrive at the practice rink too.

By the time lunchtime rolls around, my big plan is to hide out in a corner of the stands. In fact, I might never leave here again.

Coach Chen refused to give me the particulars of what people are saying, but between overhearing Stacie and Meredith gossiping this morning (they weren't exactly keeping it down), and from the kinds of things the reporters were shouting as

Coach Chen maneuvered me through the throngs, last night I was apparently "cozying up to Hunter Wills," and he and I were "stargazing on a wintry night" as well as "hoping for some alone time, away from the prying eyes of Jennifer Madison's two best friends" — aka Stacie and Meredith. The worst one, though, was the "America's Hope for Gold Is Hoping for Some Action."

Really? Seriously?

I wonder if Danny Morrison is aware that the speculation around our made-up relationship is dying down due to my brand-new made-up relationship with Hunter Wills.

If he knows, he's probably relieved.

Then I wonder why I'm even thinking about Danny Morrison at a time like this. I mean, what is my problem? Coach Chen is right: I don't need this sort of distraction right now. I have other things to attend to. Olympic-sized things, for example.

My stomach grumbles from hunger.

"I brought you a sandwich."

I look up. Tawny Jones is standing there in all her willowy beauty, a toasted veggie panini in her outstretched hand. Like she has read my mind. Or heard my stomach from across the rink.

I take it from her. "Thank you." Suddenly, I feel a little starstruck. Ice dancing gets a bad rep because they don't do big jumps or lifts, but I like it. And it's *hard*. All that fancy footwork? They may make it look easy, but it is *not*. And Tawny Jones and her partner are unparalleled on the ice.

Tawny sits down next to me. "I figured you weren't going out there again today with all those paparazzi after you."

"No way. Not until I go home for the night." I sigh. "And maybe not even then."

She unwraps her identical sandwich. "Don't worry. It'll die down. You've just got to ride it out."

I open my panini. "You sound like you know from experience."

"Most of the skaters here have gone through what you went through this morning at some point. Some of us more than others," she says, nodding in the direction of Hunter, who is talking to his coach over in the corner. "My moment was during the last Olympics when my old partner and I did abysmally, which disappointed everyone I knew and apparently half the country. And then we broke up, both as a team and as a romantic couple. It was a PR disaster, a career disaster, *and* a personal disaster all rolled into one. Try that one on for size."

I look at her guiltily. "I remember that."

She sighs. "You and everybody else."

"It did seem really romantic, the two of you going to the Olympics together."

"Yes, well. It was, and then it wasn't. But I survived."

We munch on our sandwiches for a while in silence, Tawny pondering her past press debacle, I suppose, and me my current one.

Then I turn to her. "You not only survived it, but you came back and now you're on top. You've got a great new partner, and you two are favorites to at least medal and maybe even win gold."

She smiles wide. "That part does feel good."

"It should. I've always been a huge fan."

"Thanks, Esperanza."

"It's true. And I appreciate the advice, and you coming here to make sure I eat."

She laughs. "No problem. I'm glad we got to chat. But can I give you one last bit of unsolicited advice before I head to ballet?"

I nod.

Tawny glances in Hunter's direction again. "One of the biggest lessons I learned during the last Olympics and with my last partner was *not* to mix business with pleasure. Or business with romance."

I open my mouth. Close it again. My cheeks start to burn.

"I'm not judging you, Esperanza. There are plenty of people who will do that all over the world during the next few weeks. I'm just giving you some food for thought. Be careful. Make this Olympics about your skating and your skating *only*, not some drama with Hunter Wills. You're new to this, and when you're new, it's easy to get swept up in situations that distract you from what really matters."

I nod. "I hear you." I sigh again. "And I appreciate the advice."

"I'm here if you want to talk, and not just this weekend. We're going to be seeing a lot of each other all the way until the Closing Ceremonies. Don't hesitate to come find me. At this point, I'm a veteran of all things Olympic figure skating, including scandal."

Tawny says this with such a friendly smile that a huge wave of gratitude washes over me. I could use a friend on this team, a friend other than Hunter Wills.

And I think maybe I just made one.

★   ★   ★

"I think we should have everyone to Luciano's tomorrow evening like you wanted," I tell my mother that evening. She is in the kitchen, having some tea before bed. "If that's still an option," I add quickly.

My mother brightens at this. "I thought you weren't into the idea."

I sit down at the table next to her. "I wasn't sure about it at first. But now I am."

"What changed your mind?"

Well, I think to myself, *my afternoon included several under-the-breath remarks from Stacie and Meredith calling me a "Media Hog," which made me feel awful and want to run away, and all Hunter said to me today was, "Way to steal my spotlight, Espi." He said it with a laugh, but I wasn't sure I bought it. People think I am trying to hog the spotlight, and I want to prove that I'm not. Maybe with a party, the other skaters will see I'm generous and not at all hoglike.*

What I say is the following:

"I just think you were right and it would be a nice thing to do."

"I'm glad," she says.

I nod. Then I stare off into space while my mother finishes her tea. It's late, and I'm tired and sore, and it's been a long and not-so-easy day. "Full of right angles," as Mr. Chen would say. Then again, it's been a long and not-so-easy couple of days. It's difficult not to wonder if they will only get harder going forward until the Olympics are over. Maybe I'm not cut out for the Olympics. Maybe this is all too much for me. Maybe this whole thing was a bad idea.

Notice this big pile of self-doubt?

I realize this is what Libby would call a Shame Spiral, which she defines as a downward descent into a black hole of negativity. Shame Spirals are really bad for you. I need to stop this one before it's too late and I'm so spiral-y I can't find my way out again.

"Espi?"

"Hmm?"

"Are you okay?"

"Sure," I say. Nothing to see here. "Why?"

"You have a look of abject horror on your face."

I smile. English may be my mother's second language, but boy, can she knock it out of the park with the vocabulary sometimes. "'Abject horror,' Mamá?"

"Yes. Just like the girls in those horror movies who aren't one of the leads, and suddenly the villain is coming to get them in some awful way, like with a chain saw, and they know it's their time to go."

"Wow. That is a vivid explanation of my facial expression."

"Well, *mi amor*, it was pretty vivid. And worrisome. There isn't some bad man coming for you. You're one of the stars, *mija*. You just need to get used to it."

"I guess so. It's strange. It's different. Maybe it's not what I'm meant to do."

My mother gets up and places her empty teacup in the sink. "I don't think anyone is meant to withstand the kind of onslaught you did today," she says.

Onslaught! My mother is racking up the SAT words.

"But with figure skating," she goes on, "I can't imagine anyone more meant for this opportunity to be in the Winter Olympics in the entire world, *mija*. And I mean that."

I get up too. "I know you do, Mamá." My voice is tight. I am trying not to cry, something I've been doing a lot of lately.

"I love you, Esperanza. But I'm not just saying all these things because I love you!"

This makes me laugh. "I know that, too." I get up and give her a big hug. She's soft and round and familiar.

"Now go get some sleep. You need to be wide awake to fight through those cameras like Coach Chen showed you today. That woman can be a warrior sometimes. It's amazing to watch."

"That she can."

"Espi," my mother says when I'm about to go down the hall to bed.

I turn back. "What?"

"You can be a warrior too. You already are one. I see it in you. You're so strong and tough."

I nod. I can't get any more words out.

"Good night," she says, and I watch her disappear into her room.

CHAPTER FIFTEEN

Secret no more

Sunday morning, I wake up sneaky.

It's one day before we all leave for the Olympics. It's also the day of the team's visit to Coach Chen's rink and the going-away party at Luciano's, so I need to make the most of it.

Therefore: sneakiness necessary.

I shower and change and get together my skating gear. I'm about to grab the Wang, then I think better of it and put on my favorite old costume of Coach's instead. I finish packing my things and am out of the house at 4:30 a.m., which is crazy early, but I'm hoping to avoid the press and I want alone time on the ice. It will re-center me around the things that matter, I think.

I hope.

Blissful quiet.

That's what this morning is made of so far. My walk out of the house and through the snow to Coach Chen's was uninterrupted. The rink is dark and cold and empty, but in a way that brings me joy. The prospect of being out on the ice by myself for at least an hour and a half with only my music is a thrill. I unlock the building and flip on the lights. At the sound system, I plug in my iPod and scroll to my favorite salsa playlist. Then I take off my winter gear, trade my boots for my figure skates, and get out on the ice to warm up.

Maybe it's Tawny's influence, but for a while, all I do is dance. I salsa with the help of my toe picks, my hips moving as though separate from the rest of my body — my feet, my rib cage, my shoulders. I was born with salsa in my blood, since my mother loves to dance and she is as good as, if not better than, any of the celebrities on those competition dance shows. I swivel and sway until I'm thoroughly inspired. In the cheesiest way, it's like I've just walked out of a feel-good movie that made me believe I can do anything.

Cheesy-inspiring can be the best, in fact, when you need energy or you need to get yourself psyched up, or when some of life's doubts have been getting to you.

Like now, for example.

The song shifts to one of my favorites.

After the opening bars, right when the rhythm picks up, I decide it's time for some jumps. First a few triple axels. I pick up speed and take off for the first triple axel, landing it and holding the back outside edge with a perfect position. Then I do it again. Once. Twice. Three times.

What has gotten into me?

Is it the salsa beat?

The press-free, drama-free morning?

The non-Wang dress?

Maybe I should stop asking stupid questions and just skate. So I do.

★　　★　　★

Two hours later, just after 7:00 a.m., people start showing up.

Coach East smiles at me, her long pretty hair hidden away in a bun. Coach Danson stares at me while pretending not to. The ice dancers, including Tawny, who gives me a wave, head into the studio for their morning ballet class. The pairs are nowhere in sight. Oliver Mason is stretching on the rubbery floor at the far end of the rink.

I don't see Hunter anywhere.

We still haven't really talked since our paparazzi debacle. And the cheek kiss. He hasn't indicated whether it has any grander meaning. Which I take to mean that it doesn't.

Stacie and Meredith strut out onto the ice. They whisper and laugh and generally ignore my presence as usual. Stacie is in blue, surely to match her big eyes. Meredith wears black, which is striking with her red hair. The fact that I notice this makes me wish, once again, that somehow I could become friends with her, because then I'd be able to say things like, *Hey, Meredith, you look great in that color!* as though she were Libby or Joya.

Maybe now is my chance.

"Good morning, Esperanza," Stacie says, in this way that I can't tell if she's being genuine or fake.

"Hi, Stacie, hi, Meredith," I say.

Stacie makes a point of looking around the rink — up into the rafters, around at the bleachers, and at the other end of the ice. "So this is Lucy Chen's famous private compound?"

"Um. Yes," I answer, feeling awkward.

Her expression changes to something approaching sincerity and I wonder if she might actually say something nice. Maybe whatever comes out of her mouth next might alter the course of our relationship.

"Lucky for you she was willing to take on a charity case," she says.

I open my mouth in shock, but before anything can come out, Meredith changes the subject.

"So you got here early," she says.

"I couldn't sleep." This sounds like an honest enough explanation.

"Yeah, the Olympics will do that to you," Meredith goes on, and she actually sounds almost sympathetic. "I'm in the same boat."

Stacie looks at her, eyelashes fluttering. "Yeah, stress about losing at the US Championships can really mess with a girl." She turns on me again. "We should discuss who among the two of you is going to be the alternate for the Team event. Or more accurately, which one of you will *not*." She rolls her eyes. They are made up with eye shadow, thick liquid liner, and mascara. "It's so stupid they're doing this event this year. I don't want to use up all my mojo on some shared gold."

Who ever says *mojo* for real?

"It's not our decision who the alternate will be," I say, since this is, like, obvious. "And regardless of whether it's shared, it's another chance to medal."

"That may be, but it's a *group* win, so it's worth less than if it's just on your own," she says, ignoring the part about how she doesn't have control of who participates and who doesn't.

Meredith shrugs. "I wouldn't mind getting a gold that way."

"That's because it's probably your only shot."

Meredith's fair skin flushes all over. Even her neck gets blotchy with shame. "You don't know that."

"Yeah, I do," Stacie snaps back. "And you know it too, so stop pretending like you don't. We're both fully aware that Esperanza almost has a quad." She nods in my direction, like what she's just said is old news, a flash of triumph in her eyes.

Oh my gosh. Did Hunter tell?

When he knew beyond a shadow of a doubt that this was a huge secret?

"But —" I start, unsure whether to deny it or give in and confirm that the quad is a potential reality.

Yet Stacie rattles on like what she's said is no big deal. "Plus there's that triple lutz–triple toe loop combination Esperanza has already been nailing forever now." She turns to me, hand on her hip. She tries to smile innocently but it only makes the evil triumph in her eyes seem more wicked. "What else have you got up your sleeve, *Espi*?"

I wrap my arms around myself, suddenly freezing. I almost don't know what to respond to first: Stacie's mean comments to Meredith, her mention of the jumps in my programs, or the way she's talking to me — first like I'm not even here, and now, like she deserves a full and honest answer. "How did you even know I was trying for a quad?" I finally manage.

Stacie smirks, her pink lip gloss shining in the overhead lights. "A little birdie told me."

The only "birdie" that could blab such information is Hunter, of course. *Stupid, stupid, stupid girl!* This is why I do not need any boys in my life right now. Boys mess with your head, which then messes up everything else.

"I don't have it yet," I croak, thinking Coach is going to kill me. "Not even close. Definitely not good enough to risk it at the Games."

Stacie's eyes get wide. "So it's true you *are* trying for a quad!"

"You didn't actually know?" I ask, flustered.

"I had my suspicions," she says.

It's my turn to flush. Meredith shakes her head slightly, and I wonder for a second if she might be coming over to my side. I'd be thinking about switching alliances if Stacie treated me like she treats Meredith on a regular basis.

"And now I know for sure," Stacie goes on. "Thanks for the heads-up, Esperanza." She grabs Meredith by the elbow and tugs her away. "Let's go tell our coaches. You've got a *lot* of work to do to have any hope of medaling now. Or a lot of praying." She giggles like this is all a game. "Come *on*," she urges Meredith when she doesn't budge. Stacie is halfway across the rink before Meredith shows signs of life again.

"Don't let her bully you," I say mostly under my breath as Meredith starts to take off, but just loud enough that she might be able to hear.

She doesn't turn around, but slows a little. For a moment I think she might be about to stop and talk.

But then Meredith skates away after Stacie.

"I'm going to go for the quad sal, okay?" I say to Coach nonchalantly. It's my last run-through of the day, just before the meeting when we'll be told who is going to be the alternate for the Team Event.

Coach Chen looks at me in alarm. "What? You can't!"

I stare down at the nude-colored tights that stretch down over my boots. I can never decide if they look better than just wearing traditional tights that show my skates. Coach likes them because I don't run the risk of my laces coming undone with them, but they are a definite fashion statement too. Some people hate them. I could go either way.

"Espi? I'm waiting." Coach has her right hand on her hip. I can feel her dark eyes focused on me. She is in white again today — her favorite — her long black hair shining like silk down the back of her warm-up jacket. We're the same height and body type, but Coach manages to seem intimidating nonetheless.

"Stacie and Meredith know about the quad," I finally blurt.

Coach is shaking her head. "I'm going to have a word with that Hunter Wills. And then afterward, I am going to have some more words with you. This was supposed to be *our* secret! Our secret *weapon*!"

I nod. "I'm not even sure it was Hunter that told, though. Stacie didn't seem to know for sure — she acted like she did at first, and I assumed Hunter must have said something, but then she tricked me into confirming that whatever she'd heard was true."

"But who else could it be?"

I shrug. "I have no idea. I haven't told anyone else in skating."

"Well, it certainly wasn't Bax."

I laugh at the thought. "So I thought, since everybody knows or is going to know if they don't already, shouldn't I just go for it? I mean, won't it help me at least get some respect among the other skaters on the team?"

"By 'other skaters on the team,' you mean Stacie and Meredith," Coach says.

I shrug. "Maybe. But is that so bad?"

Coach gets a faraway look, which means she's thinking. Debating, really. "Go do it," she says after a moment. "And nail it. It will put you ahead of Meredith. And it will be good practice at making history, Espi. You'll join the ranks of the very few women who've landed quads in public."

The thought of knocking Meredith out of the running stabs me with guilt. But the possibility of making history — even just a little bit — is incredible even to contemplate.

"Okay," I say, and before I can turn all Esperanza Pollo on myself, I skate out onto the ice, skirting the edges of the rink as I take the far curve, adrenaline pumping through my body, warming me even as the chill of the ice rushes along my cheeks and my arms as I pick up speed. Out of the corner of my eye I see Stacie and Meredith chatting in the corner, their attention trained on me.

Then I block them out.

I block *everything* out.

And I go into the second curve, faster still. When I come out of it, I race down the center of the ice, every stroke sure and strong and ready.

I'm *ready.*

And I go for my quad sal like never before, realizing that there's nothing about being watched — no, being watched by *my competition* — that has to psych me out. That instead I can use the attention to drive myself to reach new heights.

Quite literally.

It's a good lesson to learn.

Because I reach the top of my jump like I'm used to defying the laws of gravity, rising higher than I ever have in my life, spinning so fast and so perfectly poised that I know — I am 100 percent *positive* — that I'm coming out of this one standing.

And I do.

I nail it and as I slow to a stop on the ice, the only person who makes a sound is Coach Chen. "Go Esperanza!" she is cheering. "I knew you could do it!"

Everyone else is silent.

Then I hear Tawny join in. "Woo-hoo, Espi!"

The sound of clapping gets thicker now. I look around and see Oliver and Jason on the bleachers, their mouths wide with surprise as they applaud. Tawny's partner and their coach cheer too. Coach East is standing next to Coach Chen and she's nodding her head as she claps, the two of them talking even as their eyes are on me.

But the best moment of all is when my eyes meet Stacie's.

She's standing there, frozen, her eyes wide and her jaw hanging open, and in her stare I see shock, but also fear. It's all over her face, really: full-on terror. She knows that if I can do that again even once at the Olympics, it's all over. I'll not only beat her out for gold, but I'll beat out Mai Ling and Irina Mitslaya too. Plus, there's that going-down-in-history thing by being the first ladies' figure skater ever to land a quad anything at the Olympics.

I smile sweetly in her direction, in that way that's also openly wicked. I can't help myself — I learned it from watching her. And, to be totally honest, it kind of feels good to give her a little dose of her own medicine.

My smile fades when my eyes land on Meredith, though.

Her cheeks shine in the light. They are wet with tears, but they're obviously not tears of joy. She and I both know, without either of us having to say a word, that by landing that quad sal, I've just beaten her out of the alternate spot for the Team Event. We don't need to wait for the meeting to follow after practice for confirmation.

"Nice job, Espi," Coach says when I come off the ice. She pulls me into a big hug. "Don't feel bad about taking that spot," she whispers. "You're here to win."

"I know," I whisper back. Then I look down at my costume, the one that Coach once wore, and can't help wondering if I'd worn the Wang today whether I would have landed on my butt instead.

Sometimes I hate being superstitious.

"Congratulations," Coach East says, a smile so genuine on her face that I find myself hugging her too, in gratitude, and before I can think better of whether or not this is appropriate. She just laughs, though.

"Thanks," I tell her.

A few minutes later, we all gather for the final Team USA meeting before we leave for the Games tomorrow — ice dancers, pairs, men and ladies too. Just before we start, Coach Danson pulls Meredith into a corner, and whatever he says to her is not good. People try to ignore the yelling that cuts into our more casual conversation — but it's difficult. After what seems like an hour, even though it probably is only a few minutes, the yelling stops and the door to the rink opens and slams shut as Coach Danson storms out. Meredith, wiping tears from her eyes, follows after him.

Everyone grows silent.

Tawny pats the space next to her and I go sit with her, grateful to have at least one ally. After all Hunter's phone calls and overtures to be a friend I can count on, he's acting like I don't exist.

Whatever, I think, even as I wince a little at this rejection.

But as the coaches confirm what we all knew without them having to say it — that it will be Stacie skating in the Team Event for the ladies and that I've won the alternate spot — I can't help but wonder: *If I'd landed on my butt today, would Hunter be sitting next to me right now?*

Maybe there's only room for one gold medalist in Hunter's heart.

And that would be him.

CHAPTER SIXTEEN

Beware the boy charmer

"*Esperanza?*"

The back door slams. My mother's home. She made it through all the press still surrounding our house, which is no easy feat.

"Mamá?" I put the party dress I spent the last ten minutes folding carefully on top of the other clothing already in my suitcase. "I'm in my room. Packing!" I'm nowhere near done, but I'm determined to finish before the going-away party this evening. I considered packing a spare costume of Coach's just in case my superstition gets the best of me, but in the end, I only pack the Wang so I can't chicken out of wearing it. One of my skating mugs, the one with IF FIGURE SKATING WAS EASY, IT WOULD BE CALLED HOCKEY, stares up at me from its place on my bureau. I've been debating about bringing it for luck, but I've already got too much stuff.

Every time I see the word *hockey*, I think of Danny.

And I wonder if he'd be more true to his word than Hunter Wills.

I hear footsteps coming down the hall. My mother pokes her head into the room. She still has her Luciano's uniform on. "I can't believe you're leaving tomorrow," she says, followed by a sniffle.

The clock has run out, and no matter how much Coach Chen and my mother have begged and pleaded and USFS has called in favors, apparently there is no rushing her visa, even when the person needing it has a daughter representing the United States in the Olympic Games.

"You're not allowed to make me cry again, Mamá."

"Oh, *mi cielo*. I don't mean to. I'm just so proud of you. And I'm going to miss you."

I turn around to face my closet, my throat too tight to talk. Maybe if I don't look at my mother for a minute, the tears will stop pushing their way into my eyes. I want to have fun tonight. It hasn't been the easiest few days. Plus, it's my last chance to see Libby and Joya and everyone else I care about.

Like Mamá, for example.

There go the tears again. I may as well give in to them.

I turn back to see her standing there, wiping her eyes. "Mamá," I say, and go to her. She puts her arms around me in a big hug and we stay like that for a while and just cry.

"Luca's making hummus. And tabbouleh," she says in the middle of all the tears.

"What?" I ask, pulling back with a laugh. The two of us go to my bed and sit down on the edge. "I didn't think Luca had ever seen a chickpea in his life."

My mother laughs too. "He wants to make sure the figure skaters have *options*, as he calls them. I think he's nervous they're not going to like Italian. He asked me whether vegetarians really would eat eggplant parm or if they'd be horrified if it was the only veggie-friendly option."

"A few of them might be," I say. "I'm sure it will all be fine."

"I'm sure it will too. He's just nervous."

I study my mother's expression. "That's sweet."

She narrows her eyes. "What are you looking at?"

"Nothing, nothing," I say innocently. "So, I have news today. It looks like I'll be the alternate for the Team Event medal. It's not that big a deal in the sense that I won't actually be skating, but it means that I'm considered number two, just behind Stacie, which is pretty important."

My mother puts her arm around my back and gives me a squeeze. "Esperanza, that's wonderful!"

"I hope so," I sigh.

She pulls back to look at me like I must be crazy. "Why wouldn't it be?"

"Because it will be me and Stacie Grant somehow having to be there for each other."

"You'll both rise to the occasion. It's the Olympics!"

"I know. You'd think that. But this morning she was talking about how she doesn't want a gold if it's a shared one. She doesn't even *want* to compete for the trophy. Then, on top of Stacie not caring, the alternate spot is something Meredith really wanted, and now I've taken her place. And I feel really bad about it."

"Espi, had someone given her the spot before?"

"No," I admit.

"Well then, you didn't take it."

My shoulders slump. "I guess."

"You should be excited!"

"I mean, I am."

"That doesn't sound excited, *mija*. But I'm going to be excited for you regardless." She gets up and goes to my suitcase. "You're bringing all of this?"

I nod. "Do you think it's too much?"

"It's the Olympics, *mi amor*. I think you should bring as much as you want."

I laugh. "I wish you'd be this laid back when we go on other trips."

"Finish up and get ready. We have a party to go to and we don't want to be late." She turns. "Cheer up, *Spiñorita*! No more tears tonight. Only celebrating."

"Okay, Mamá."

"Now put on a pretty dress."

"Yes, Mamá."

"I love you."

"Love you too," I say. Then I mark the final X on my Olympics countdown calendar before doing as I'm told.

"Esperanza!" the press is shouting when we arrive at Luciano's. "How does it feel to be dating Hunter Wills?"

I do my best not to roll my eyes, since I don't want them to get that particular photo op. You'd think they'd ask me about the Olympics and skating, but instead all they want to know is what it's like to be attached to a famous boy. I allow myself to be grateful for a moment that the press has not yet figured out how to combine our names. Esperanza and Hunter are pretty hard to mash together. Esperanter? Hunteranza? Hespi? None of these are good options.

"Esperanza! Is it true you've broken Danny Morrison's heart?"

My jaw drops a little hearing this, but I quickly recover.

"Come on, *mija*," my mother says, and we both smile as we push our way through the throng of reporters, just like Coach Chen showed us.

Luca is waiting outside the door in the cold. He's set up a velvet rope at the edge of the parking lot to keep the press away. A big banner outside the restaurant says, GO TEAM USA FIGURE SKATERS! He seems excited, from the smile on his face, but he seems nervous too, given that he's wringing his hands. His breath makes little white puffy clouds in the cold air.

"So good to see you, Espi," he says, giving me a big hug.

"Hi, Luca. Thanks for doing this. That's twice in just a few weeks. You are too good to me."

"You are like family," he says. "Come on inside so you can get away from these people."

"One second," I say, and turn back to the press. "There is one thing I'd love to comment about," I tell them, and a shocking thing happens.

They get quiet.

"I'm so honored to represent the United States at the Olympics," I go on. "I just wish someone would help my mother and me get her a visa so she could come see me skate. Without her, I wouldn't be leaving for the Games tomorrow, and the thought of her missing this breaks my heart. Thank you for listening," I finish, and turn around again, ignoring the rest of their shouts.

My mother's eyes are glistening. Luca gets between the two of us, taking one arm each, and ushers us inside. The door shuts, blissfully muffling the sounds of the reporters.

The restaurant is already full of skaters and coaches mingling and eating. Marco, Betty, Anthony, Gino, and Marcela are crowded together by the buffet table, oohing and aahing. Marcela has powdered cocoa all over her apron, which means there will be tiramisu tonight, and Gino's chef pants have a light dusting of flour, so I know there will be homemade pasta too. Likely ravioli. Marco is bounding up and down on his toes, wine glass in hand; Anthony is nodding; and Betty's cheeks are flushed. Her hair is as Proud Southern Lady style as ever, pouffed and styled to perfection.

It's not the food that has everyone impressed, however.

Hunter Wills is holding court.

Betty primps the bottom of her curls, her eyes steady on his gorgeous face. "So is it true that you and Esperanza were having a romantic moonlit night out on the pond?"

"Betty!" I protest.

Betty sees us and covers her mouth guiltily, trying to hide her laugh.

Hunter Wills turns his megawatt smile around, straight onto me, and I am nearly blinded. "Hi, Esperanza."

"Espi!" the waitstaff and the cooking staff all say more or less at once, since I've caught them red-handed trying to gossip about me. There are hugs and extra-big *forgive us* smiles exchanged before they slink away, leaving Hunter and me by the buffet table.

It's our first time alone since our paparazzi debacle, which was followed by the completely confusing cheek kiss. I don't know what to think of him now. Especially after he maybe — or maybe not — shared my secret with my archenemy, Stacie.

"Hello, stranger," I say, like we are in some stupid movie.

He laughs, but doesn't say anything.

"Still not talking to me?" I go on.

"I never stopped," Hunter says, a big grin on his face.

"Yes, you did." Nothing like being direct.

"No," he says, going for a plate and some silverware. He hands it to me before getting some for himself. "*You* are the one who stopped talking to *me.*"

"Not true."

"Absolutely true."

I ponder this. Was it me? While I consider, I pile my plate full of chicken parmesan on one half, eggplant parm on the other, not a green vegetable in sight.

Hunter stares at the Italian food mountain I've constructed. "So you're a girl athlete who actually eats real food and not only raw garden materials."

"Why wouldn't I be?" I ask, watching as he builds his own mountain with pesto raviolis on one side and steak *pizzaola* on the other. Neither one of us goes near the healthy part of the buffet. "We burn, like, gazillions of calories."

"Exactly," he says.

For a moment I think this is going well, and Hunter and I are starting to have another moment like we did last Thursday, but then he grabs a napkin and says, "I've got to go talk to Miff a second." Miff is short for Jason Mifflin. "We'll talk again in a bit, yeah?"

"Sure." I'm nodding.

But will we? Luckily, before my brain can become overly addled with boy confusion, Libby and Joya arrive. I am awash with relief and gratitude. I'm practically floating on it.

"I can't believe you're leaving," Libby says. Tonight she's wearing a blue sweater that brings out the color of her eyes.

"Me neither."

Libby twirls a blond lock around her finger while her eyes drift to Hunter and Jason talking in the corner. "I hear Vienna is nice."

"I'm kind of excited to see it," I say. "For the entire five minutes we'll be there."

That's right: The entire figure skating team has to go to Vienna for "processing." Like we're all slices of Kraft American cheese. USFS keeps what they call a "safehouse" there, as though we are in witness protection and about to testify against hardened killer mafiosos. After processing is over, we go on to the Games for the Opening Ceremonies.

"Make sure you eat some schnitzel for me," Libby says.

"I think that's like the Austrian version of chicken parm," I say. "Speaking of chicken parm." I wave my hand in front of Joya's eyes, which have been fixated on the long table of buffet food this entire time. "Hey, how's the show going?"

She tears her eyes away and sighs. "They miscast Tony, I think."

I smile. "That's great to hear."

Now she looks at me funny. "Why?"

"Because before you were worried that you were miscast for Maria, which you totally weren't, so I think it's a step in the right direction that you're worried about someone else being miscast now."

She shrugs. "I guess. It's still not a great situation."

"You'll find a way to fix it. Or at least fix him."

But Joya is distracted again by the food. She reaches for a plate and utensils and begins moving down the line. Libby and I chat while I eat. "You're not hungry?"

Libby nods. "I am. I'm just biding my time."

"For what?"

"I don't know, really. But I am."

"I'm really going to miss you guys." I look around the restaurant. In between all the skaters and their various coaches and trainers are the people in my life who actually matter. "I'm not cut out for the figure skater crowd."

"You never have been, though," Libby says. "Which is why you have us."

I smile. "I know. But it would help my chances of medalling if I understood better how to relate to the high-level figure skater species."

"How do you think I'd relate to that Jason Mifflin species?"

"Libby," I say. "Don't you think he's a little old for you?"

"I like older men."

"Since when?"

"I like all boy types."

"I suppose that's true."

"Besides, he's only *twenty-one*."

"Like I said before, way too old for you."

Joya rejoins us and we stuff our faces while Libby catches me up on the gossip from school. My mother and Luca are deep in conversation in the corner, just the two of them. Coach Chen and Mr. Chen arrive fashionably late, along with the skaters and their coaches previously unaccounted for. I crane my neck, trying to see everyone who's here. I spot Stacie and Coach East, but Meredith and Coach Danson are nowhere in sight.

As the night continues, I realize they're not coming. Even though I've basically gotten zero sign from Meredith that she and I could be friends, and even though my mother was right when she said that I didn't technically take anything away from her, I still feel pretty awful that she wasn't chosen as alternate for the Team Event competition.

Something else becomes clear as well: Hunter *is* avoiding me. Or ignoring me. Or he just wasn't that into me and our phone calls and magical night skating and the cheek kiss were all a misunderstanding on my part. No matter where I go in the restaurant, he always seems to be on the opposite side.

Then, to make matters more confusing, Hunter suddenly heads toward me. Joya and Libby see this happening and mumble something I can't understand before conspicuously heading off to the dessert table.

"I've been trying to get back to you all night," he says when he gets here. "I'm glad you're finally alone."

"I am," I say, since this is obvious.

"You were right. I did kind of stop talking to you."

My eyes get wide. I didn't know we were about to have an honesty chat. "All right. Why?"

"I'm embarrassed that I got you into this awful situation. You know, with the paparazzi and the press camping out around your house. I'm used to it, but you didn't need this right before taking off for the Olympics and having to say bye to your mother and all of these nice people who love you."

"Oh. It's okay," I say, all those hard feelings I had softening to mush, while thinking to myself, *especially when you say it that way.*

He sighs, taking in the team mingling with the waitstaff of Luciano's. "But now they're stuck dealing with the press too, when what they really want to do is spend time with you and psych you up and stuff."

He can be really sweet sometimes. He's about to open his mouth to keep going, but I stop him before he can.

"Hunter," I say. "It's really okay. And thanks for telling me the truth. But you don't have to avoid me. It's not your fault the press followed you to the pond Thursday night. They are vultures. Hyenas even."

Hunter looks at me funny, then laughs. "Like in *The Lion King*?"

"Exactly," I say, unable to hide my grin.

"Let's make a deal, Esperanza."

"What kind of deal?"

"Wednesday night after processing, you and I are going to check out Vienna together and help each other ward off the jet lag. The press shouldn't be as bad there. Or this time, we'll just be better at outrunning them."

"Okay," I say. "That sounds great."

"It's a date, then," he says, then gestures toward Libby and Joya, who are staring blatantly in our direction. "I'm going to go over to Miff so your friends feel like it's okay to come back."

My cheeks flush. I try and push away the nagging feeling in my middle that we still haven't addressed the part where he maybe betrayed my trust and announced the news about my secret weapon to Stacie.

Then Hunter leans toward me. "Don't be embarrassed," he whispers in my ear. "I'll take your friends leaving us alone as a sign that you might actually like me. Or at least think I'm cute," he adds, then gives me a big grin and walks away. "She's free now," he says to Libby and Joya as he passes by.

Their eyes get wide and they practically run toward me, but before I can relay each and every word Hunter and I exchanged, Tawny comes up to say hello and I have to do introductions.

"Tawny, this is Libby and this is Joya," I say, gesturing between everyone. "Joya and Libby, this is Tawny."

"Hi, I totally love you," Libby says, then covers her eyes with her hand, embarrassed. "I mean. Ack. You know what I mean?"

Tawny just laughs. "Thank you for the compliment. It's nice to meet you too."

The four of us chat for a while and eat some dessert. We talk about all kinds of things — the food, Betty's southern accent, growing up in Rhode Island versus living in Detroit, Michigan, which is the ice dancing capital of America, believe it or not, and where Tawny has spent the better part of the last ten years in training. Anything except for Hunter and whatever is going on between the two of us, even though that is what I am thinking about between all the other stuff.

Before the end of the evening, Tawny raises her eyebrows at me. "I see you watching Hunter, Esperanza."

"What? Me?" I ask innocently, hand to my chest.

"I'm not judging. Just remember what I told you about him."

"Of course I do," I say with a sigh. "How could I forget?"

She gives me one last *be careful* look before walking away and leaving me to ponder whether Hunter's last comments to me were him being friendly, or romantic, or a bit of both.

I decide that they are both.

Even though his behavior is confusing.

And maybe not entirely dependable.

Which is exactly the problem Tawny is warning me about.

In the car ride home later on, my mother and I don't talk. It's the last time it will be just the two of us until after the Olympics.

We can't talk, I don't think. At least I can't.

But she holds my hand tight and I squeeze hers back.

Enough said.

PART THREE
Olympic Dream

"I think what every skater dreams of is not only skating the

best program they can possibly skate, but, you know, having the

crowd roar at the end. And it was just so loud I couldn't even

hear my music."

— SARAH HUGHES,

Olympic gold medalist, Winter Games 2002

CHAPTER SEVENTEEN

Fancy meeting you here

Saying good-bye to my mother and Libby and Joya and everyone from Luciano's at Boston Logan Airport was so sad I can't really think about it without crying again, and the lady I got stuck next to by the window is sick of my hiccuping and sputtering. On the other hand, the ginormous knitting needles she's using to make a seriously ugly mustard-and-brown-colored scarf keep poking into my arms and once even my head.

Before this flight is over, one of us is going to lose an eye.

The press was there to film the whole thing, which was insane. We all wanted to ignore them even though there were cameras rolling and flashing the entire time, which was really difficult to pretend not to see.

My mother tried to be brave, especially when the press was asking her how she felt about not watching me skate at the Olympics. Betty was wearing a kerchief over her curlers in the middle of the afternoon, which for some reason made me even sadder, and the rest of the staff from Luciano's are an emotional bunch in general, so it was a big weeping-willow festival. Libby brought me double chocolate peanut butter chip cookies, which are my favorite, and Joya sent me off with her Good Luck/Break a Leg teeny tiny sparkly stud earrings that are shaped like stars.

"Trust me," Joya said, handing them to me. "If you wear these, you'll medal."

"But what about *West Side Story*? What are *you* going to wear for that?"

She jutted out a hip and planted a firm hand on it. "When I'm on Broadway, you can make sure to give them back."

I was touched. "I'll wear them every time I get out on the ice, Joya."

"You'd better. I'm going to be watching on TV, and I expect to see them sparkling on your ears."

Just remembering this makes me teary again. I check to make sure the star earrings are secure, then I sniffle and dab my eyes with a tissue while Knitting Lady harrumphs. Then I munch on more of Libby's cookies, which are permanently melty, even when you don't put them in the microwave to warm up.

I wish I was sitting next to Tawny, but she's about ten rows ahead. The entire figure skating team is spread out over three different airplanes because the US Olympic Committee holds random seats on commercial flights for us, and then just drops us into them when we qualify. Coach Chen is in first class. She got upgraded because of her super fancy million-miler status. Even though she offered to get me upgraded too, I didn't think that traveling in first class when the rest of the team is in economy was a good idea, and she agreed.

Stacie is in business class, though. All by her lonesome. Of course she and I ended up on the same flight.

Hunter is surprisingly traveling in coach. I'm not sure why, since it's not like he doesn't have the money or the status.

Meredith is here with us too, but in the way back, almost next to the bathrooms. She hasn't spoken to me since the Team Event debacle. I wish she'd shown up at the party last night, because a crowded plane is not the best environment for us to talk. Despite this, I decide to make a trip to the bathroom to see if I might catch her eye, which could at least give me an opening to say something to her. For some reason, I really believe there's hope for us as potential friends.

On the way to the back of the plane, I get a nod from Jason Mifflin and a cheerful "Good evening" from Coach East. Hunter smiles and waves me over, and I gesture that I'll see him on my return trip. In the line to use the bathroom, I practically stand next to Meredith in her seat for ten whole minutes and she doesn't even look up from her iPad. It's like I'm invisible.

I'd rather have her react in anger than keep ignoring me.

I give up hope when the little old man who was the last person ahead of me comes out of the tiny bathroom. I head inside even though I don't even have to go. I spend five minutes touching up my hair, my lip gloss, and whatever else needs fixing, before I reemerge.

On my way back to my row, out of the corner of my eye, I spot Danny Morrison in a window seat. My heart does a little dance, though this might just be the bout of turbulence shaking us around. He and I haven't seen each other since the embarrassing hockey game spotlight incident. I head down the aisle, minding my own business, looking everywhere but at Danny, who's staring so hard out the window that his face is practically pressed against it.

But then the man in the seat next to him puts his hand out and stops me.

"Esperanza Flores!" he exclaims. Half the plane hears him yell my name. "I thought that was you! Danny's told me all about his fellow Rhode Island Olympian! I'm his dad!"

If it was possible to disappear through the floor of an airplane at thirty-five thousand feet, it's clear that Danny would do just that. He gives me a nod, which I guess is his version of hello, but doesn't say anything else.

"It's nice to meet you," I say to Mr. Morrison, taking him in. Danny and his father look nothing alike. His father has black eyes when Danny has blue ones. His father's features are softer and rounder and friendlier, too — easier to read — under his wildly curling gray hair.

"It's wonderful to meet you! I'm looking forward to seeing you out on the ice at the Games."

"Oh! You have tickets to the figure skating . . ." I start, but then I see that Danny is shooting his father *would you calm down!* looks. He seems mortified by our whole interaction. So I don't finish my question. Instead I say, "That's really nice you get to go with your son to the Olympics."

Mr. Morrison grins. "Well, I'm Danny's manager. It's important that I'm here. He needs me."

"Oh," I say, surprised. His father doesn't look like the manager type.

Danny rolls his eyes. "You are not," he says to his father. Then he looks at me. "Hello, Esperanza. Nice to see you. FYI, I don't have a manager." His voice is pained.

I smile. I can't help it.

I love parents.

Meanwhile, Danny's father is grinning like a maniac. I never would have guessed that a goofy, harmless man such as Mr. Morrison could have spawned such a broody moody hockey player type.

"Regardless, consider yourself lucky your dad gets to be here," I say. "I wanted my mother to come but we . . . she's . . . um, not here." I stumble on this last bit because the sadness hits me all over again.

"Sorry to hear that," Danny says, his expression shifting from embarrassed to sincere. "She must be disappointed."

I nod. "I am too."

"Well, Esperanza," Mr. Morrison says, his expression changing to match that of his son's, "you can count on me as someone to lean on for any and all of your parental needs over the next ten days. I'll do what I can."

For the first time I see the resemblance between them. It's in the eyes, even if they're different colors. "That's sweet of you to offer," I say, touched.

"Dad!" Danny protests right about the same time. "Don't force yourself on everybody." Before I can respond, he is up and getting out of their row. "I'm going to take a walk," he says, propelling himself over his father's knees by grabbing on to the backs of the seats, brushing by me without looking me in the eye.

Mr. Morrison moves over and pats the aisle seat he's just vacated. "Why don't you join me for a few minutes, Ms. Flores?"

"Sure," I say, watching as Danny hurries away. Then I sit down and ask Mr. Morrison how he "manages" his hockey-playing son, and he, in turn, asks me all about my program and the kinds of jumps I do. Mr. Morrison, it turns out, is a big fan of skating.

It isn't long before Danny has returned from his trip around the airplane and is standing next to me in the aisle.

"Maybe you could come to one of my practices," I suggest to Mr. Morrison as I get up and move out of the way so Danny can sit. "Since you like to watch skating so much."

"I'd love that," Mr. Morrison says. "It's a plan. Why don't you work out the details with Danny? I'll give you two some privacy now," he adds, and puts on some earphones. He turns to the window and stares outside at the night sky.

Danny is still standing there, his hand on the top of the empty seat in front of his. He blinks. "You don't have to invite my father to see you skate. I'll talk to him."

"No, I want to," I say quickly. "Your dad is great."

"Sometimes he's a bit much."

"I like him," I say. "Your dad is staying with you at the hockey team's safehouse, right? So, um, maybe you can give me the safehouse info and I can drop off a few passes for your father?"

"Sure," Danny says distractedly. He keeps glancing at something behind me. When he goes to get a pen out of his knapsack, I turn to see what it is.

Who it is.

Hunter Wills is staring at us from the other side of the plane. He quickly looks away and pretends like he wasn't. If I didn't know better, I would say Danny and Hunter were being territorial. Over *me*.

Huh.

I look from Hunter back to Danny again, and, though I'm not proud to admit this, the first thing that passes through my mind is the following: *I wonder who's cuter, Hunter or Danny?* Then I remember that I was supposed to go see Hunter and say hello. Oh well.

"Here," Danny says, handing me the information.

"Thanks," I say, mind racing.

"So I guess we'll see you Wednesday after processing? When you come to drop off the passes?"

I nod, even though I feel like I'm forgetting something. "Okay."

"Why don't you come by around six p.m.?" Danny says, wiping the hair away from his eyes. "I'm sure we'll be fighting jet lag anyway."

"Sure," I agree.

"See you then," he says, a little smile appearing on his lips. "I'm going to try and get some sleep."

"Me too," I say, and start down the aisle toward my seat. There is absolutely no way sleep is in the cards now that I apparently have two maybe-dates in Vienna, with two boys, all three of us headed to the Olympics.

Which is totally surreal.

And also kind of fantastic.

I wake up a few hours later, cramped and curled in my seat, when the airline attendant is trying to give me breakfast and coffee and the pilot is explaining that we'll be landing within forty-five minutes. The knitting needle lady is snoring next to me, her mustardy-brown scarf curled in her lap like a snake.

It's Tuesday morning already.

I crane my neck around behind me and meet Hunter's eyes all the way on the other side of the plane. I wave. He raises his coffee cup in a toast, then immediately looks away.

I wonder if he's mad I never went to visit him.

Then again, he could have visited me.

It isn't long before the pilot comes over the loudspeaker to say that we are about to land.

Vienna, Austria. Soon on to the Games.

Dios mío.

My days as a US Olympian have officially begun.

CHAPTER EIGHTEEN

Fancy free

The train from the airport into Vienna is silent — except for the loud Americans like me and Coach Chen.

"Why isn't there any noise?" I whisper to Coach.

"The Austrians are very well-behaved and good at self-control. They're much like the Germans." Coach Chen rubs her eyes. "It's kind of nice after the plane."

I should be tired too, since sleeping at thirty-five thousand feet is not exactly a comfortable affair, but I'm too amped up with excitement and nerves.

We get off the train right in the center of the city.

Vienna is jaw-dropping. I mean, I've seen all kinds of beautiful in my life, especially the pond in my backyard on a pretty night or the beach on a summer's evening. But this is a whole other kind of beauty with which I've previously been unfamiliar.

First of all, it's snowing. Everywhere you look, everything's covered in white, and we are in the old part of town where there aren't many cars. People walk around, looking in shopwindows and stopping at cafés to warm up with coffee. The buildings are big and majestic and gleaming, their lights providing a soft glow in the gray day. They kind of remind me of the fancy government buildings and the Smithsonian in Washington, DC, but they're way more beautiful. Probably because they're like hundreds of years more ancient.

"We need to turn left here." Coach Chen consults the GPS on her phone and leads us down a little side street with one quaint shop selling soaps, another selling fancy sheets, and the next one all teas and jams. Then she stops abruptly and peers at the little screen again. "I think this is it."

Coach Chen and I stare up at the beautiful five-story stone townhouse where apparently we are going to be staying for the next two nights until we go on to the Games.

I blink and blink again, expecting it to disappear. "This is the safehouse? Seriously?" Our safehouse is not at all like those rinky-dinky ugly broken-down places where they hide people on FBI shows. It's more like a small, beautiful mansion. "Wow."

We ring the doorbell, and a member of the housekeeping staff ushers us inside and to our rooms. Mine has two sets of windows that open out like French doors, and big thick drapes. There are two beds in the center and a fireplace against one wall. I drop my bags to the floor. I don't know why it didn't occur to me before, but I wonder if I'll have a roommate. Maybe Tawny?

Oh no. What if it's Stacie?

I take the bed farthest from the window, so whoever else is staying in the room will have the best one. The fluffy pillows and the warm room finally start making me woozy, so I go into the bathroom to brush my teeth and change into my pajamas.

Today is a day of rest for us. Probably the last one I'll have before everything gets crazy.

I crawl into bed and look at the clock, which says 3:00 p.m. here, so it's 9:00 a.m. in Rhode Island. I call my mother, hoping to catch her before work. She picks up on the first ring.

"Mamá?"

"*¡Mija!*" She shouts into the phone so loudly I have to hold it away from my ear.

"I just wanted you to know that we got here safe and I'm in Vienna and everything is beautiful."

"Oh! I'm so glad. I miss you already."

"I miss you too, Mamá. Are you headed to work?" I ask just as I hear Betty's voice yelling "Hi, sugar pea!" in the background. "Tell Betty hi."

"I will. I love you, *mi cielo*."

"I know. Me too."

"Are you tired?"

"Exhausted. I'm going to take a nap."

"Okay, *mi amor*. Sleep well. We're all thinking of you at home and sending you gold medal thoughts."

This makes me laugh and tear up all at once. "Thanks, Mamá. Have a good morning."

"You have a good rest," she says, and we hang up.

I look around at the plush chairs and the thick rug on the old wooden floor. No one else has shown up to claim the other half of the room. Suddenly everything feels a little lonely, so I turn down the bed and get inside to get some sleep.

When I wake up later on, it's dark.

I grab for my phone.

Two a.m.!

Dios mío. I've slept for eleven hours.

On the coffee table by the couch is a covered plate and a note sitting on top from Coach Chen. "Get sleep while you can! Tomorrow is a busy day. Here are some leftovers in case you need a midnight snack."

I peek underneath the lid and see something that resembles macaroni and cheese but isn't. I don't eat anything unless I know what it is. In this darkness, everything is mostly a bunch of shadows, so I get up and turn on the light.

"Hey!" someone yells from by the window.

It's Meredith. She's sleeping in the other bed.

"Sorry," I whisper and flick the light off again.

"Whatever," she mumbles into a pillow.

Then she tosses and turns a little and doesn't say anything else.

I think to myself: *I hope she falls back asleep.*

And also: *This is not the best make-up scenario.*

Though then again: *We have nothing to make up since we were never friends in the first place.*

After a while, when I'm pretty sure Meredith is sleeping again, I sit back down by the food and break my rule of not eating what I can't really see.

It's tasty, whatever it is. There's some sort of cheese. And bacon.

Then I get back into bed and stare at the ceiling until I get sleepy again, my mind on repeat the whole time, going *Esperanza! You are at the Olympics! Stop it with the drama!,* hoping that my head and my heart get in sync with each other sometime in the near future.

Like by tomorrow.

At the US processing plant for Olympic athletes, which is what I'm calling it, Coach Chen and I are each given a giant shopping cart when we walk in the door.

"Is there food shopping involved in this experience?" I ask, looking at the athletes and coaches and trainers milling about all around us. I wonder where Meredith is. She was already gone this morning when I got up.

"Not exactly," Coach Chen says, unfazed and already maneuvering toward our first stop in the various lines.

I push my cart after her. It has a squeaky wheel and seems to want to ram into people of its own volition. This place is like a giant warehouse of Olympic madness, and I soon learn why we need shopping carts for the experience.

It's because of all the free stuff.

There's more Team USA paraphernalia here than I've ever dreamed of. They have warm-ups and jackets and pants and hats and gloves and socks and even hair ties for the girls — all of it some combination of red, white, and blue so everyone looks patriotic. We can wear whatever we want when we're just walking around Olympic Village, but for anything official, the US Olympic Committee wants us in its attire. There is Nike gear galore and Polo clothing and tons of cool shoes, all for the taking. There are Olympic mementos everywhere too, like pins and bracelets and key chains. To top this off and help us carry our swag home to the United States, we get free Nike duffel bags and backpacks and giant Polo suitcases. I pick up one of each of these and start fitting all my goodies inside as I push everything around in the shopping cart.

Coach eyes me as I reach for yet another mug. "Control yourself, Espi!"

Reluctantly, I pull my my arm back. I've already picked up two mugs to add to my collection at home. One is just a basic Team USA mug, and the other has the Olympic rings on one side and a figure skater on the other. I end up passing on the patriotic underwear too, but only because my cart is so full and so out of control with all the extra weight that I fear it could knock someone over. Plus, who wants to be maneuvering a shopping cart through large crowds of one's fellow Olympians with red, white, and blue bikini underwear sitting on top? Or underwear with the Olympic rings on the butt?

Not me, I can tell you.

There are even free tickets we can pick up for other events. I grab tickets to the first US hockey game.

Coach Chen's eyebrows go up. "Hockey? Why the sudden interest in hockey?"

"What? What do you mean? I grew up in Rhode Island. Everyone loves hockey in Rhode Island."

"Hmm," is all she responds.

On top of the free stuff there is also the stuff we need: credentials for getting into the Olympic Village, plus the ones for the Ice Palace, which is where the figure skating events are to be held, plus our official schedules. And there's lots and lots and lots of paperwork to fill out. Finally, we get in line for our costumes for both the Opening and Closing Ceremonies.

Coach gets a faraway smile as we stand in line for our turn. "I remember all of this."

"Were you nervous too?" I ask.

We move a couple of steps closer. "Yes," she says. "And excited and thrilled and scared and in awe."

When we reach the front, the woman at the booth hands me a box with my name on a paper taped to the outside. I open it up to find a white velour tracksuit with bright blue lines running down the sides of the pants and the seams of the jacket. There is a matching blue scarf and white hat with a red, white, and blue pom-pom on top. Even though the outfit is completely hideous, I still feel a thrill at the thought of walking into the Olympic Arena for the first time, wearing my official Opening Ceremonies costume with all the other US athletes, behind a giant American flag.

I actually get chills thinking about it.

Underneath this is the Closing Ceremonies outfit. It's a blue down jacket with a matching white wool turtleneck underneath, blue fleece pants, and a matching blue hat with cool red boots. This one is only half hideous, especially since I'm totally going to wear the boots again to school when I get home.

"Over here, Espi," Coach beckons, and I follow her into the dressing room area, where the tailors will adjust everything so that all we US Olympians look the same when we wear them.

Coach Chen inspects each item while I get fitted. "You'd think they would pick a more attractive material. In my year they were ugly too. We had to wear orange down parkas and matching pants, and we all looked like poufy Michelin men and women, shivering in the freezing cold. At least you'll get to be inside."

"Probably sweating. These look really warm," I say as the tailor finishes up. I change out of the Closing Ceremonies outfit, and Coach and I leave the dressing room area to get into the next set of lines. My cart gets heavier and heavier by the minute.

Our next stop is the one I'm most excited about.

Medal ceremony outfits!

That's right. *The* clothing I will wear if I medal at the Olympics. I hold my breath when we reach the front of the line and I get the box.

"Please don't faint on me, Espi," Coach says, but she is smiling. She's excited as I am.

Inside are a gorgeous blue and gray jacket, navy waterproof pants, a navy shirt, and matching shoes. Unlike the Opening and Closing Ceremonies outfits, these are sleek and stylish. We go back to the dressing room to have these fitted too.

Once I have them on, I model everything for Coach. "I can't believe that the next chance I'll get to wear this is if I medal," I say, my voice filled with awe.

"*When* you medal," she corrects.

I study Coach's face. She is tearing up. That almost never happens.

It makes me tear up too.

Soon we are both sniffling and laughing as the tailor tries valiantly to do her job.

When we're done with all the fittings, Coach and I head for our last stop before we're done for the day — my official Olympic commemorative ring. You can choose regular gold, white gold, or platinum, and with each one, there is an option to get them with diamonds, believe it or not. The design changes every Olympics, and this year it has a round face with the words OLYMPIC and TEAM along the top and bottom curves, with the Olympic torch in the middle. They look like big class rings.

I ask for mine in white gold, no diamonds. Diamonds are a little flashy for me.

After we're done putting in my order, my eyes land on Stacie and Coach East a ways off in the corner. They are too far away to say hello, which is a relief. Several of the hockey players are congregating to my right by the table with the free drink cozies, but Danny isn't among them. Most of them are much older than he is. Early to mid-twenties, maybe. I wonder if it's weird to be the youngest person by a lot on an entire team. At least in figure skating there are people close to my age.

Coach Chen is taking stock of our carts. "This is crazy. What are we going to do with all of this?"

But sheer joy shoots through me when I look at all our booty. "We're going to wear it to school after the Olympics and feel really cool. Or at least, that's my plan."

This makes Coach Chen laugh. "Let's get out of here."

Just before we are about to leave, my shopping cart somehow wills itself into the left leg of a very cute boy. Hunter Wills. His face lights up when he sees it is me who has rammed him.

"Hey, Esperanza," he says.

There must be romantic interest here if he looks happy after I've hit him with a large, metallic object on wheels. "Hi, Hunter," I say while Coach Chen pretends to be interested in a display of Team USA baseball hats. "I didn't see you at breakfast this morning."

He grins. "I didn't see you either. But here we are now."

"Yes. Um." I glance at Coach.

"And you said you'd let me walk you around Vienna."

I eye Coach again. She's studying a hat with the Olympic mascot on it — a girly bunny rabbit wearing a blue scarf. "I did," I say. I remind myself that I've also made plans to go by the hockey safehouse and meet with Mr. Morrison and possibly Danny too.

"Well, let's go, then," Hunter says.

"But we have all this stuff."

"I'll have my assistants take it all back."

"Your *assistants*?"

Hunter shrugs. "Yeah." He turns and points at three men hovering nearby. "They come with the endorsements." He laughs, but I can't decide if he's kidding. "Just you wait until you get them too."

"They look like bodyguards."

"They're a little like bodyguards. But they'll get our stuff back to the house if I ask them to, which is what I'm going to do right now," he says, and heads their way.

"Coach Chen?"

She sighs and returns the baseball hat to its table. "You can go with Hunter. But don't stay out late. We have the Olympic Games to get ready for."

"Like I could forget," I say with a nervous laugh. "Are you sure you want to let me go with him?"

She looks at me funny. "Are you looking for a way out of this?"

"No. Um. I just. No."

"If you don't want to go, just tell him you don't."

"I do want to go."

"Well, go, then. I'm saying you can. And I already heard about his minions, so don't worry about your stuff." She rolls her eyes.

"You don't like him," I state.

She shrugs. "I think Hunter Wills is one of the greatest male skaters to ever be on the US Olympic team."

"But you don't like him."

"What I think doesn't matter. You obviously *do* like him, so don't worry about anyone else. What I *don't* like is drama. You need to focus on your programs and medaling, and *not* on the rumors going around about you and some hot teen skater. Just don't cause another scandal in the press, please. And don't tell him anything else he doesn't need to know."

But I'm laughing. "You think Hunter's hot?"

"Espi! I could be his mother. I'm repeating what I read in *People* magazine." She glances behind me. "No, go have fun. Here he comes. Bye," she sings with a little wave, and takes off, leaving Hunter and me alone.

On our maybe-date in Vienna.

CHAPTER NINETEEN

Two dates are better than one

Hunter and I walk around the center of the city. It's cold and snowy and dark even though it's afternoon, but I don't care and I don't think Hunter does either. We go in and out of shops, and in one of the famous Viennese cafés, we share a Sacher torte, which is basically a really dense chocolate cake. We talk about our families and our friends and where we grew up and not once do we mention figure skating or the Olympics. We don't see any press, which means we can relax and have fun and talk without worrying. It's like I'm suddenly in a movie and this is the part where the girl and the guy get to know each other and you see flashes of them laughing and walking around some beautiful city and sharing a dessert, after which they realize they are in love.

Though, I've never been in love and I'm not now. At least not yet.

And here is the other thing: We are both on our way to the Olympics.

We need to focus on things like our routines and landing quads.

The Winter Games is priority number one.

"Hunter?" I whisper.

We've just walked inside an enormous Gothic cathedral. It's in the center of Vienna and it's the kind of church we don't have in the United States. It's gloomy and quiet but in the coolest way, and, like everything else here, jaw-droppingly beautiful.

"Espi?" he whispers back, smiling.

We sit down in one of the pews toward the back. The ceilings soar high above. There are stained glass windows two stories tall along the walls. I feel tiny and insignificant, but not in a bad way. Tourists are in groups here and there, talking about the history and the artwork, so it doesn't seem like a bad place for a conversation.

"You haven't said anything about the quad sal I nailed at practice before we left for Vienna," I say.

His face is blank. "I haven't? Well, it was great. Incredibly impressive."

"Thanks," I say, but his ambivalence has me uneasy. Shouldn't he be really happy for me? Shouldn't he be more excited and encouraging?

"So you're going to go for it at the Games?" he asks.

I shrug. "I don't know," I say honestly. "It might be too big a risk. I still haven't mastered it yet."

Hunter is looking everywhere but at me, his blue eyes an ocean of avoidance. "No?"

"Is something the matter?" I say.

"Why do you ask?"

"Because you won't look directly at me."

"It's a nice church."

"You're being evasive."

"Why would I be evasive?"

"I don't know. You tell me."

Hunter sighs. "Maybe you should just forget about the quad sal."

"I can't just forget about it. It could win me gold! Don't you *want* me to land my quad?"

"Of course," he says, running a hand through his wavy dark hair.

But he doesn't sound convincing. "Then why aren't you help-ing me anymore?"

"I gave you all the advice I have already." He finally looks me in the eye with all the arrogance I've read about in the past on the gossip blogs, before Coach Chen forbade me from going on them.

"You told Stacie, didn't you?" I say, anger growing in my voice.

"I told Stacie what?"

"You know what? Don't even answer, because I already know what you're going to say." I stand up. "You might be the Quad King, Hunter, but as a friend, you couldn't even qualify for the top ten." Tourists are starting to turn around. I shake my head and make my way out of the pew. "I need to go. I'm supposed to be somewhere else."

"Esperanza, wait!" Hunter yells after me. "Don't go! I didn't mean to upset you!"

But I'm already walking away.

★　★　★

The hockey safehouse isn't at all like the figure skating one. It's sleek and modern and boxy, on the outskirts of the old part of town. There are guys congregating out front, talking and laughing. I remember one of them from processing earlier today. All at once they look at me.

No, they *ogle* me.

And I want to yell, "Hey, cradle robbers, mind your own business!"

Inside, the house looks like what I imagine a frat house would look like, with guys lounging around everywhere. Joya and Libby would love this, especially Libby, since she adores hockey players. There are soda cans and sandwich wrappers on every surface, and the staff looks frazzled as they try to figure out which things they can throw away to maintain some semblance of order.

"Oooh, a high school girl," says a meaty guy who stops to check me out. "How can I help you?" he asks in a tone he must think is seductive.

My cheeks are red. "I'm looking for Danny Morrison. And his dad."

"Lucky him. I'll go see if they're here."

He disappears up to the second floor while I stand there awkwardly, aware that there aren't any other girls or women in the vicinity, including among the staff. After five painful minutes, I see Danny make his way down the stairs. He's wearing jeans, black boots, and a black leather jacket.

Okay, so he's really attractive.

"I thought you weren't coming," he says when he reaches the

place where I've been standing in the corner, waiting for him. Well, hiding, really.

"I'm sorry I'm late," I say. "I got caught up in something and didn't realize the time." I take out the guest passes I shoved in my bag earlier in the day. "Here are the passes I promised your dad. Where is he anyway?"

Danny takes them. "Thanks. But my father crashed already. He doesn't do well with jet lag."

"Oh." A wave of disappointment floods through me. While I was spending time with a person who doesn't necessarily have my back and brings with him a whole host of drama, I don't bother to show up for someone who actually wants to be supportive. "That's such a bummer. Maybe I'll see him when we get to the Games?"

He shrugs. "Sure. Maybe. I'll ask him."

"Please tell him I'm sorry."

One of the other hockey guys walks into the foyer. "She's cute, Morrison," he says casually before heading away again.

"Oh, to be young and in love," another one calls out from the other room, and the rest of them laugh.

Danny rolls his eyes. "Shut up, D'Amato," he shouts back. Then he looks at me. "Let's go outside."

"They're out there too."

"We'll take a walk, then."

"Okay. You're not tired?"

"No." He opens the door. "After you."

The whistles of the other hockey players follow us as we leave and don't stop until the door shuts and cuts off the sound.

Danny puts his hands in his jacket pockets. "They may be college graduates, but they act like small children."

"They're definitely different from the figure skaters."

He looks over at me as we walk. "What are figure skaters like, then?"

I try to think of how to describe so many types of people. "Well, even though technically we're all figure skaters, there are four different sports we compete in — pairs is really different than ladies' and men's, for example, which are different from ice dancing. And I think each category attracts a certain type."

"And what type are you?" he asks.

I think about Meredith and Stacie and even Jennifer Madison. "I don't know. I'm not sure I can say that I'm a typical ladies' figure skater, to be honest."

Danny and I turn the corner and head toward the old part of town. "I don't always feel like I fit the typical hockey player image either."

I laugh. "You definitely don't."

"Oh?"

I've sparked his curiosity — and potentially revealed that I've given this some thought. "Look at all those pastries in the window," I say, trying to distract him.

He doesn't take the bait. "You're not getting out of answering. So quit stalling."

I adjust my scarf tighter around me so that it comes up higher, almost to my mouth. "You know the kind of hockey player I mean," I say finally. "The big meathead arrogant guy with thick legs, a chest as wide as a truck, and an even thicker neck topped off by a crew cut. Kind of like the other guys in the safehouse."

Danny bursts out laughing. "That's quite an image. I'm relieved I don't fit it."

"Me too," I say, trying to hide the giant smile on my face.

For another hour we wander the streets, talking and getting lost, since the roads go round and round in circles that twist and turn. The cold and snow doesn't seem to dissuade the Austrians or the tourists from being out, and the evening is crowded with people headed to dinner and packed in cafés and shopping in the glitzy stores everywhere in this part of town. Vienna is full of life, and I am swept up in the excitement of being in Europe on my way to the Olympics, and getting to do all of this with a guy from home, who turns out to be really nice once I get to know him a little.

Much to my chagrin, the evening goes by fast and soon I have to get back, so we turn around.

"Are you with that Hunter Wills guy?" Danny asks when we reach the figure skating safehouse and we're about to say good night. "Romantically, I mean."

I'm standing on the first step, so I'm just about the same height as Danny. Maybe still even a little bit shorter. I shake my head. "No. I'm not."

"Interesting" is all he says, and turns to go.

"Interesting good or interesting bad or interesting neutral?" I call after him.

"Definitely not interesting neutral," he says cryptically. "See you at the Olympics, Esperanza," he adds, and then walks off into the snowy Vienna evening.

When I enter the room, my cheeks are flushed from the cold and my heart is racing. I pull off my scarf and coat and heap them onto a chair before I realize I'm not alone.

"Hi, Meredith," I say.

She's sitting on her bed, facing the window. Her shoulders are hunched over and shuddering.

I move closer. "Meredith, are you crying?"

"Why would you care if I was?"

"I care."

"Well, you shouldn't," she says with a sniffle. "It's not like I've ever been nice to you. And now this is karma, isn't it?"

"What are you talking about?"

"Me having to room with someone I've been mean to. Me not being the alternate for the Team Event. Me falling behind on everything. *I* was once America's Hope for Gold, you know. I just never came through."

"Meredith," I say. "Don't talk like that. You're going to the Olympics! You could still win," I add, even though a part of me is thinking, *Wait a minute, Esperanza! You want gold too!* But the thing is, I'm not that girl who plays mind games with the competition and does whatever it takes to win — not if it includes kicking someone when they're down. I don't want to become that girl either.

Meredith turns a little, enough that I can see her profile. "You shouldn't say things like that. You're supposed to enjoy this moment, because it's going to help you beat me."

I get a little bit closer but stop short of sitting down next to

Meredith. I'm not sure I'm really the company she wants right now.

Then she wails for me not to come any closer and starts crying again. Harder. So I have my answer.

"Do you want me to get Stacie?" I ask gently.

"Noooo," she howls. "Her seeing me like this is even worse than you."

I take a step back. "I can go. I won't tell Stacie a thing."

Meredith turns again. Even with her face blotchy from crying, she's still really pretty. All that cascading red curly hair. "You won't?"

I laugh a little. "No way. It's not like Stacie and I are besties or something."

Meredith laughs, but it comes out more like a snort from all the crying. "Definitely not."

"Can I get you something? Water? Food? Schnitzel? The famous Austrian chocolate cake?"

She laughs some more and turns around on the bed to face me. She crosses her legs and leans forward, looking at me with an openness I've never seen before. "I'm okay."

"Are you sure? I could go find whatever you want," I offer, as though she is Joya or Libby, because the thing is, I would do it for them, since that's what girlfriends do for each other, and maybe Meredith and I have a chance at something like friendship. You never know.

Meredith gives me a weak smile. "You're not so bad, Esperanza."

"I like to think that I'm not overly horrible."

Her smile gets bigger. "Maybe sometimes you are. Like when you beat me out for stuff."

"Yeah, well. Same to you," I say, then do something I'm not expecting. "Can I ask you something?" When she nods, I go on. "I've always wanted to braid your hair. It's kind of amazing."

"My hair?" She seems startled by the request. "My hair is a frizzed-out mess."

"No, it's not. Have you ever looked in the mirror? I'd die for your hair."

"It's so hard to take care of. I'd rather have your sleek long locks."

This makes me laugh. "Sleek long locks are boring."

"Sleek long locks are pretty and people who have them shouldn't complain."

"Yeah, well, people with long curly red hair shouldn't either."

She pats the bed. "Come try and braid it and you'll see exactly how difficult it is to have on your head."

"Okay," I say, and join her. She turns around so I can start. We chat about nothing much while I work on her hair, but still, we chat. About her brothers and my mother. About leaving for the Olympics tomorrow morning and what it will be like when we get there. About how weird it is that the competition for figure skating starts the day before the Opening Ceremonies this year.

I don't talk about Hunter or Danny or landing my quad.

Meredith doesn't talk about Stacie or her coach or whatever else she refrains from telling me.

And it isn't quite like when I'm with Libby and Joya, but it's definitely a start.

"Is it true that you're cracking under pressure? That the Olympics is too much for you to handle?" a reporter asks Meredith the next day at our pre-Games figure skating press conference.

My mouth widens in shock at the audacity. Meredith blinks quickly, and I wonder if she's holding back tears. If I was sitting next to her, I would nudge her or squeeze her arm in solidarity. But I'm not.

Hunter is to my right, which means I lean to my left, which unfortunately is occupied by none other than Stacie Grant. She is as perky as ever on our last morning in Vienna, her blond hair blown out and sprayed to perfection, her makeup professional and perfect, highlighting her big blue eyes.

"I'm as focused as I've always been," Meredith responds, but her voice cracks.

The press corps murmurs and I worry they're going to ask a follow-up, but they move on to a question for Tawny.

"Is there romance in the air for you and your partner this time around?"

Tawny laughs good-naturedly. "I've learned my lesson from last time, so *no*," she says authoritatively, ever so poised and articulate and somehow friendly too. "My partner and I are close, but just as friends."

"Stacie?" a woman from one of the television networks pipes up.

"Yes?" she says in her sweetest voice, the one she only reserves for press conferences like these, since I've never heard her use it outside this sort of situation.

"It's rumored that your teammate, Esperanza Flores, is going for a quad," the reporter says, then pauses as though she wants what she's just revealed to sink in with everyone around her.

I gasp.

Stacie's face pales.

Meredith's jaw drops.

It's one thing for the figure skating team to discuss what's possibly going into my program, and it's a whole other thing for the rest of the world to be gossiping about it. What if Mai Ling decides to go for one too now? What if I decide to leave it out because it's too risky? Then everyone will know I've failed. That I'm Esperanza Pollo!

The reporter gets a little triumphant smile on her face. She was obviously eager to unnerve all of us and now she has. Her eyes are still trained on Stacie. "Are you worried that she's going to beat you out for the gold because of it?"

Stacie shifts in her seat. "No," she finally answers. "Of course I'm not worried." She straightens up, shoulders back, chin up. "No ladies' figure skater has *ever* landed a quad at the Olympics, and it's simply not going to happen this year either. I'm sure my teammate Esperanza knows better than to risk a fall in front of the world during the most important moment of her skating career. Right, Espi?" she adds, turning to me, batting her eyelashes and smiling sweetly as ever.

"Um," I say, because I don't know how to respond.

But I'm saved from answering. Sort of. Stacie's acknowledgment seems to have opened the way for the reporters to fire their questions at me.

"Esperanza, is it true that one of the US senators from Rhode Island is getting your mother a visa so she can come see you skate?"

I blink, surprised. "I don't know," I say immediately, looking around for Coach Chen, who looks as shocked as I am. "Is she? I mean, that would be wonderful!" I add, excitement puffing me up like a balloon.

A lot of the reporters laugh, but one man looks at me hard. "Esperanza, is it true that you and Hunter are on the outs? Rumors are flying that you've broken up."

My eyes go wide. "Um. Um," I stutter. "We aren't —"

"No, those rumors are false," Hunter answers before I can get any more words out, putting his hand over mine on the long table where we sit. "We've made up and we're going strong," he adds, and gives me that megawatt smile from his photos in *People* and *Us Weekly*.

I am too stunned to speak right away.

"That's not —" I start once I find my tongue.

But I'm too late. The reporters are clamoring for one of the pairs to answer questions about *their* rumored romance, and soon after, the press conference comes to a close.

Coach's hands cover her face. When she finally meets my eyes across the room, she's shaking her head. The one thing she wanted me to do was to stay away from the drama, and I just got pulled back in. What's more, Hunter gets up quickly without even looking in my direction and stalks off like I don't exist. So why in the world would he say that we're together?

Then I think of something else that makes my heart sink like a stone.

Danny.

I wonder if he'll see what just happened on television.

He's going to think I lied to him about Hunter.

Dios mío, I think to myself as Coach and I drive in silence to the airport to catch our flight to the Games.

CHAPTER TWENTY

Drama queens

The Olympic Village and its arenas and hotels and residence halls for athletes are in a quaint seaside town pressed right up against the snowy mountains. From the airplane we can see the giant bubble domes the host city has built in the middle of all that quaintness, just inland from its long stretch of beach. The Ice Palace looks like a silver spaceship, and the blue-windowed Skating Arena swoops and curves. The ski slopes and jumps are farther off up the nearby mountains, and I barely catch sight of them as the plane heads in for a landing at the local airport.

Happily, Coach Chen and I seem to have a silent agreement not to discuss what happened at the press conference. In fact, we talk about everything but that as we sit in traffic for two hours before we pass through security at the entrance to Olympic Village. This time it's only the two of us, since Mr. Chen went back home to teach. He won't return until the ladies' finals event.

Once we are through the gates, the Olympic Village is a chaotic zoo. It's even colder here than it was in Vienna, with snow and ice covering the ground and frost coating the edges of the car windows. People mill about everywhere, athletes proudly wearing their country's colors and going a little crazy with their, well, enthusiasm about being here. The guys especially run around grunting and groaning and high-fiving each other like madmen.

Coach Chen looks at me hard when we get out of the car. "I know you're a little boy-crazy lately, Espi, but these *men* are off limits. Understand?"

"I'm not boy crazy!"

She waves me off. "Right, Mrs. Hunter Wills."

"But there's nothing going on!"

"Hmm" is all she responds.

Even if I am the teensiest bit boy crazy, most of the athletes are older than me anyway. I forgot I'd be spending two weeks living in close quarters with hundreds of people at least six or seven years my senior, and many of them more than a decade. A lot of the athletes here seem to be looking to party too, which is something else I'm not expecting. It makes me long for Danny and Meredith, who are at least closer to me in age.

Not Stacie, though. I don't long for her. And she's the closest in age of all.

Coach leads me up toward the athlete dormitory where I'm slotted to stay. "So you and Meredith seemed kind of chummy this morning at breakfast."

"We had a heart-to-heart last night."

"And what did your heart say?"

"That's she's not so bad."

"Great news," Coach Chen says, opening the front door so we can check in and go to my room, "since Meredith is going to be your roommate while you're here."

"She is? How come you're just telling me this now?"

"Vienna was a trial run," she says. "But you made it through without killing each other."

"Thanks for the heads-up," I say sarcastically. "Did Coach Danson arrange this with you?"

She shakes her head. "*I* did. Coach Danson hasn't been very nice to Meredith since she's dropped in the rankings. I thought she could use a friend." She looks thoughtful. "If I had to bet, I'd say it was Danson who leaked the rumors to the press about your quad sal."

I open my mouth, but words don't emerge.

"Espi, while I'm glad you're making friends with Meredith and I think she needs some good company right now, ultimately the only person you need to worry about out there on the ice is *you*. You need to focus on yourself a hundred percent. Okay?"

I nod.

"No more drama, please," she says. "Stay away from it."

I nod again.

Coach takes the keys from front desk security and we find our way to the suite where I'll be staying for the next couple of weeks. We unlock the door and pass through a kitchen and lounge area that has two bedrooms connected to it.

Coach eyes the one to the left. "At least you're not rooming with Stacie, right?" she whispers.

"Oh no," I groan.

"You'll hardly ever see her. Either she'll be in her room with her door shut or you'll be in yours." Coach keys into the bedroom on the right, which is basically a white-walled box with two beds. The furniture is the same bright blue as all of the official Olympic paraphernalia, and there are welcome baskets for each of the women staying here, plus bottles of water and snacks stocked in the fridge and the cabinets.

As in Vienna, I'm the first one to arrive. I drop all my things on the bed and suddenly feel a little light-headed. I'm really here! I'm at the Olympics!

"Settle in, but be quick," Coach says. "We have ice time in an hour and we have a lot of work to do."

Before Coach leaves me to unpack, I ask her one last question that's been on my mind. "Do you think there's really a chance my mother will get to come see me skate?"

Coach's expression softens. "I hope so, Espi. I'll look into whether it's just a rumor or if it's true."

"Thanks," I say.

When Coach is gone, the first thing I do is take out Joya's star earrings from my bag and put them by the dresser where I can see them. I smile as they sparkle in the light. I can't wait to wear them.

Then I pick up my phone and call my house.

"Hello," Mamá says sleepily. "Espi?"

"I'm at the Olympics, Mamá," I say, which wakes her up.

Even though I'm far, far away in another country halfway around the world, hearing my mother's voice makes this place feel like home. During our conversation I wait for her to mention that she's getting a visa and heading here, but she doesn't.

I decide she just doesn't want to get my hopes up.

★　★　★

The Skating Palace is enormous. It seats twelve thousand people, but it's nearly empty right now, except for the workers sweeping and cleaning and the sound techs testing out the speakers. One of the figure skating pairs is down on the ice now.

Coach Chen and I watch from the edge of the rink. A vivid image of me in my newly fitted medal outfit standing on the top podium dances in my head.

"Coach, it's possible I extended an invitation to a couple of friends for practice today," I confess.

"Espi! Who?"

"Danny Morrison and his father."

Coach Chen gets an exasperated look on her face. "Now is not the time for you to be flirting with another boy. Now is the time for you to focus on winning gold!"

My cheeks burn but I plow forward. "I'm not going to do any flirting. I was just trying to be nice. Danny's father is a skating fan, and he sort of offered to be a stand-in parent while I was here since Mamá isn't, and I figured the more support the better, right?" Coach opens her mouth, but I rush on before she can say no. "Please! I'm not going to get involved in any more boy drama."

Coach ponders this. Then she sighs. "Fine. Now get out there and warm up," she says when the ice clears.

I smile at her. "Thanks." I'm about to step onto the ice, but I turn back and give her a hug.

"What was that for?" she asks after I let her go.

"For getting me here," I say. "I can't believe I'm about to skate in the same place where I'll be competing in the Olympic Games."

Coach Chen smiles back. "I *can* believe it. Now off you go."

I speed around the edge of the rink a few times, because going fast always gets me psyched up and helps me get a feel for the ice. Then I warm up my legs and my footwork before I start in on the jumps, the easiest ones first. Single axel, double loop, double axel, then triple salchow, triple loop, triple flip, triple lutz in that order. I love how these jumps are second nature to me now. I don't even have to think going into them — my body just knows what to do from memory. I move on to a series of single jumps, simply because it's amazing to feel like I'm just hanging in the air when I don't have to worry about so many rotations. Then I gear up again for more doubles and triples so fast they blur my vision.

Even though the harder jumps require every ounce of energy I have, they leave me more revved up than before. I feel like I can do anything.

Not bad, given that this is my first practice on Olympic ice.

I pass close to Coach, her eyes intent on me. "Let's see some series and then a few spins," she says with a nod.

So I go into some jump combinations and a few mini sections from my free skate, then some of the tougher elements in my short program. Next are the spins, which give me a rush. Now that I'm feeling good and warmed up, I head around the rink a few more times before doing a big Ina Bauer through the middle of the ice. It's like a gliding backbend where your primary leg is bent and the other is stretched out behind you, and your arms reach back, back, back as far as your body will let you go, so it shows off your flexibility and grace. Some people don't like doing them because you need to be able to open up your hips, but I mastered that position long ago, and for me, they feel easy. Well, except for the part where the arch in my back is so severe it's difficult to breathe.

"Nice, Espi!" Coach calls from the edge.

I skate over. "Thanks. That felt great." I'm on cloud nine. Practice is going so well, and I'm even wearing the Wang today. I shouldn't have been superstitious about it after all. I'm excited, yet my mind is calm and focused, exactly the state a skater needs to win.

She gestures behind her. "Your friends are here."

Danny and his father are coming down the steps. The bubble I'm on threatens to pop as I suddenly worry if Danny is angry about what Hunter said at the press conference.

Now is not the time to clarify things, though.

"That was wonderful, Esperanza!" Mr. Morrison is as enthusiastic as ever. "You're so graceful! How do you bend like that? And the spins!" He turns to Danny and nudges him. "Isn't she great?"

Danny is blushing. "Um, yeah. Yes."

I smile, relieved to see that he's not giving me an evil glare. "It's nice of you to be here," I say, pushing the drama thoughts away. I need to stay focused.

"I'm Lucy Chen." Coach holds out her hand to Mr. Morrison and they shake. "Hi, Danny, nice to see you again," she adds, nodding at him and then turning back to his dad. "Espi says you are a big skating fan."

"I am." There is excitement all over his face, and his eyes

are shining. He's like a big kid. "We'll go watch over on the side so we can be out of your way." He glances up at me. "Good luck, Espi."

"Thanks, Mr. Morrison."

A smile plays at Danny's lips. "Let's see if you've gotten any faster."

"Like you could beat me," I say, and watch as Danny and his father head to the place where they'll watch.

Coach Chen turns back to me, all business again. "The speed you get on the way into your triples needs to go up if you want to consistently land the quad. You do love to go fast, Espi. Give it all you've got."

"Okay," I say, and get going around the edge of the rink until I feel like I'm flying. Then I head straight into the quad sal. I *almost* make it the four rotations, but I'm about a quarter turn short when I land on the ice again. I have more height than ever, though. I'm just not rotating fast enough.

I skate over to Coach.

"Again" is all she says.

"Sure." I take a deep breath. Glance up at the place where Danny and his father are standing. Danny is watching me intently. There's something about the way he's looking at me, maybe with a little awe, that makes me giddy inside. "Here goes nothing," I say, and take off around the rink again.

On the second jump I end up a quarter spin short once again.

But you know what they say: The third time's the charm — because on my third attempt I come out of the quad sal flawlessly.

I squeal. This quad is my best yet. Better even than the one I landed in front of the entire figure skating team before we left for the Olympics.

"Nice, Espi!" Coach Chen calls out.

Mr. Morrison is clapping wildly and Danny is smiling that half smile of his. Between landing the quad so perfectly and having Danny watch me do it, my body is humming with more nervous energy than ever. I wonder how much this gives me some added speed and height that has nothing to do with technique.

I go for the quad sal again and again. I nail it once, twice, three times. On the fourth I'm short, but my confidence is up, and on the fifth I make it like I've been nailing it my entire life.

"Enough for today," Coach calls out.

I skate over to my audience of three. Coach Chen is beaming. She pulls me into a giant hug. "Esperanza Flores, that was amazing. Beautiful! Bax is going to love this when I tell him."

I squeeze her back. "I'm kind of excited too."

"You should be," she says with all the giddiness in her voice that I've been feeling since Danny and his father showed up. Coach and I let go of each other. "If you land your quad sal like that during the Games, you're going home with a medal."

"*If* Mai Ling doesn't go for one after hearing the rumors about mine," I point out, crossing my fingers.

"We're going to think positive," Coach says, then turns to Mr. Morrison. She holds out her hand. "Maybe you and Danny are good luck."

Mr. Morrison is beaming. "Glad we could help!"

"We'll make sure you have good seats for the figure skating events that don't conflict with Danny's games," Coach offers.

"That would be wonderful," Mr. Morrison says. "We'll be there cheering really loudly."

"Speaking of Danny," Coach goes on, "I know Espi picked up some tickets to the first US hockey game. Maybe we'll both have to go." She smiles at Danny. "Show support to Team USA."

My cheeks burn.

"Sure," Danny says awkwardly. "So, I've got practice and I gotta run."

"I'll leave with you," Mr. Morrison says, putting a hand on Danny's shoulder.

Danny nods, then he turns to Coach Chen. "Bye, Ms. Chen."

"Oh, you can call me Lucy," she says. "Good luck at practice."

He looks at me. "See you later, Esperanza. You were . . . pretty great."

"Thanks. See you," I say, like it's no big deal if we do or if we don't, even though inside my heart is pounding.

And not because of all the time I've spent on the ice.

That night, I have my first opportunity to Skype with Libby and Joya. Joya talks about how *West Side Story* is going and I listen to Libby gush about her newest crush. Then my two friends grow strangely quiet on their end of the screen.

"What, guys?" I press. "What aren't you telling me?"

"Um. Well." Libby is stalling. She blinks her blue eyes guiltily.

"Oh, no," I say. "Joya, you say it, then."

"Well, how are things with you and Hunter?" she asks.

"They're not. We had kind of a falling-out in Vienna, and then Hunter made some stuff up at a press conference about us being together. Why?"

Libby's eyes grow wide. "So you two *did* get in a fight!"

"Please tell me you two haven't been reading awful gossip about me," I say with dread. "Please tell me that rumors about me and Hunter have disappeared."

"Well, um, we can't really tell you that, despite your 'please,'" Joya says.

Libby vies for more screen space. "The headline in TMZ was: 'Olympic Spat! America's Hope for Gold Gives the Quad King the Cold Shoulder.' And there was a picture of you glaring at Hunter in some kind of church."

"Oh no," I say.

Joya wants her share of the screen space now. "Oh yes. But now the headlines are all, 'Hunter and Espi, This Year's Olympic Golden Couple?'"

My cheeks flush with shame. All I can think about is Danny seeing this stuff and thinking less of me. "That's horrible, both because it's cheesy and also because it's untrue. What else have you seen?"

"Why don't you just go look for yourself?" Libby asks. "Maybe you'll feel better knowing what's out there."

"Or you'll feel worse," Joya says.

"I can't," I say. "I promised Coach Chen I wouldn't, and if I break my promise, I might jinx myself."

Joya rolls her eyes. "Superstitions aren't real."

"They are in my Dominican household."

Libby wraps one of her blond locks around her finger and lets it go. "Maybe you should stay away from Hunter Wills. Between the insane press and the fact that maybe he's still with Jennifer —"

"What?" I interrupt. I admit: My heart does a little loop and then a big dive upon hearing this.

"Um," Libby says. "I forget you're not caught up on all the gossip. There are actually two sets of rumors around Hunter, only one of which is about you."

"And the other?"

Joya looks at Libby, and when Libby doesn't keep talking, she jumps in. "There are some people who think he's back together with Jennifer."

"But he's been flirting with me every chance he gets!"

"Espi," Joya says. "You need to get focused. Your only worry is the Olympics. It's like being an actress — you can't get caught up in all the offstage drama or you'll mess up the drama that really counts, which is the one that happens *on*stage."

"I know," I say. "But I have to see Hunter all the time. He's not the easiest to avoid."

"So don't avoid him," Joya goes on. "Just don't give him another in to mess with you. Focus on something else. You'll get over it."

"There's nothing to get over," I say, even though that's not entirely true. The twisting and turning in my stomach assures me of this. "I should go," I add, because I've lost steam for gossiping.

"Are you sure you're okay, Espi?" Libby asks.

"Yeah. I am. I'll talk to you guys soon."

"We love you," Joya says.

"Love you too."

"Bye, Espi." They wave, and then the screen goes black.

I go into the kitchen to get some water and a snack. Stacie is sitting in the lounge with Meredith.

"Hi, guys," I say, straining to open the water bottle.

"Hi, Esperanza," Stacie says in that snotty tone that seems to be her only one.

"Hi, Espi," Meredith says quietly, but then Stacie shoves her foot into Meredith's leg, and Meredith turns away from me.

Stacie stares over the back of the couch, her eyes narrowed. I roll my eyes and try to ignore the smug expression on her face.

"You know, Esperanza," she says. "You may think you're all high and mighty and above the drama, and that deep down you're just a nice girl who just wants everyone to like her, but really, you're the biggest drama queen of all of us."

"I am not," I protest.

"Oh, believe me, you are. And good luck with that. Wait till the press gets hold of you. Before you know it, you'll go from America's Hope for Gold to America's Queen of Drama," she says, then gets up from the couch and flounces out of the room, dragging Meredith with her.

And I am left behind all alone.

The next day, everything starts to fall apart.

I try to chalk it up to Stacie's glaring presence in the stands.

But really, it's my fault.

I lose my ability to focus. And worse still, to land my quad sal.

"Espi!" Coach is shouting. She skates out onto the ice. "What has gotten into you? Yesterday you were on fire, and today, well . . ." she trails off.

My shoulders slump. I can't decide what to mention first. Should it be the fact that Meredith is now ignoring me, maybe to get back into Stacie's good graces? Or should it be the rumors swirling around about Hunter and me? Or should it be the reality that my mother isn't going to make it to see me compete at the Olympics, which I found out officially this morning when I asked her straight out and she started to sob?

"I'm feeling kind of overwhelmed," I say finally, my voice cracking.

Coach pulls me into a hug. "I know you're under a lot of pressure, but you've got to rise above it."

"How?" I cry.

"You can do this, Espi. I've seen you do it."

"I can't."

Coach looks at her watch. She sighs. "Our time is up for today anyway. We've got to get off the ice for whoever is next."

I sigh, then follow her to the exit. To make matters worse, Mai Ling is waiting to warm up. Her face is blank as she watches me skate toward her. It's like she doesn't even see me, like I don't exist. I step through the door and she heads straight into the center of the ice, picking up speed.

Then she goes straight for a jump.

A *quad sal.*

I gasp.

Coach's eyes practically fall out of her head. "Oh no."

Mai doesn't make it. She's a half rotation off.

But still. She almost does.

"Forget her, Espi," Coach says. "You absolutely must forget her. She'll only psych you out even more."

"But how? It's *Mai Ling*. She's even more of a favorite to win gold than Stacie!"

"You need to stop."

"What if I can't?"

"That's not an option here," Coach says, and starts up the stairs right next to the row where Stacie is sitting with a smirk on her face, her eyes on me.

"You can't handle the pressure, Espi," she hisses as I pass. "You don't belong with world-class skaters like us."

And I have to admit, I worry whether she might be right.

CHAPTER TWENTY-ONE

The thrill of victory and the nerve of defeat

The Opening Ceremonies are amazing and they are agony.

All the athletes from the United States stand around in our white velour outfits waiting to enter the arena. The noise from the show outside is muffled backstage. The thumping beat of the music starts up and stops again as the announcer takes the audience through the various acts. The energy among so many Olympians waiting to get let out of the gate is electric and there are moments when I light up with it, but then the current fizzles inside me. Today's failed practice has really gotten me down. Coach Chen is flustered and annoyed too.

Not to mention, between my time on the ice and now, the following has occurred:

Hunter has decided he wants to talk to me, but I won't talk to him.

Danny Morrison has stopped talking to me, but won't tell me why.

Meredith is also not really talking to me, even though she's my roommate.

Stacie talks to me all the time, but only to say mean things.

The worst part is this little voice inside me that won't shut up, which says that Stacie is right and I'm not on her level.

And then it keeps reminding me that Mai Ling is attempting a quad too.

I'm letting all this drama get the best of my Olympic dream.

I look around at the gazillions of Americans. Out of the corner of my eye I see Hunter talking to Jason, probably about how awesome he skated last night for the Men's Team Event Short Program. Danny is nowhere in my vicinity, though I avoid looking over at the mass of US hockey players, so maybe that's why I don't catch a glimpse of him.

Then Tawny appears next to me. "Esperanza, why so glum?"

"I'm not glum. Not exactly."

"Good, because you are about to participate in the Opening Ceremonies of your first Olympic Games! It's going to be one of the most exciting and fun nights of your life so far. Don't let anyone else ruin it for you." She puts an arm around me. "Okay?"

"Okay," I agree, but not in a very convincing way. "Though if it gets ruined, it's my own fault. I skated abysmally this afternoon."

"Come on. Forget about that for now. This is going to be so wonderful! How about you and I walk in together?"

This makes me smile. "I'd like that."

"Excellent. Especially since my partner is flirting with some skiing chick."

"Oh no! Are you upset?"

"Nope. Not a bit. I told you: no more mixing business with pleasure. It's a good rule to follow, especially since there's enough Olympic drama without adding romance to the mix."

"Tell me about it," I say.

It's almost time to start. The athletes from the Ukraine are ahead of us, dressed in bright yellow with blue stripes to match their flag, and a small group of Uzbeks are behind us in green. I'm not sure which among us drew the shortest straw as far as ridiculous costumes go, but the bright yellow pants of the Ukrainians might have our white velour beat.

Tawny adjusts her thick scarf, which we have to wear even though the Ceremonies are indoors. "Hunter really set us up last night for the Team Event. Janie and Johnny did well too. The US is off to a great start."

I sigh. "We are."

"It's a good thing, *chica*," she says. "Now all the rest of us have to do is get on the ice and ride the momentum they started."

I laugh. "You make competing in the Olympics sound so easy."

"It is. Just don't fall on your butt."

"Don't worry, I never fall," I say, then cover my mouth in horror.

"What? What happened?"

"I just jinxed myself!"

Tawny is unfazed. She fixes her ponytail. "You did not."

"I said I won't fall, and I'm superstitious." I blink back disbelief. "I should *never* say 'never.'"

"You're wrong about that, Esperanza," she says, and brushes this off like it's no big deal.

But now I'm thinking about this jinx and about the Wang, which I'll be wearing for the first time in competition — the first time I've ever *not* worn one of Coach's altered costumes.

Aside from yesterday, when I skated really well, every time I've worn the Wang things have gone either mediocre or flat-out horrible.

What if I'm doubly jinxed now?

"Let's go," Tawny says, nodding toward the organized line of Americans that's forming. She leads me over to our place.

I don't have any more time to fret and stress, because the march into the arena has begun. The wide line of athletes surges forward a little and comes to a halt. Surge. Halt. Surge. Halt. There are a lot of us and the United States is at the very back of the line because the participating countries enter in alphabetical order. The only exceptions are Greece, which always enters first, and the host country, which always enters last.

The closer we get to entering, the more the air around us crackles with excitement. It's difficult not to get swept up in it, and so I do.

"The Olympics are starting!" I whisper to Tawny.

She smiles. "Isn't this amazing?"

I nod.

Tawny takes my hand and squeezes it. "Remember this very moment, when we are about to walk in to the Opening Ceremonies. The slate is clean. Anything is possible, Espi. *Anything.* It's all ahead of us, and our only job is to take it now that we are finally here. It's our job to *make* history."

I squeeze her hand back. "This is such a dream."

"Well, get ready," she says as we near the entrance, which is tall and wide and thick with athletes. "Because the dream is about to be a reality."

We crest the hill, and suddenly we are entering the arena, heading down the long, gently winding path in a giant parade of athletes from so many different countries. All of us are the best in the world at our sport.

And somehow, I'm one of them.

I take in the scene around me. Together we are a rainbow of color from our different flags and costumes, everyone obviously swelling with pride to be here and in awe that we are. "I can't believe this!"

The crowd goes wild with cheers and the camera flashes are blinding. So much is happening at once, plus the announcer is talking over all the noise from the audience and the live music blares from the center of the field, where we are headed. A woman with long black hair, dressed in sparkly white and blue, holds a microphone on the stage.

I want to dance, I want to sing, I want to scream for joy. A lot of the athletes ahead of us are clapping and waving and blowing kisses at the fans.

"I think we need to acknowledge our public," I say to Tawny.

She nods and the two of us whistle and wave and even skip a little bit when we can. "I could do this forever," she says, grabbing my hand and lifting it high.

"Me too."

"Do you feel it, Esperanza?"

I stop waving a moment and look at Tawny. "Feel what?"

"History calling out to us! History saying, 'Come here, Tawny! Come here, Espi! I want to include you in the list of Olympic gold medalists!'"

I laugh at the possibility. "My ears aren't quite picking it up in all this craziness, but I trust you that history is making a plea."

"Good. Because it is."

I blow a kiss at the crowd, smiling bigger than I've ever smiled in my life. I imagine that my mother is watching me, that she is seeing this — seeing *me* — and I blow another kiss with her in mind.

I hope she catches it.

The thought makes my eyes sting with tears.

"*Hola*, Mamá," I say softly. "You're right here with me in my heart."

Our grand entrance finally comes to an end as the athletes are directed to create a giant ring around the center stage and sit down on the glittery floor so we can enjoy the rest of the show. Once all the Americans are seated, I look around to see who is nearby. Meredith and Stacie are like two peas in a pod all over again, squished together and giggling. Danny Morrison is about ten people away and a few people back. I have a direct line of view to him, but he's not looking at me, either because he doesn't want to or because he doesn't know I'm nearby. But I won't let the quick sad flutter of my heart take over how I feel tonight. There are too many amazing things happening all around me to let this one small disappointment ruin the moment.

As I continue to look around, I turn right into the staring eyes of Hunter on my other side, just a few feet away. Somehow, he still looks like a god in the ridiculous outfits we have on, and my heart flutters all over again. And when Hunter smiles wide at me, like he's never been happier to see me than right now at this very moment, I even smile back.

How can I not?

I'm so giddy I could fly away, like the hundreds of blue balloons floating up into the arena above us.

The Olympics have officially begun!

One of the places a person can fail most spectacularly in the entire world is at the Olympics. There are enormous crowds of people watching. Tons of press from every country across the globe. Your athletic peers, who are the best in their sport. To even land a spot in this show, you have to have reached a level of competition and a standard of performance that is not only beyond average but that reaches the stratosphere in terms of exactly how good you are. What's more, you and your family have likely sacrificed for just about the entirety of your childhood and young adulthood for the mere opportunity to show your face in competition at the Olympic Games.

Talk about pressure.

Talk about anxiety.

Talk about the possibility of astounding, tear-inducing triumph!

After all that it takes to get here, to this place that is every competitive athlete's ultimate dream, to *not* to live up to all those hopes and expectations pretty much borders on Shakespearean tragedy.

But it happens all the time during the course of Olympic competition.

It has to, right?

Only three people win, and the rest of us lose — and lose big.

I think about all of this when I wake up the next morning in my narrow little bed after the glitter and gorgeousness of the Opening Ceremonies. It runs through my mind when Meredith snubs me first thing and stalks off to Stacie's room, probably to psych her up for her participation in the Team Event today, and all through the early morning as the two girls proceed to ignore me. My brain goes over it while I'm brushing my teeth and looking in the mirror and remembering how I jinxed myself in conversation with Tawny.

Why do I have to be so superstitious?

I look at the clock and take a deep breath. Speaking of Tawny, she's going to be skating soon. The Team Event has a busy schedule today: the Ice Dance short dance, the Pairs free skate, and the Women's short program.

It's time to get to the rink to watch my fellow skaters go for gold, so I grab my stuff and head to meet Coach. She is already waiting for me outside the arena doors when I arrive.

"I wonder if Tawny is nervous," I say first thing.

"Tawny has been around for a long time. She'll do fine," Coach says as we head inside, straight through the Mixed Zone to the place where teammates can watch each other backstage. The stadium is packed, the audience cheering the Canadian ice dancers now coming off the ice.

We're just in time to see Tawny and Malcolm skate out to the center of the rink to take their opening pose. When their music starts, their grace is immediately apparent, their footwork beautiful, and their lifts just stunning. I hold my breath as the crowd oohs and aahs each new element in their program. Even if Tawny isn't nervous, I'm nervous *for* her.

But it turns out I have no reason to worry. Coach is right. Tawny and Malcolm not only do fine — they do amazingly well.

"Tawny! Malcolm!" I'm cheering as they wave to the crowd and get ready to come off the ice to the Kiss and Cry.

While Coach is still clapping, she leans toward me. "The US is still in contention for a medal. Everyone is coming through so far." Then she looks at me. "Do you feel better now that Tawny is done?"

I smile and give another cheer before answering because Tawny and Malcolm's scores are posted, and they're excellent — enough to bump the US up to third place overall. "Definitely better. Fantastic!"

"Now all Stacie and Janie and Johnny need to do is keep up the momentum, ideally the *upward* momentum."

When it's time for the pairs to do their free skate, Janie and Johnny do well enough to keep the US in a holding pattern at third, but not enough that we move up in the rankings. Between my teammates' programs, I spend time in the skaters' lounge, picking at all the food, and hang around with Tawny once she's done with her press interviews. At one point, she starts bouncing up and down on her toes and her eyes get big.

"I don't think I've ever seen you so excited," I say, laughing, following the line of her gaze to see what the fuss is about. Then I know why she's freaking out. "Is that Katarina Witt?"

Tawny can barely speak. "Mm-hm." She gathers herself before going on. "I love her. The way she skates — all that grace — she's one of the reasons why I got into ice dancing."

"Should we go say hi?" I ask, even though obviously this is what we need to do.

"I think I'm too nervous to talk to her."

"You? Nervous? Never," I say with a laugh. "Come on." I take her hand and drag her toward the small crowd around the famous East German Olympian, and we wait our turn to get her autograph.

The next time I look at my watch, I realize we're due to watch Stacie. It's already time for her short program.

"Stacie could really pull us up to silver, or even gold," Tawny says, the hope obvious in her tone.

"It's kind of weird to root for Stacie," I admit as we head back out to the place where athletes can watch their teammates again. We go stand next to Coach Chen, who nods at us briefly, then turns her attention back to the ice. "I'm used to rooting *against* her."

Tawny raises her eyebrows. "I think a lot of skaters are used to rooting against that girl, including her friends. *If* they actually show up."

I look around. There are a lot of coaches and other skaters here, including most of the Americans, but a couple of people are conspicuously missing. "Hunter isn't here," I observe, though I'm not totally surprised. But there is someone whose absence does surprise me. "Meredith isn't here either."

"Exactly," Tawny says under her breath.

Coach turns to me. "Don't worry about that now. Stacie is about to start. Pay attention."

The crowd hushes. Everyone else near the entrance to the ice quiets down to watch.

Stacie is going to nail this. I know she will. She might not be the nicest teammate in the world, but she's going to wow the judges like she always does, and raise the US to gold for the Team Event.

I would never admit this openly, but in this moment, as I look at Stacie out there at the center of the ice, all alone, waiting to begin, knowing that the entire world is watching her and that the entire US team is relying on her, a part of me is so glad — relieved, really — that it isn't me with this responsibility.

Being the alternate is kind of nice. You get to be number two, without all the pressure of being number one. It also means that you still get to be an underdog for the singles event, and have everyone rooting for you to come from behind to win.

The initial bars to Stacie's music fill the arena and she is off. But her trademark smile is missing, which is weird, and her strokes seem almost — I don't know — sluggish?

Maybe it's just me, I think. *Maybe I'm just being overly critical.*

But it isn't long before something becomes clear — something no one could have predicted on Team USA, and something very unfortunate for all of us. Though I do remember a certain conversation about the value — or *non*value — of the Team Event medal, according to a certain athlete named Stacie Grant. About how she couldn't care less about a shared medal.

Because here is the thing: Stacie looks as though she couldn't care less about her short program either. She's doing all the footwork and making all her jumps, but she's going through the motions like a robot. There isn't any glimpse of the charming skater who earned the nickname "America's Darling on the Ice." There's only the nasty, selfish girl I've come to know over the last few weeks, who stabs her friends in the back and says mean things and obviously doesn't intend to share a medal with anyone else.

At least, that is what *I* see. And it isn't just me.

"How could she do this to everyone?" I say to Coach and Tawny, my mouth dropping wide as Stacie makes her way off the ice with only a very lukewarm reception from the crowd. She's smirking and rolling her eyes like none of this matters. "It's the *Olympics*!"

"She obviously doesn't care," Tawny says in a small, disappointed voice.

Coach Chen is shaking her head. "She did every element as though she couldn't be bothered. I can't get over the level that girl will stoop to. Her coach must be mortified."

In fact, Coach East has a look on her face I've never seen before — an *angry* one. She is livid. Her arms gesticulate wildly as she talks to Stacie, but Stacie doesn't even seem to care. She barely even pays attention as the two of them sit down in the Kiss and Cry to wait for the monitor to flash confirmation of what everyone already knows: Stacie's scores will be lackluster at best.

But when they do come up, the disappointment still stings.

"She knocked us back into fifth," Tawny cries. "I can't believe this!"

Our eyes — and everyone else's for that matter — are on Stacie in the Kiss and Cry, to watch for her reaction. What makes matters even worse is that all she does is shrug. *Literally.* Stacie shrugs off her scores, a smirk on her face the whole time. When she heads off to the Mixed Zone, where the press will definitely have questions for her after that performance, we follow after her.

"I want to know what she has to say for herself," Tawny says.

It isn't long before we find out.

The press starts in right away. "Was there something on your mind tonight, Ms. Grant? Did something happen behind the scenes that's distracting you?"

Stacie rolls her eyes — she *actually rolls her eyes.* "Nope."

"Am I imagining this?" Tawny whispers. "Or is she actually acting this way on camera?"

"You are absolutely not imagining this," I whisper back. "It's real and it's live."

Another reporter's voice rises above the rest. "How do you account for tonight's . . . *unusual* performance for a skater of your caliber?"

That's a polite way of putting it, I think to myself.

Stacie leans toward the bouquet of microphones in front of her. "It doesn't matter what happened tonight. The Team Event is *not* why I'm here. Group medals are *not* what I've trained for. I don't know why they even added this event, but they did, so here I am, doing what I'm told. Trying to be supportive and all that." Then she rolls her eyes again.

Again!

"Stacie acts like it's *such* a burden to have to skate for the US," I whisper to Tawny, thinking she is done speaking.

But she isn't. "I'm definitely not upset about my performance. This was just, like, a trial run for the singles event. Wait until you see how I skate when I'm doing it just for me."

Now she's done — this is evident because she gives everyone in the room one of her trademark perky smiles and then trots off. I'm left to wonder if that shockingly awful speech might tarnish her reputation. I kind of hope it will. Is that horrible of me?

I don't have long to wait to find out, because suddenly the press and everyone else around me erupts in shock, some people shouting additional questions after Stacie, who's already long gone. Others are just talking to each other about whether or not a world-class figure skater really just had the nerve to announce her arrogant thinking about the Team Event like that in public, live, and on camera.

Tawny's cheeks are pale, her face drained of all color. "I can't believe we just witnessed that."

"I can," I say. "If I've learned anything about Stacie Grant since I've started to run into her at competitions, it's that *nice*, she is absolutely *not*."

"Well, I'll tell you something else," Tawny says as we watch the crowd around us dwindle. "She's not America's Darling anymore."

CHAPTER TWENTY-TWO

Make way for Esperanza Pollo

Early the next morning, I wake to the urgent buzzing of my phone. I don't even look to see who it is when I pick up. "Mamá?" I say drowsily.

But it's not my mother.

"Espi, I need to see you immediately," Coach says. She doesn't sound angry, though. She sounds *excited*.

"What is it?"

"I don't want to discuss this over the phone. I'm outside your door. Put on a robe and meet me here. We need to talk in private."

"Oh. Okay." I rub my eyes, then lift my head from the pillow to see that Meredith is indeed in the room now, even though she was nowhere to be found yesterday or last night when I got back. She's an unmoving lump in the bed, sleeping soundly. "I'll be there in a second."

"Hurry," she says before ending the call.

I throw on one of the Olympic sweatshirts I snagged at processing and decide my pajama pants are good enough for now. Then I shuffle out of the suite in my flip-flops, closing both doors behind me as quietly as I can. The moment I reach the hallway, Coach grabs both my arms.

"Espi, I have huge news. Scandalous but huge."

A pit opens up in my stomach. I'm almost afraid to hear whatever comes next. "Okay," I say.

"USFS is horrified by Stacie's performance yesterday — both on the ice and with the press afterward. They are mortified she acted so badly, and they've revoked her position as ladies' representative for the Team Event as a result." Coach is looking at me expectantly. "You realize what this means, don't you?"

I swallow. "Um." I'm still trying to shake the sleepiness off. My head feels like it's stuffed with cotton. "I think I'm slow this morning."

Coach smiles wide. Her eyes dance. "You're up, my dear!"

Now I almost fall over. I have to lean against the wall to stay upright. *"What?"* I gasp.

"USFS has decided to put in the alternate for the free skate today. The alternate who happens to be *you*."

My stomach is suddenly nauseous. My heart swoops and dips in fear. "So it's suddenly my turn? Just like that?"

"Well, first it's the men's free skate, then the ice dancers are up again, and *then* it will be your turn."

All I can think about is how yesterday I was secretly relieved that it was Stacie's responsibility to help carry the team and not mine. It's like I jinxed myself for having the thought. "But . . . but . . ." I can't get the words out to express everything going on inside me right now. My brain is spinning. "But I'm not ready! I'm not prepared to skate today! I thought I still had a week before I was up!"

She puts her arm around me. "This is what it means to be the alternate. You need to be ready to sub at a moment's notice. You've always known that. And yes, you *are* prepared. You've been training for this your whole life. You can do this, Espi. Now get dressed, because you have an important day ahead of you."

"Okay, sure," I say, nodding, still in a daze about this turn of events. Then, "I hope you're right," I add under my breath as I go back inside the suite, not at all sure I agree with Coach about being ready. I certainly don't *feel* ready. And whether I can do any better than Stacie is still a very open question for me. The last couple of days have not been the best in my career, but over the next several hours until the free skate starts, I need to do my best to forget that.

Dios mío.

Whatever Stacie started yesterday with her *couldn't care less* performance and her public negativity seems to have infected the entire US Figure Skating team. It moves through each one of us like a virus.

Hunter gets through his program without too many flaws — but he scowls the entire time. His scores reflect this attitude, and the US stays stuck at fifth in the rankings. Then Tawny and Malcolm — so gorgeous yesterday, so elegant — today have lost their confidence, or at least their flair, since not once, but *twice*, they skip over the more complicated lifts that are supposed to bump their GOEs above the competition.

Meanwhile, everyone, absolutely *everyone* — my fellow skaters from countries all over the world, skating fans far and wide, and even your average viewer of Olympic competition — is up in arms about Stacie Grant. Coach had it right: Stacie getting bumped from this event and USFS deciding to put in yours truly, the alternate, is scandalous indeed. I don't need to go online to find this out. I overhear people talking backstage, for one, but it's the newspapers people have left lying around the skaters' lounge that give me the gist of the conversation. The headlines are intense:

AMERICA'S DARLING GETS DUMPED BY USFS

STACIE GRANT: SHOULD SHE BE GRANTED A REPRIEVE?

MAKE WAY FOR ESPERANZA FLORES! AMERICA'S *ONLY* HOPE FOR TEAM GOLD!

Reading these ties my stomach into knots.

I don't have enough time to process this — all of it — the surprise change in the roster, the world's reaction, the way it's upset everyone on Team USA figure skating — because suddenly I'm up for my free skate.

"Stop tugging at the elastic, Espi!"

Coach Chen is shaking her head at me while a seamstress is sewing me into the Wang before I head out onto the ice. I know that sounds a little strange and maybe even torturous, but it's a normal thing that happens in the dressing rooms of major figure skating competitions everywhere. It basically involves someone sewing the edges of your dress to your tights along your hips and butt so nothing rides up while you're out on the ice in front of millions of people all over the globe. It would be really unseemly to pick a wedgie in the middle of a program, which is why we all submit to the sort of practice you'd think only fancy runway models in Paris would have to endure.

But being cute is part of our job.

Skating through a long program with half a butt cheek exposed is definitely not.

"This is really happening, isn't it?" I ask.

Coach Chen puts her hands on my shoulders. "Esperanza, you need to try to be calm."

"Okay." I can't stop fidgeting, though. The poor nice seamstress lady has to keep pulling out the thread and starting over. Knowing that I'm backstage at *the Olympics* is challenging my ability to get my head in the game. Knowing that the whole world is talking about the *scandal* of Stacie getting pulled from this event and wondering if this was fair, if it was the right call, and if I can do any better, also isn't helping much. All I can think about as I look around me is that everyone else who is here is way more experienced at this than me. "Look over there," I say to Coach, pointing through the crowd of skaters and trainers and coaches milling around the dressing room. "It's Mai Ling again."

Ever so gently, but ever so quickly, Coach Chen pushes my arm down and makes me focus on her, not Mai Ling. "I know it's chaotic in here and you are surrounded by all the competition. But you *cannot* focus on everyone else" — she comes closer, her eyes intense on mine — "or they *will* psych you out."

I nod. The seamstress sighs.

Out goes the thread and we have to start again.

After two more tries, I am finally sewn in.

"Thank you for your patience," I tell the seamstress sincerely, and I follow Coach Chen through the door that leads into the arena.

"This is really happening, it's really happening," I mutter under my breath as we push through the crowd of skaters. Many of them have headphones on, doing the very thing that I should be doing, which is trying to block out all the madness and pretend like we're not actually at the Olympics. I'm so nervous my heart is practically jumping out of my body. But the relief I feel that the quad sal isn't a part of my program today is intense. At least I have this reprieve to hold on to.

"Stop tugging at the neck of your costume," Coach Chen says. "You're going to stretch it out!"

"Maybe I shouldn't have worn this. I wish I'd brought another dress from home so I would have had options."

Coach Chen sighs. "Espi, stop worrying about what you have on and worry about your long program. Mitslaya is up next. Then it's Mai Ling, and you. Despite whatever it is that Stacie started, you guys are still in fifth, which means that *you*, Esperanza Flores, could bump up those scores and position the US for a Team Event bronze."

"But China and Russia —"

"— are not your concern at this moment. Focus on your program and block *everyone and everything else out*."

"Okay," I say, but in truth, I'm terrified. I'm all out of sorts. I'm basically 100 percent Esperanza Pollo right now — that's what those headlines *should* have said. And I hate how the ladies always go last. Everyone loves to leave the worst pressure to us, so if we fail, they can get good shots of us sobbing on camera.

That sounds bitter, doesn't it?

It might, but the thing is, it's true.

Then to make matters worse, my hand brushes my earlobe and I gasp.

"What now?" Coach wants to know, exasperated.

"I forgot to put on the good-luck star earrings Joya gave me," I cry. "I'm triply jinxed today."

Coach looks like she wants to kill me. "Forget about jinxes. Now is not the time." She points to the center of the rink.

Irina Mitslaya is already out on the ice. Rather than burrow into myself and go over all the elements in my program in my mind, I focus on her. I can't help it.

She's mesmerizing.

Graceful. Gorgeous. Nearly perfect.

The crowd adores her.

When Mitslaya finishes, it takes the sweepers a long time to clear all the stuffed animals away for Mai Ling. As Mitslaya passes by me, out of the corner of her still smiling mouth, she says, in perfect English, "Take that, Miss Quad Queen."

I take a step back as though I've been slapped.

Then I wonder whether she might be related to Stacie. They're both blond, after all.

I turn to Coach. "Did you hear Irina —"

But she gives me the death stare. "Focus, Espi. *Focus.*"

I nod. Yet I just can't.

Watching Mai Ling out there next only makes matters worse. She's absolutely flawless. The height of her jumps would make Mr. Morrison get up out of his seat. Her spins are so fast that she's a tiny blur on the ice. My one consolation is that she doesn't go for a quad anything.

This isn't enough to quell the nausea I feel, though.

I grip my middle. My face goes pale, I can tell.

Coach looks at me in alarm. "Get yourself together. You're up."

My head spins with all sorts of things that it shouldn't, number one on the list being that Stacie essentially threw our chances of Team Event gold in the toilet.

Tawny emerges from the dressing room. "Knock 'em dead, Espi," she says, giving me a quick hug. "I'll be right here rooting for you."

"Hmmm," I say distractedly, pulling at the Wang again.

"You can do this, Espi," Coach Chen says, though there is a frantic pleading in her tone.

The Olympic official opens the door to let me through, but I don't move. I don't think I can do this. I really don't. So many negative thoughts are having a party in my head just as I step onto the ice.

Focus, Espi, I think as I skate to my starting place.

This is it, Espi, I think as I take my pose.

You are competing at the Olympic Games! I think as my music starts.

It's happening now! I think as I falter and almost trip, but ultimately manage to save myself from what could have been a major bobble.

Oh no. I'm already off to a horrible start. *You're not going to do worse than Stacie*, I console myself as I round the edge on my way into a series of jumps.

But I *am* going to do worse.

Because right then, I choke.

I choke hard.

I choke like I've just tried to swallow an entire piece of chicken parm from Luciano's in one bite.

I choke in such a way that I cannot be resuscitated.

Because what happens next is that I fall spectacularly on my triple axel, and in the process take the Team Event medal hopes of the whole United States down with me, single-handedly and once and for all.

"Oooooh!" goes the crowd as I sprawl there, arms and legs spilling everywhere.

Everything else that follows occurs in slow motion. I can barely hear my music. My hand and my arm are cold, but it takes me a moment to realize it's because they are still on the ice.

"Go Esperanza! Come on, Espi!"

Tawny's voice pulls me back to myself.

I finally get my bearings, pick myself up, and finish the rest of my program. But the whole time, my brain is going, *You blew it, Esperanza! You blew it for everyone! Now there won't be a Team Event medal for anybody! You blew it at the Olympics!*

Your official Olympic debut is an all-out Disaster! Capital D!

By the time I come off the ice, I'm sobbing even as I'm trying to smile. I give a whole new level of meaning to the Kiss and Cry.

I'm embarrassed. I'm mortified. I've let *everyone* down.

The crowd claps sympathetically. I can't even wave my thanks for their support because my hands are over my eyes.

Coach Chen pulls me into her arms the minute I reach her. "Oh, Espi." She hugs me tight as I sob into her shoulder, shielding my face from the cameras that are filming all of this live. My cheeks burn from shame. To know that everyone I love and everyone from school and half the state of Rhode Island just watched me fail myself, fail the United States, and fail my fellow skaters, makes everything worse.

I'm no longer America's Hope for Gold.

I'm more like America's Failure for Everything.

I hate the Olympics.

"I can't handle all of this pressure," I say to Coach through my sniffles and hiccups. "I choked! I choked and now no one will get a medal because of me."

"Esperanza, look at me," Coach Chen says. She hands me a tissue and I wipe my nose and my face. "Sometimes we fall. It's a part of life and it's part of being a skater at this level. It happens to the best of us."

"Sometimes we fall? That's all?"

"Yes. If you remember correctly, I fell once too."

I nod. I do remember. Probably half the world does.

"And then what happened afterward?" Coach wants to know.

"You lost."

Coach Chen sighs. "Yes, I did. *That* year I did. But then what happened the next time?"

"You won an Olympic gold medal."

"Yes, I did. Because sometimes we fall." She takes my chin in her hand and looks at me intensely. "And sometimes we don't."

"Sometimes we don't?"

"Yes, Esperanza. Sometimes we don't fall, and that's when we win."

Just then, the scores come up from the judges. The crowd sighs and groans.

My scores are bad. But then, we knew they would be. The total is a full four points lower than Stacie's, which means I'm the anchor of the team, and not in a good way. I'm dragging everyone down to the bottom.

"I can't do press right now," I wail, thinking about just how badly I'm going to get swarmed by cameras and microphones the second I leave the Kiss and Cry.

"Espi," Coach Chen says, forcing me to look at her as we go to a private space backstage. "You can smile, you can cry, you can do whatever you feel. Be honest and be yourself. Just remember, the Olympics are not over for you. They're far from over. You're going to skate two more times before the Closing Ceremonies! You still have a shot at individual gold. And now you've got your fall over with."

"Maybe."

"You have. I know it."

"So you're not mad I choked?"

Coach Chen smiles. "Oh, I'm mad at you, Espi. I'm mad you let all the figure skating drama get to you instead of focusing on what you're really here for. But I have faith that you're going to turn it around. It's a setback, but it's that and nothing more."

"No?"

"You can't let it define you."

"I can't?"

It seems like I can only repeat what Coach says right now.

"No," she says forcefully. "You are not going to be remembered for this fall this Olympics, Esperanza Flores. You are going to be remembered for being the first female in history to land a quad sal at the Olympics."

"But you said I shouldn't do it. You said after my practice the other day that I wasn't ready."

"Well, I changed my mind. You're going to put it in your free skate for the ladies' singles, and you're going to nail it with the entire world watching. We have almost a week before the event starts and before you skate a fantastic comeback."

I swallow. "Okay. Okay." My voice is hoarse from the crying and the sobbing.

"We're going to have to work hard these next few days. The new plan is that we're going offsite to practice, and we're going to stay offsite until it's time for you to skate your short program. I don't want you in the middle of any more drama."

My shoulders droop even farther. "But that means . . ." I trail off, trying to blink back the new tears that want to come.

"I know it's not what you want, but it's what I think is best." I cover my face with my hands again. Coach peels my fingers away from my eyes. "Espi? What? What's so important that you're going to miss? Hunter? Because I think it might be a good idea if you didn't see that boy —"

I'm shaking my head vigorously. "It's not Hunter." I know Coach is 100 percent right, but it's still difficult to accept. "It's everything. I'm going to miss all the stuff that happens at the Olympics when you're an athlete but not competing. I'm not going to get to hang out at any of those cool pavilions they've set up for recreation, or see any other events. The hockey games, for instance. I have tickets, remember? I really wanted to go. And I want to see Tawny skate, and the ice dancers go before the ladies' finals, which means I'll miss her too."

"I see," Coach says slowly.

"Tawny's been so good to me. I want to be there to support her. And I don't want to miss Danny's big Olympic moment."

A little smile appears on Coach's face. A tiny seed of hope plants itself in me.

"All right," she says. "*Maybe* we can make an exception for Tawny and for the first hockey game."

"Really?"

"Really." Coach Chen puts her arm around me and gives me a squeeze. "But you can hang out at the pavilions *after* you win, and trust me, there will be plenty of celebrating at the Closing Ceremonies and all the parties afterward. Now, though, you're going into seclusion. Do you think you can manage this?"

I nod. My throat is too tight to speak.

"Good. Now let's go deal with the press."

When we emerge into the storm of camera flashes and the thunder of the reporters' questions, tears are running down my cheeks, and they capture it all on tape. I'm still crying because of what happened on the ice, but not only because of that. Now the tears are from Coach Chen's kindness, her willingness to forgive and to not lose faith in me, even when I worry that all is lost.

For the Americans in the Team Event, it certainly is.

Needless to say: We do not medal.

And when the entire team has its press conference with American reporters about what just happened, at first, it's excruciating. I avoid looking at everyone else, even Tawny, but especially Hunter. I don't have to worry about seeing Meredith, though, and looking her in the face after blowing my moment as the alternate who gets called upon and fails, because she is nowhere to be found. Stacie doesn't show up either.

"What do you think happened?" asks a TV reporter. "The United States was a contender for Team Event gold, and now you are walking away without a single medal." The reporter looks directly at me. "Do you blame Stacie Grant?"

My heart is pounding. Despite the fact that I *do* blame Stacie — at least partially — for how we all imploded today, it's not entirely her fault. I pull one of the microphones toward me. "It's no one person's fault," I begin, trying to be generous to Stacie as I can manage. "We all had a difficult day today, me especially. It's my first time at the Olympics, and I admit I had a really hard time getting my head around going in as a sub. I can't say that I did my best. This was probably one of my worst performances in an international competition." I pause a moment and turn to look at my teammates, who are sitting on either side of me at the press table. "And I want to say I'm sorry for that, to everyone who was depending on me to come through."

After I finish, no one speaks. Not at first.

Then Tawny grabs the mike. "Esperanza is right that it's no *one* person's responsibility — but there isn't any need for apologies. The Team Event was an incredible opportunity. We didn't finish in one of the top three spots — this is true, but it is *also* true that the Olympics are far from over. What's most important for everyone to remember right now is that, while the US figure skaters didn't medal today, there are United States skiers who did, and the bobsled team, and the women's speed skaters. *We* didn't shine for this event, but there are *plenty* of athletes who did shine. I am going to let those medalists inspire me as we move forward from here."

Wow.

Tawny is amazing.

She should be America's Darling *and* America's Hope for Gold, all rolled into one.

I reach over and squeeze Tawny's shoulder. She looks at me and I mouth, *You are awesome.*

She smiles. *You too,* she mouths back.

I shake my head no. Because I'm not.

Not tonight, at least.

Then a reporter asks, "Esperanza, do you still feel like you've let America down?"

"Yes," I say. "I know I have. And regardless of Tawny's generosity, I know I've let my team down too." Before anyone can ask me another question, I try to muster the positive attitudes of both Coach and Tawny, and add with a smile, "But I'm still hope-ful. The Olympics aren't over yet."

Meredith isn't in the room that night, so I take advantage of the privacy to curl up in bed and call my mother. I don't need to put on a brave face for her.

"Mamá, I'm so sad and so tired and so, so overwhelmed," I say when she picks up.

"Oh, Espi."

"I need you. Really, really."

"I know, *mija*. I know," she says. "I'm doing my best. We're making progress with my visa, you know."

I start to cry. "I want you to hug me right now and make it all better."

"Oh, Esperanza, I wish I could. I love you so much."

"I can't do this without you," I tell her.

"Yes you can, *mi cielo*. You are stronger than you know."

I hiccup into the phone. "I don't want to be, though."

"But you are. It's early. There's a long way to go before the Olympics are over."

"That's what Coach Chen said."

I can hear my mother breathing. She's trying not to cry. "Your coach is a smart lady. You listen to her and you lean on her too."

"I know. But I want my mamá here."

My mother's sigh is long and sad. "She wishes she was there. So does everyone else from the restaurant. They all say hi. Betty and Luca send hugs and kisses."

After a while, when I've gotten my breath a little and the tears have slowed, I bring up one last thing. "I think the Wang is jinxed."

This makes my mother laugh. "It's beautiful, *mi amor*. Of course it's not jinxed."

"I'm serious. I should have brought one of Coach's dresses, but like an idiot, I didn't."

There is a long silence. "If it's that important to you, I could mail you one," she says finally.

"It won't make it in time. And if you sent it express, it would cost more than if you brought it yourself on an airplane."

There is another silence. Even longer this time. "You're probably right, *mija*."

I sigh. "I should go."

"I love you, Esperanza."

"Me too, Mamá. Good night."

She hangs up on the other end, and I pull the covers tight around me, all the way up to my chin. I try to focus on the positive attitudes shown by Coach and my mother and the one I did my best to give to the press tonight, despite all that has happened so far.

But it's not easy.

CHAPTER TWENTY-THREE

Retreat, regroup, return

When I wake up the next morning, Meredith is sitting up in bed, reading. I have no idea when she got in last night.

"Hi, Meredith," I say.

Meredith responds with . . . total silence.

I'm sure she thinks she could have done better as alternate for the Team Event.

She's probably right.

Just about anybody could have done better than I did. And Stacie too, for that matter.

"I know you're not talking to me," I say. "And you have a right to be mad that you weren't included in the Team Event. If you had skated instead of me, maybe the US would have won a medal because I wouldn't have messed everything up. For whatever it's worth, I'm sorry it was me and not you. It deserved to be you."

I hear an intake of breath. For a second I think she might say something back. It seems like maybe I've gotten to her.

But then all she does is roll away onto her side and not say a word.

After Coach picks me up to take me offsite for training, I watch from the car windows as the Olympic Village recedes into the background, taking all the chaos and excitement with it. As we drive, I am still mourning how the rigorous schedule at the Games has so far prevented me from even entering one of the big pavilions set up for the competitors to enjoy in our free time, like USA House for all the United States athletes, and the gigantic one put on by the big Olympic business sponsors.

Tawny says it's amazing. You can go there to do your laundry or have people do it for you. They will dry-clean your skating costume. Or your ski pants. Or your speed skater outfit. Whatever you have to wear for Olympic competition. There are flat screen TVs everywhere, apparently watched by a lot of husbands of women athletes, who go there to veg out. There are video games and a huge gourmet dining hall. There is even a spa! You can have your hair and makeup done and get manicures and pedicures so you look your Olympic best.

As the car starts to wind its way through the mountains, everything to do with the Winter Games disappears from view, taking my hopes of a makeover and some free gourmet smoothies with it. But after the two-hour route to the rink where Coach has reserved us practice time, I realize that she is right. Getting away from the madness and the drama is not a bad idea.

I already feel different. Less wound up.

The ice is fresh, and as I warm up, I forget the cold and everything else that has happened so far. The old Esperanza Flores starts to return — the one who doesn't get shaken by her opponents and who isn't worried about boys and who is simply this girl who loves figure skating more than anything else in her life.

I work on some spins and then move on to my jumps.

"Nice, Espi! Nice!" Coach calls out as I nail triple axel after triple axel.

I skate through all the elements of my short program and my free skate flawlessly. Then I do them again. And again. And again. The only thing I don't go for is the quad sal. I decide that it's important to get my confidence back before I attempt another one.

It won't be long now, though.

"I feel so drama-free," I say to Coach after skating over to edge of the rink, where she is beaming at me too.

"You look it too." She studies my face. "Do you really want to go all the way back to Olympic Village for a hockey game?"

I nod.

"All right. Into the car we go."

The hockey arena is packed to bursting by the time we arrive. I don't talk to Danny before or afterward, but I watch him play and he's amazing. He even scores.

Coach Chen and I sit with Mr. Morrison, who either doesn't know his son is avoiding me or doesn't care. He chats with us happily about the rules of the game and why some violence is okay while other violence will get you sent to the penalty box.

"Sure, I'd love come to another practice," Mr. Morrison tells Coach Chen after she invites him. "I'd be honored! Maybe Danny will come too, if he can get away!"

My cheeks burn. "Um, I'm not sure he'd want to." I think back to the Opening Ceremonies, and how I haven't heard anything from him in a long time. "It's possible he's not talking to me."

Mr. Morrison's eyebrows go up. His eyes are so open and vulnerable. "Oh, I doubt that. And why wouldn't he want to go to a practice? You're amazing to watch!"

"He is too," I say quietly, not thinking.

"Oh, I'll definitely tell him you said that! I bet he'll be happy to hear it."

Surely, my skin is on fire. "You don't need to. Really you don't."

"But I will!"

Coach Chen is trying not to laugh. I glare at her and mouth, *Not funny,* which only makes her laugh harder.

The United States wins 3–1, and I hurry Coach Chen away so we don't have to see Danny, even though Mr. Morrison wants us to wait with him outside the locker room.

It's back to seclusion for me. Coach has rented us rooms in a hotel and she won't let me communicate with the outside world, even with Libby or Joya. She's afraid they might ply me with press rumors again, which always seems to throw me off. The only exception to the rule is my mother. I get to talk to her.

"I'm rooting for you, *mija!*" she keeps telling me.

I hear her. I do. But I can't get it out of my mind that she's rooting for me way far away in Rhode Island when what I really want is for her to be rooting for me right here.

"Thanks, Mamá," I say back. "I love you. Things are getting better. Little by little, but they are."

I tell her this because it's true.

☆   ☆   ☆

Over the next few days at practice, I do my usual dance training and conditioning. I get my mental state in order. And I nail my quad sal time after time.

"Woo-hoo," Coach actually cheers at one point. Something I've never heard her do before.

She sounds giddy.

Mr. Morrison comes out to one of our practices, but without Danny. "He has a game tonight," he explains apologetically. "That's the downside of winning everything. You never get time off."

"That's good that they're winning," I say.

During a break, Mr. Morrison says something that catches me off guard. "Danny thinks you're pretty special."

My eyes go wide. "He does?"

Mr. Morrison nods, then he takes a bite of his sandwich. "I did some digging and I think he might be jealous of whatever is going on with you and that Hunter Wills fellow."

"There's nothing going on, though," I confess.

"Are you sure? The press —"

"— loves to invent romances where there aren't any."

He swallows another bite. "But you and Danny obviously have something romantic between you two, so they were right about that the first time around."

Do we? Do we "obviously"?

"Well, they aren't right about Hunter and me."

"Interesting. Good. You should tell Danny that."

"Maybe I will if he gives me a chance." Would I, though? Or would I just chicken out?

"He will. He's just getting up the nerve, I suppose. My son can be shy."

I nod. "Thanks, Mr. Morrison."

"Anytime, Esperanza," he says with a smile. "America's Hope for Gold!"

After a few more minutes, Mr. Morrison leaves, and Coach Chen does the two-finger point from her eyes to mine and back and forth again. "Espi, you need to focus. You are doing amazing. You are nailing your quad sal like you've been doing it since you were in baby-sized figure skates. If you keep this up, you are going to take home the gold."

My heart flutters in a way that has nothing to do with boys or drama. It's purely about the possibility of being at the top of that podium, watching as they lower the American flag above my head. "You really think it's possible?"

"I do," she says. "You just need to not freak out when we're back on official *Olympic* ice."

"Right."

"Seriously, Espi."

"I wish I hadn't been so stupid and only brought the Wang."

She rolls her eyes. "This is *not* about the Wang."

But it is. At least a little.

"Wang or no Wang, you can take the gold, Espi," Coach goes on. "Have a little faith."

"Sure. Of course," I say. "No big deal."

The trick, obviously, will be to do everything I've been doing out here in seclusion in front of an Olympic-sized crowd at the center of the drama that seems to follow me and everyone else who skates everywhere.

Easy as cake.

Right.

"Hurry up, hurry up!"

I am bouncing one leg and then the other, fidgety and anxious. The security to get back into the Olympic Village causes a three-hour traffic jam.

"Esperanza, we're not in a tank," Coach Chen says. Her black hair is sleek down her back because she keeps taking it down from the bun she usually wears and then putting it up again while we wait. We're in a pre-bun phase at the moment. "We can't roll over the cars in front of us, so we need to try and be patient."

"But if we're not back soon, I'm going to miss seeing Tawny skate!"

Coach looks at the clock on the dashboard. "We have time."

My knee is bobbing like the needle on a sewing machine. "Do we?"

She doesn't answer, so I shut up. While we continue to wait I call my mother again and again, but she's not picking up. "Where is Mamá when I need her?"

"She's probably at work," Coach says.

"But she always answers! I'm her daughter. I'm at the Olympics!"

Coach smiles as we pull forward a whole ten yards and stop again. "Maybe she's doing something where she can't pick up."

Panic runs through me. "What if something bad happened to her?"

Coach reaches over and stops my knee from its frenzy. "Esperanza, your mother is fine."

"But how do you know?"

"I just do. Be calm. You're too nervous." She looks at the clock again. "And we're definitely going to make it for the ice dancing."

Coach is right, but just barely. After what seems like forever, we are through security and running across the Olympic Village toward the figure skating arena. We get through security there much more quickly because of our badges, but they still won't let us anywhere near Tawny before she gets on the ice. Security is super strict about who gets backstage. No one other than the coaches and skaters on deck can get anywhere near the Kiss and Cry.

Coach and I practically fly to the place in the stands reserved for skaters who want to watch their teammates. When we reach our seats, Tawny and her partner are about to go out on the ice.

"Go Tawny!" I scream at the top of my lungs, and clap like a maniac.

"You really like her," Coach Chen states as they take their pose.

My eyes are glued to Tawny and Malcolm. They make a beautiful couple, even if Tawny isn't interested in him romantically. "She's been so nice to me. And she's so poised and smart. If anyone deserves gold, it's Tawny."

"You deserve it too."

"Not like her. She's been through a lot. Tragic loss. Tragic scandal. This is her chance at a comeback!"

Their music starts and I almost can't watch. I alternate between covering my eyes and peeking through my fingers.

Coach Chen reaches over and gently pulls my hands away. "She's doing great, Espi. They are both doing great."

I swallow. My stomach has so many butterflies for her, there's practically a butterfly convention in there.

"Look at that footwork," Coach Chen says with appreciation, before she realizes I'm not actually looking so I can't see what she's admiring. "Esperanza, watch!"

I take a deep breath, return my attention to the ice, and force it to stay there. Within thirty seconds they finish, their final pose beautiful and romantic — two figure skaters wrapped in an embrace, their arms and legs making gorgeous lines.

Coach Chen and I jump up, screaming and clapping. "Woo-hoo," I yell. "Do you think they did it?"

"It's going to be close, but they certainly have a shot. The judges loved that Russian pair that went before them, from the looks of their scores. You never know, though."

"Tawny!" I shout as she skates toward the Kiss and Cry. "Tawny!"

She looks up and all around to see who is screaming her name. When our eyes meet, she smiles and waves.

I wave back like a crazy stalker fan, which makes her laugh. At least she's happy. "She seems confident."

"Tawny's a professional," Coach Chen says. "She has lots of experience. She's going to hold it together for the Kiss and Cry and for the press afterward, no matter what."

"That's no easy thing."

"No, it's not."

The two of us quiet down to wait for their scores. They flash up onto the board.

"She did it!" I scream, and even Coach is caught up in the moment. "They won the gold!" We jump up and down, and when Tawny turns our way to wave before heading off to talk to the press, I shout, "Tawny! Tawny!"

So maybe I am a crazy stalker fan. There are worse things.

I can't stop beaming. I'm so happy for her.

Coach Chen walks me back to the residence hall shortly afterward. Snow falls gently through the darkness, and the world seems beautiful and perfect.

"Bax will be here tomorrow to see you skate," Coach Chen says.

I nod. "I can't wait to see him. It's weird to go so long without hanging out with him."

She laughs. "Tell me about it. He's excited to see you too. He wants to watch you win gold."

"At least someone won gold for US figure skating tonight," I say.

"Well, let's win another."

"Okay," I say, smiling. I can't stop thinking about Tawny and her amazing comeback. "Let's," I add, and then we hug and say good night.

Danny Morrison is standing outside my residence hall in the snow. He has a Team USA winter hat on his head, but he's in his usual jeans and black leather jacket, even though it's freezing out.

"Hi," I say. "This is a surprise."

He looks around nervously, avoiding my eyes. "Is it?"

I decide to get right to the point. "You haven't spoken to me in, like, a week."

"I know. I'm sorry."

"Really?"

He nods. "I'm not good at this."

My eyebrows go up. "Good at what?"

"This being in the public eye thing."

I laugh a little. "Me neither. Is anybody?"

Danny stares at me full on. "Hunter Wills seems all right at it."

"Oh, him. Maybe."

"Are you with this Wills guy or not?"

"No," I answer quickly. Maybe too quickly. "I promise I'm not."

"But you were with him in Vienna, right? You were supposed to come see my dad and me, but you went to see him instead. Some of the guys on the team showed me all the gossip about you, which is how I found out. I normally stay away from that stuff."

I let myself focus on the snowflakes falling through the sky, hoping that Danny won't see the guilt on my face. "Yes," I admit. "We weren't *with* each other, though. Not in the way you're thinking — or that the press is always implying. Hunter and I have never been together like that."

"No?"

I shake my head. "I don't really trust him."

"Interesting," he says.

"So you guys are still in it for the gold," I say, shifting the topic.

"Yup. Two more games and we could win it all."

"That would be amazing."

"You've still got the possibility of gold ahead of you too," Danny says. "No matter what happened in that other event."

I shrug. "A girl can hope. I'm glad I at least get a second chance."

Danny takes a step closer. Looks at me hard with those expressive blue eyes. "You're going to do great tomorrow, Espi."

"That's the plan," I say, suddenly shy. But I don't take a step back. "I hope it works out."

"It will."

"You sound so sure."

He takes another step closer. "That's because I am. And I'll be there to see it all happen."

"You will?"

He nods. "I wouldn't miss it. My game will be over before you skate."

"I'm going for the quad sal."

Danny's eyes get wide. "You should. It's an amazing trick you've got up your sleeve."

I smile at him. I can't help it. "I'm glad you'll be there. Whether I land it or not." The snow is falling harder now. "I should get some sleep," I say reluctantly. "Tomorrow is a big day. For both of us."

Danny hesitates. "There's something else I wanted say before good night."

"Oh?" I study his face. Snowflakes glide toward the earth between us. "What's that?"

Slowly, and ever so gently, Danny leans toward me and kisses me on the lips. His hair falls forward and brushes against my cheek. It's soft and cold in the icy air. Then he pulls away.

I'm giddy with surprise. My cheeks flush. "I thought it was something you wanted to say."

"A kiss says something, doesn't it?" His eyes are big and intense and all for me. "Probably more than words would."

"Probably you're right," I say. Then very quickly and before I can lose my nerve, I lean forward and kiss Danny back. "Good night, hockey phenom," I say. "See you tomorrow at the rink."

"Definitely, Spiñorita," he says with a big grin on his face.

Then I go inside.

I think my smile just might be permanent.

CHAPTER TWENTY-FOUR

Surprise, surprise, surprise

I open my eyes to find Meredith staring at me. She's watching me from her bed, her head still on the pillow, her red curls bright and sprawling against the white sheets.

"Good morning, Espi."

I blink. Then I sit up. "You're talking to me now?"

She sighs. "I have to talk to someone."

"About what?"

"Just in general, I guess. I'm feeling kind of lonely."

"Oh. What about Stacie? Why don't you talk to her?"

"Stacie's got other friends she likes better. Go take a look in the lounge."

Now I'm curious. I get up and throw on a sweatshirt over my tank top, put my hair in a ponytail, and peek my head outside the room.

I'm definitely unprepared for what I see.

Jennifer Madison and Stacie are sitting on the couch whispering to each other and giggling. Stacie is still in her pajamas. The left leg of Jennifer's jeans has a knee brace over it. They stop talking and turn my way.

"Well, look who's joined us!" Stacie says.

"It's America's Hope for Gold!" Jennifer's tone is so sarcastic that if she and Stacie had a mean girl contest, I'm not sure which one of them would win.

Stacie gets a smirk on her face. "More like America's Natural Disaster on Ice."

I try to think of a comeback, but I can't. Joya would come up with something witty and biting to say back in a second, but I don't have her dramatic talents. I stumble a couple of steps closer to them instead of backing out of the room like I should. I open my mouth. Then shut it again.

Nothing.

Finally I find some words, but they aren't the ones I want. "What are you doing here?" I ask Jennifer.

Her eyes narrow. "What? I'm not allowed to watch the Olympics?"

"No. I mean, yes, of course you are. I just didn't know you'd be *here*."

She smiles, but not in a friendly way. "My boyfriend needs my support," she says, drawing out *boy* and *friend* long and loud.

"Boyfriend?" I ask before I can stop myself.

Her eyelashes flutter innocently. "You know him, don't you? Hunter Wills."

"Yes," I say stupidly.

Stacie eyes me. "You know you were just a game to Hunter. He's been with Jennifer this whole time. He just wanted to psych you out, inexperienced innocent little girl that you are. Mess up your precious *quad sal*."

Jennifer laughs. "You made it too easy for him!" She holds up her pinkie. "You just let him wrap you right around his little finger. *Oh, Hunter! You're so amazing!*" She puts on a high, false voice that is supposed to sound like mine but doesn't. Not at all. *"Oh, Hunter! You understand me like no one else! Oh, Hunter! Watch me jump and help me win!"*

I try to make like Gore-Tex and let their comments roll off of me, but I can't. Tears sting my eyes. Even though I was on cloud nine last night after my romantic moment with Danny, it's awful to think that the entire time Hunter was acting like he was interested, he was really lying to me and laughing behind my back with Jennifer and Stacie. "But why would he do that? Why would he lie? How do you even know what's between Hunter and me?"

This question sends Jennifer and Stacie into a fit of giggles. "Do you really have to ask? Why, *Esperanza*," she says, exaggerating each syllable of my name in a mock Spanish accent. "You stole what was mine! You stole *my* spot on the Olympic team!"

"But I *didn't*. You got injured," I say.

She's not listening. "You didn't think I was going to let you get away with it, did you? It was so satisfying to see you choke the other night." She turns to Stacie for confirmation. "Wasn't it, sweetie?"

"Oh yeah," Stacie says. "I was glad to help the cause." Then she covers her mouth and her eyes get wide. "Oops!"

It takes a moment, but then my brain starts to put two and two together. "You can't mean that you threw your program for the Team Event," I say, my eyes on Stacie. "You did *not* actually do that at the Olympics!"

Jennifer's laughter is loud. "It's not *that* big a deal. Everyone has other chances to medal. But we didn't want *you* to go home with gold, coasting on the backs of all the other people who have been working so hard to get here — including Meredith, who didn't even get to skate!"

Stacie pinches Jennifer's arm.

"Ouch! Why did you do that?"

But Stacie only shushes her.

I look from one to the other. "That's crazy," I say. "And horrible. I might not be one of your figure skating buddies, but I've worked hard to get here too. And I think all our coaches might be very interested in what you just said."

"Please don't tell," Stacie whispers, her voice suddenly full of fear.

"Right. Of course I'd never do that. Because you've been *oh* so nice to me, I should definitely keep your dark, nasty secrets from the rest of the team."

"Esperanza, wait —" Stacie is saying.

"Also, just to remind you, the Olympics aren't over yet," I interrupt, and storm back into my room. I glare at Meredith, who is sitting on her bed with a shocked expression on her face. "Thanks for the warning before I went out there," I snap at her. "It's great to know that you were so mad you didn't get picked as alternate for the Team Event, you were willing to help them try to sabotage the gold for everybody else, especially *me*. And I stupidly thought you and I were going to be friends!"

"But we are! And I didn't . . . I'd never . . . I had no idea what they were up to! I swear!"

"Save it for someone who cares," I say, and slam the bathroom door, locking myself inside. Meredith is still trying to talk to me, but I turn on the shower and get under the hot water. I close my eyes and wish it could wash away all the mixed-up feelings surging through me. Once again, I'm pulled right back into just the kind of drama Coach wants me to stay away from.

The question is, can I find my way out of it in time to skate tonight?

"Why won't you pick up?" I shout at my phone.

Sadly, it doesn't say anything in return.

I can't get in touch with my mother. It's freaking me out.

I'm crossing the Olympic Village, bag bouncing against my hip, my mind going everywhere at once. Mamá. Stacie. Jennifer. Meredith. Every once in a while it scrolls to Danny, which makes my heart flutter, but then inevitably it lands on Hunter Wills, which makes my skin burn. The idea that I'm the target of my figure skating teammates' viciousness is humiliating.

I have to stop letting the drama get the best of me.

But how can I?

It's so huge, it's practically the size of one of those Olympic domes!

I don't want to be Esperanza Flores, Queen of Drama, though. I want to go back to being America's Hope for Gold. The Cinderella story of this year's Olympic Games. The Spiñorita of everyone's heart.

I call my mother one more time and it rings straight to voice mail.

"Ahhhhhhh!"

"What has gotten into you?" Coach Chen says the moment she sees me. We fall in step on our way to the rink. "I left you last night and you were calm and happy. Now you're a disaster."

"America's Natural Disaster on Ice," I say, remembering Stacie's words.

Coach studies me. "What happened?"

"When I got up, I found Stacie Grant and *Jennifer Madison* in the lounge."

"And? So?"

I can't meet Coach's eyes. "And they eloquently expressed how much I'm hated by everyone. What a failure I am. That I'm a laughingstock to the whole Olympic team."

Coach Chen squeezes my arm. "What those girls think doesn't matter. And you are not a laughingstock."

"But I *am*, apparently. There's something else I learned too. Something *horrible* and *shocking* and *wrong* about the Team Event and why we didn't medal." The words are spilling out of me before I can think.

Coach looks alarmed. "What are you talking about, Esperanza?"

"I'm talking about —" I start, but stop midsentence.

I'm about to say the word *sabotage*.

I'm about to tell on Stacie. Confess to Coach what she did. How she's conspired with Jennifer and Hunter this whole time and intentionally jeopardized the Team Event medal.

But then I don't.

If I tell on Stacie, I'll be stooping just as low as she has. Coach

Chen would have to tell Coach East, who would have to tell the US Figure Skating officials, and they could decide to not let Stacie skate tonight. And if Stacie gets disqualified, I won't get to compete against her for gold.

Which would mean I won't get to beat her fair and square.

Which would also mean that if I actually do medal, she could always claim it was just because she didn't skate. Just like Jennifer wants to claim that I don't really deserve to be here. That I'm only here because of her injury. Which *is* partly true, but not entirely.

Coach Chen is waiting for me to explain.

"You know what? Nothing," I say finally. "Nothing happened."

"Esperanza . . ." Coach is suspicious now. "If something is up, you need to tell me what it is."

I shake my head. "Nothing's up. Really. There isn't. I was just being melodramatic."

"Why don't I believe you?"

"I don't know. But you should."

"Well, get your head in the game, then."

"Okay. I will."

Coach studies me, eyes narrowed. "I mean it, Espi."

I breathe deep. I nod. "I know you do."

"Tonight is the short program. You'll do your triple axels. Tomorrow is your free skate. You'll do your triple axels again and you're going for the quad sal. Right?"

I swallow. "Yes."

"You've got to let go of whatever is bothering you — whatever it is you won't tell me." A lightbulb goes on in Coach's eyes. "Is this about Danny Morrison? Did something happen with him?"

My cheeks flush. "Um."

"Something did happen!"

The flush deepens. "Um."

Coach Chen puts her hand to her hip. "I'm going to kill that boy if he's upset you."

"No, no," I say quickly. "He didn't upset me. I promise. He made me feel better."

"Humph." She looks up at the dark gray sky a moment. "I need you to block the bad drama, whatever it is. You can't go out there again and let it get the best of you. Focus on Danny if you need to. On Tawny. On me and Bax. Your friends Libby and Joya at home. Your mother, who adores you."

I nod. We are almost to the rink. I pull out my phone and dial my mother. For the millionth time, it goes straight to voice-mail. Mamá would *never* let the phone ring like this, not on the day of my short program. "Something has happened to my mother. I can't handle this. I'm starting to get scared. How can I focus if I'm petrified about my mother?"

"Espi —"

"I mean, where is she?! I need her! I'm worried!" I look at Coach in despair. "Why aren't you more worried? It's been over twenty-four hours since she and I have talked, and that is not like her!"

Coach Chen puts her hands on my shoulders, the thing she always does when she wants to calm me down and reassure me that everything will be okay. My heart rate automatically slows. "Espi, be quiet and follow me."

Coach leads me through the glittering glass entrance to the arena. She takes my hand and pulls me toward the stands, not toward the door to backstage, where we should be headed.

"Where are we —?" I start, then stop.

Because I see where we're going.

Because I see why too.

"Mamá!" I cry.

My mother is standing there beaming at me. Her eyes are tired and her hair is sticking up in the back like she slept on an airplane all night.

Because she did. She must have. That's why she didn't pick up the phone. She was on her way here!

She puts her arms out. *"¡Mija!"*

I run and give her the biggest hug I've ever given my mother in my entire life. She squeezes me tight and kisses the top of my head, and it's in this moment that I know that no matter what, everything is going to be okay.

"I can't believe you're here," I say, taking a step back to look at her again.

"I can't believe it either." She hugs Coach Chen. "It's good to see you, Lucy."

"You couldn't have gotten here a moment sooner," Coach says, shaking her head. Then she turns to me. "Surprise, Espi!"

"You knew?" I ask.

"Since three days ago. The visa came through."

I look at my mother and all around us. That's when I see

Luca hovering a ways off by the seats. "Luca's here too?" He waves at me and I wave back. Mr. Chen is next to him and gives me his mad mathematician face, like always. It's strangely comforting.

My mother smiles a little bit shyly. "Luca insisted on coming." She glances behind her at him and Mr. Chen, then turns back to me. "The three of us flew together. We wanted to see your dreams come true in person."

"Being here is definitely a dream," I say. "But I don't know that my dreams of Olympic gold will ever be a reality. Please don't expect too much tonight."

"Esperanza Flores," my mother says sternly. "I did not raise you to be a doubter! Your name means hope. Don't go losing it now." She picks up the small carry-on bag at her feet and holds it out to me. "I brought you something that might help."

I take the bag and unzip the top to see what's inside. The smile on my face reaches ear to ear.

"So, there's been a change of plans," I say to Coach Chen. "I'm not wearing the Wang." I pull out her old costume and hold it up between the three of us. "I've decided I'm going to wear the Chen. For good luck."

When I get backstage before the Ladies' Short Program event, Tawny is deep in conversation with Meredith.

I didn't know those two were friends.

Meredith waves her arms around as she talks. Tawny has a look of horror on her face. I hang back. I don't want to talk to Meredith right now.

Stacie and Coach East are a little ways off in the corner. I don't see Coach Danson anywhere, and I almost wonder if he's simply abandoned Meredith altogether. The thought sends a pang of sadness for her shooting through my middle.

I turn the other way and see Jennifer and Hunter coming toward me, holding hands, both of them wearing smirks. Hunter's silver medal is dangling around his neck.

It kind of makes me want to barf.

But at least he isn't taking home the gold.

I'm surrounded on all sides by major figure skating drama. It doesn't matter which way I go, I'll have to contend with somebody I'd rather avoid.

Then suddenly, everyone is headed in my direction.

Stacie is on her way to talk to Jennifer and Hunter, I think. Tawny and Meredith are on their way to me. Tawny glares at Stacie and blocks her path. "I can't believe you'd do that to us!"

She rolls her eyes. "Do what?"

"Sabotage the Team Event!"

Stacie's face goes white. Her eyes go to me, even as she answers Tawny. "Who told you?"

Meredith snaps her fingers to get Stacie's attention. "I did."

"You'd betray our friendship —"

Meredith huffs. "Friendship? What friendship? You're nasty to me. You boss me around. You make me feel bad about myself. You psych me out, not up. And you call that friendship?" Stacie opens her mouth, but Meredith halts her by putting up a hand. "Don't even try to fix this. It can't be fixed. You and I are done."

"But I —"

Tawny snaps her fingers in front of Stacie's face to get her attention. "My turn now." She screws up her face in disgust. "Don't bother with excuses, Grant. Tell them to the USFS! And to Janie and Johnny, whose only hope of medaling depended on the Team Event!"

Tawny is so sweet all the time that I didn't know she was capable of such rage. It makes me glad I'm not on her bad side.

Stacie points a finger at me. "Esperanza fell! And Esperanza —"

"Don't you dare blame Espi. She didn't do it on purpose. *You*, however, *did*! And you threw everyone off in the process!" Tawny looks over her shoulder at Jennifer and Hunter, who've been hovering in the background, listening this whole time. Then she turns back to Stacie. "You do realize that sabotaging Esperanza wasn't the only item on Jennifer's agenda, right?"

Stacie twirls her blond hair around a finger nervously. She lets it go, then does it again. "What are you talking about?" she asks, her tone uncertain.

"Did it ever occur to you that by convincing you to botch your programs for the Team Event, Jennifer was sabotaging what might be *your* only chance at gold? And when she let it slip in front of your other teammates that you agreed to this, she was sabotaging *you* for the individual medals too? Maybe she *wanted* people to find out your secret so she could pull you into a drama and psych you out. Or worse, even jeopardize your ability to compete. I mean, why would someone like Espi, after the way you've treated her, *not* get you in trouble with the US Figure Skating officials? What reason have you given Esperanza to protect you? Or me, for that matter? Or your former best friend, *Meredith*?"

Stacie's mouth opens wide. She clearly hasn't thought of any of this.

Coach East approaches. "What's going on here? Why are you girls fighting?" Her voice is sweet, but I can hear the tone underneath that says she doesn't mess around and isn't happy to hear us bickering.

Tawny and Meredith open their mouths at once, ready to speak, but I get there first.

"We were arguing about one of the hockey boys," I pipe in cheerily. "Silly girl stuff. You know how it is."

Coach East looks at me hard. "You're arguing about boys *now*?"

"Mm-hm." I turn to Meredith and Tawny for help. "Aren't we?"

Tawny shoots me a *what are you doing* look. "Um. Sure," she says. "I guess."

Meredith stays silent. She gives Stacie a glare as sharp as a knife.

"Cut the drama," Coach East says to all of us. "Three of you are about to skate tonight." She eyes me. "I thought you were an exception to this sort of ridiculousness, Esperanza."

"I'm sorry to disappoint you, Coach East," I say in a small voice, honestly sorry to lose some of her respect, especially at the expense of protecting Stacie.

Coach East shakes her head and walks away, leaving the three of us alone again.

Stacie's lip quivers. "Why didn't you tell on me?" she asks.

I stare straight into her eyes for a long time before I answer. "Because I'm not a mean person like you. And because I'm going to beat you fair and square. No one is going to be able to say that Esperanza Flores only won Olympic gold because Stacie Grant didn't compete."

Before she can say anything else, I walk away.

"Wait up," Tawny and Meredith call out behind me.

So I do.

CHAPTER TWENTY-FIVE

America's hope for gold, at your service!

My short program goes flawlessly.

I do my triple lutz–triple toe loop combination. I do my straight line step sequence for the sake of the judges. I do the flying sit spin with its death drop that makes the crowd ooh and ahhh. My triple axel goes off without a hitch.

I do it all with pizzazz and confidence and with Joya's good-luck star earrings sparkling brightly from my ears. I hope she sees them shining there on television.

"¡Qué bonito, mija!" my mother screams from the stands.

Before I skate a victory lap around the rink, smiling and waving at the crowd, I pause a beat in front of the spot where Mr. Chen, Luca, and my mom are jumping up and down like lunatics and I blow them a kiss. When the little girls sweeping the ice of teddy bears and other stuffed animals bring them over to the Kiss and Cry, I give each one of them a hug instead of turning away from them in tears like I did last time.

"Nice job, Esperanza," Coach Chen says, giving me a squeeze followed by a kiss on the cheek when my scores come out, the two of us smiling and celebrating on camera for all the world to see. "No tears for you tonight."

I brush my left hand along the shoulder of my costume. "It must be my lucky Chen," I tell her, and she laughs.

I start to feel a little redeemed. Like I might even have a shot at gold. Mai Ling is a full point and a half ahead of me, and Irina Mitslaya is two tenths of a point in front for the silver, but I'm still totally in this thing.

If Mai Ling doesn't go for a quad in her free skate, I *could* pull off gold.

Then again, so could Meredith. She came out onto the ice tonight with her arms swinging, ready for battle. We're only one tenth of a point apart.

Stacie, to everyone's shock and dismay, is trailing far behind at number 10. She actually fell. Landed on her butt not once, but *twice*. I would be lying if I said I felt bad for her. I just don't.

As the clock ticks down the last twenty-four hours until my final Olympic performance, my only job is to stay focused.

Confident.

Drama-free.

Esperanza Flores, Queen of Drama, has left the building for good.

America's Hope for Gold is back.

"Espi?"

Meredith is sitting cross-legged on her bed, reading a magazine when I walk in the door. My cheeks are flushed from standing outside for the last hour saying good night to Danny.

Yes, it took a whole hour.

It was mostly talking, though. His final game is tomorrow, so gold will be decided for the both of us on the same day.

"Hi, Meredith," I say, sitting down across from her. "Your short program was amazing tonight."

"Thanks. So was yours." She sets the magazine aside. "I admire the fact that you didn't say anything to Coach East about Stacie."

"It's not *that* admirable. I almost ratted her out to Coach Chen before I thought better of it. And I seriously did *not* do it for Stacie. I meant what I said earlier. The only reason I didn't tell was so Stacie couldn't say that whoever wins does so only because she didn't skate."

Meredith gets a happy, faraway look in her eyes. "Well, either way, Stacie is now the victim of her own evil ways."

"You're really glad she choked, aren't you?"

She nods. "I've spent years in Stacie's shadow. It's about time I go out on my own."

I take my hair out of its topknot, bobby pin by bobby pin. "You may have distanced yourself from Stacie, but you're not on your own exactly. And I don't mean that in a bad way," I add quickly.

"No?"

I shake my head. "You still have me as a friend. If you want."

Meredith smiles. "I want."

"You do?"

"Yeah. I definitely do." A cloud passes over her. "Promise me something, though."

"Okay," I say cautiously.

"Promise me that regardless of what happens tomorrow night, regardless of whether you and I both medal, if only one of us medals, or if neither of us do, you'll still be willing to be friends."

I laugh. "Of course. That's an easy promise to make."

"Really?"

I nod.

"Good," she says. "Now let's talk about the important stuff. I want to know what's going on with you and Danny Morrison. I mean, it's not like I didn't look out the window tonight and see you two making out. And I met this short-track skater boy and he's totally cute."

I sit across from her on my bed and the two of us dish happily about boys and the Olympics so far and a million other things.

When we finally go to sleep, I'm still smiling.

"Time to warm up, Espi." Coach Chen ushers me out of the dressing room after I'm all sewn in, straight toward the official who's waiting to let me onto the ice. "Impress those judges during warm-ups," she goes on. "Give them a little preview of what they're about to see — but hold back the quad sal. Make sure the technical panel sees your footwork. And finish off with a nice Ina Bauer or one of your spins."

"Yes, Coach. Will do."

"Nice dress," she adds with a smile.

I give her a big smile back. "Did you know? Someone wore it to win Olympic gold a couple of decades ago."

"I *did* hear that."

"Maybe its luck will rub off on me."

Still smiling, I skate out onto the ice. Warm-ups at international competitions are for showing off. I do a quick lap, a back spin, and then go straight into some jumps, with a little footwork in between. The technical panel always wants to see a step sequence a couple of times before they can give it a level three or four grade of execution, and tonight is not the night to be holding back. I focus on my spins next. Jumps are easy for the judges to score, but the spins require a high GOE, so they're worth doing a few times in front of the panel. I do my best to stay out of the way of the other skaters and try not to notice who is doing what, since I don't want to psych myself out. I don't even look to see if Mai Ling is attempting a quad. I stop to stretch my arms and shoulders, grateful for the television holds that give us a precious few minutes off camera to get ourselves ready. Then I do one last fast lap around the rink and finish off with an Ina Bauer before curtsying to the judges and the audience. The curtsy is a sign of respect and gratitude that they watched you.

I use the last minute of warm-ups to try to relax a little and talk to Coach. I'm practically made of nervous energy by the time I reach the place where she waits for me with a bottle of water.

"You're almost there, Espi," she says, and gives me a great big hug. "In less than an hour, this will all be over."

"I know," I say, butterflies erupting in my stomach. "Don't remind me."

I shake out my arms and legs just to have something to do.

I wish they gave parents credentials to wait by the ice entrance so I could hang out with my mother, but they are really strict about these things at the Olympics. To see her, I'm going to have to go into the stands afterward.

While I wait to get called, I stay away from the skater's lounge. The last thing I need is to be around food, which I think would make me nauseous at this point, or hear the television commentary and the scores as the other skaters compete. I always hate listening to the announcers during people's programs, because then I start to imagine what they must be saying about me to the entire world while *I'm* skating. Besides, I'd rather see the competition from backstage, where I have a direct view of the ice.

Mai Ling is up, and I hold my breath.

She skates like a machine.

Perfect.

Powerful.

But lacking a little in the pizzazz department.

And no quad sal.

I'm practically bouncing up and down on my toes about this.

When she comes off the ice, there are no smiles for her from her coach, and she doesn't smile for the crowd either. She waves, but she's more like a girlish figure-skating robot than someone you watch and think, *She really loves this sport.* She's gracious to the sweepers, though, and gives each of them a hug when they hand her the gifts they've picked up off the ice.

Her scores are great.

But they're not unbeatable.

Irina Mitslaya is as perky as perky gets. She almost reminds me of Stacie with her blond hair and her sparkling smile. She messes up some of her footwork, though, which is going to affect her GOE. And she's off by half a rotation on her triple lutz.

The crowd loves her regardless. They jump to their feet while she blows kisses and waves.

Her scores open up a wide gap between gold and silver, however.

There is room to squeeze in between her and Mai Ling.

"Espi, you're on deck. Meredith's up now."

"Come on, Meredith," I yell. "You can do it!"

It turns out that Meredith has some tricks up her sleeve too. She does a perfect triple axel, though her balance on the landing was a little off. But then she does another going into one of her jump combinations.

I thought *I* was the only one other than Mai Ling with a triple axel. I guess not.

"Did you know she had that?" Coach Chen leans in to whisper.

"No idea."

"You've got to land that quad sal, Espi."

"I know."

When Meredith finishes, the crowd leaps to its feet. She skated a nearly flawless program, but she also showed the kind of personality that only someone like Irina Mitslaya usually manages. Stuffed animals litter the ice.

When she exits the rink, her lungs are heaving and her cheeks are flushed.

Before she enters the Kiss and Cry, I give her a big hug. "You were amazing, Meredith. Those triple axels were so high!"

She looks at me a little guiltily. "I should have told you about them."

But I smile back. "It's okay, and no, you shouldn't have. Then I would have had to tell you about my amazing quad sal — and that I'm totally nailing it tonight."

Her eyes get wide, then she starts to laugh. "May the best skater win."

I nod. Then Meredith joins Coach Danson in the Kiss and Cry to wait for her scores. It's the first time I've seen him in a long time.

Meredith doesn't have to wait long.

The crowd gasps.

Her scores are really high.

High enough by a tenth of a point to knock Mai Ling into second.

Meredith squeals. Coach Danson picks her up and twirls her around. At least when she wins, he's nice.

As she heads into the Mixed Zone where the press is waiting for her comments, and where they'll film her watching me on the ice, she's literally biting her knuckles. She takes her hand away long enough to look at me and say, "Good luck, Espi." Then she disappears through a door into a frenzy of camera flashes.

"Going last is intense," I tell Coach, trying to remember to breathe.

"Going last means you know exactly what you need to do. So go out there and do it."

"You got it," I say, and skate to the center of the ice.

The crowd hushes.

Just before the first bars of my music sound through the arena, I hear a few familiar voices.

"Go, *mija*! I love you!" This from my mother, obviously.

"Esperanza Flores! America's Hope for Gold!" This from Mr. Chen.

"Break a leg, Esperanza Flores!" This from Jennifer Madison, who I am sure means exactly what she says.

I almost roll my eyes. But instead I just block her out.

Then I hear one last, "Go, Espi!"

It's Danny's voice.

By the time the first notes float through the speakers, I'm smiling wider than ever.

I feel like I can do anything right now.

And that quad sal in my program?

Let's just say I nail it.

"Espi!"

Coach Chen is actually jumping up and down when I come off the ice to the Kiss and Cry. I've never seen her do that.

The crowd is on their feet too, screaming so loud I can't hear anything. I put my hands on my knees, trying to catch my breath.

"I've never skated that well in my life," I say when I look up again at Coach Chen.

"You skated like your life depended on it," she says.

"I skated like an Olympic gold medal depended on it," I correct.

Coach laughs and pulls me into a hug. "I'm so proud of you. You'll definitely medal. We just need to see how much the judges reward you for that quad sal. And those two triple axels. You got so much height on all your jumps!"

"Honestly, the more I skated, the more it felt like I was flying. The jumps almost got easier as I went along, so by the time I got to the quad sal, I knew I was going to make it."

"It showed, Espi. It really did." Then Coach looks over at the judges. "Here they come."

My scores flash all at once.

Then a split second later the total comes up.

Dios mío.

"You did it, Espi!" Coach Chen is screaming, tears pouring down her cheeks.

But it takes me a minute to realize what she means. "I did it?"

"You won the gold!"

Excitement surges into my heart and chills run through my body. I lean into Coach as she bounces me up and down in a hug. "I can't believe it," I say.

"Believe it, Espi! You're an Olympic gold medalist!"

"*We* are," I say with a smile. A sense of peace floods through me, followed by joy.

So much joy.

When it's time for the medal ceremony, Meredith comes over and gives me a giant hug. "Congrats, Espi. You deserve gold after that quad sal."

"Thanks, Meredith. It was really close, though. It could have been either one of us. Congrats on the silver."

She nods. "I'm happy it will be the two of us up there."

"Me too," I say.

We stand there, arm in arm, until she has to go out onto the ice to accept the silver and climb up on the podium.

Then, finally, after all this time, it's my turn.

CHAPTER TWENTY-SIX

Gold medalist, potential girlfriend, Latina figure skater, unofficial Luciano's spokesperson, friend

The elevator doors open into the arena stands.

I step through and look around the crowd, trying to locate my mother, my phone to my ear, where Libby and Joya are practically bursting my eardrum from all their screaming.

"You did it," Libby is yelling.

"I'd like to think that those lovely star earrings you're wearing helped," Joya says, which makes me laugh.

"Thanks, guys," I tell them, my heart swelling so big it feels like it might burst. "I couldn't have done it without your support."

"We know," Joya says, all matter of fact.

I turn one way, then another, still unable to find my mother or Luca or Mr. Chen.

Then to my left, someone cries, "That's Esperanza Flores!"

And suddenly, I'm mobbed with fans.

"Can you sign my program?"

"Will you autograph my T-shirt?"

"Over here!"

"No, over here!"

"Me!"

"Me!"

"Not her! Me first!"

I'm totally surrounded. "Um, guys," I tell Libby and Joya. "I've got to go. I'll call you tomorrow. Love you," I say, and click END.

Pens and notebooks and various articles of clothing are thrust in my direction. The only way I'll make it to the other side is to wade through the mob. Good thing they're friendly. I smile and hug and sign and sign and sign.

"Thank you, Espi!" says one little girl.

"I want to be just like you some day," says another.

"I've never seen anyone jump like that," says yet another, her voice filled with awe.

By the time the crowd dwindles, there are tears rolling down my cheeks at all the emotion of the day. I wipe my eyes with the back of my hand, and when I look up again, the people I came to see are waiting for me.

"Mamá," I cry, and leap into her arms, almost knocking her over.

"I knew you could do it, *mi hija preciosa, hermosa, bonita.*"

"I'm so excited you were here to see it."

"Oh, me too, *mi cielo.* Me too."

When I hug Luca, I whisper, "Thank you for coming with her," into his ear.

He nods, but he's too teary to talk.

I hug Mr. Chen next.

"No right angles today, huh, Espi?" he says.

"All smooth, like a circle," I say back. "I'm glad you're here. It wouldn't be the same without you."

Finally, I get to my new friends: Tawny; Meredith, who's standing with her parents; Mr. Morrison; and Danny.

My smile turns to a grin. So maybe one of them is more than a friend.

The four of them surge forward. Meredith and Tawny talk over each other as we hug. "We're going to have to be on the *Today* show, like, the second we get back," Meredith is saying.

"Rockefeller Center all to ourselves," Tawny cries.

"I've never actually been to New York City," I confess.

Meredith rolls her eyes. "That explains why you need a wardrobe makeover."

"I do not!"

Tawny smiles. "Um, you kind of do. We'll take you shopping."

As they plot what stores we should hit first, I turn to Mr. Morrison.

"Nice height on that quad, Espi."

I smile. "Thanks for your support."

This whole time, Danny has been waiting patiently at the back of the group, but now he steps forward. "Hi, Espi," he says.

We don't hug. It's like, now that we've kissed, we can't touch each other in front of other people. But I see a medal hanging around his neck. "Congratulations on winning gold," I tell him.

He grins ear to ear. "You too."

"I bet you'll be busy celebrating with the hockey team tonight."

"I might go for a while. But I have other ideas about celebrating."

My eyebrows go up. "Oh?"

He nods. "You up for it?"

Tawny and Meredith are pretending not to eavesdrop, even though they totally are. "Definitely," I tell him.

I'm about to say something else when I notice Hunter out of the corner of my eye. He's alone, but it's obvious he's looking for someone. I go up and tap him on the shoulder.

He spins around. "Oh. Hi, Esperanza."

"Congratulations on medaling, Hunter."

"Oh yeah. Thanks."

There's a little silence.

"Really? Is that all?"

He looks annoyed. "Well, what were you expecting?"

A little congratulations, I think to myself.

"Nothing," I say. "Never mind."

Hunter can barely even look at me. I wonder if it's because I won gold and he only got the silver. When his eyes finally focus on me again, I say, "You're one of those guys who's easily emasculated, aren't you?"

Confusion crosses his face. "Emascu*what*?"

"Look it up." I point across the stands. "There's your girlfriend over there glaring at you. See you on the *Today* show, Hunter. I'll be with the gold medalists," I add, even though it's a little obnoxious. I just can't resist pointing that out.

Then I walk back to the place where my family and friends are waiting for me. I give Danny a quick peck on the lips.

"Awwww," Tawny says.

Luca puts his arm around my mother like it's no big deal. My eyes get wide, but I don't say anything.

"Believe it or not," Luca says. "I found an Italian place just outside the Olympic Village that's supposed to be delicious. I was thinking we should go."

"I'm up for that," Mr. Chen says.

"Me too," Coach says, appearing from behind everyone.

"I'm in if my parents can come ," Meredith says.

I smile at everyone. Then I look at Luca. "I think that's a great idea. The chicken parm will never be as good as yours, though."

Luca starts blubbering again.

"He's a sensitive man," my mother says. "Very emotional."

"I'm famished," I say. "Everybody ready?"

I get a chorus of yeses in answer.

"Good. Let's go."

"What are you thinking right now, Esperanza?" the reporter asks at the end of the morning press conference the next day.

I hold out my medal to the camera and take a deep breath. "That this gold should really go to more than just me. That if I could copy it, I'd give one to all the coaches and the rest of my teammates from the United States, because they've earned it. That if there are any other figure-skating-loving Latina girls out there with Olympic-sized dreams, that this medal is for them too."

I look into the camera. "I wouldn't have survived this without my best friends, Libby and Joya, who are watching this from home and who are as good as gold at heart. I *never, ever* could have done this without the most incredible, generous coach in the entire world, Lucy Chen, a gold medalist in figure skating herself. And if they gave out gold to parents of athletes, my hard-working, amazingly supportive mother would definitely be first in line."

My mother smiles through her tears when I say this. She's just a few feet away by the giant cameras, with the rest of the people I care about, who are sharing this moment with me.

I grin and make my final announcement. "And for anyone out there who likes Italian food, come to Luciano's Restaurant in the great state of Rhode Island for dinner. My gold medal will be on permanent display there, thanks to the kind support of my career by its owner. And if you *do* come by, maybe we'll get a chance to meet. I'm there all the time."

The reporter seems surprised by this offer. "I bet you'll have a lot of takers on that one."

"I hope so. And the chicken parm at Luciano's is worth the trip, medal or no."

This makes Luca laugh. He wipes his eyes and puts his arm around my mother.

The reporter laughs too. "One last question, Esperanza," she says.

"Sure."

"Are your Olympic days behind you?"

I shake my head. "No way," I say to her.

Then I look from Coach to Luca and from Luca to Danny, then from Danny on to my mother, as they're all beaming back at me.

"I'm just getting started."

ACKNOWLEDGMENTS

First I want to thank Rachael Flatt, the 2010 US National Champion and member of the 2010 Olympic team, for all of her help with this novel. Rachael, your generosity and willingness to talk on the phone and answer all of my email queries, big and small (and while you were finishing out your year at Stanford!), was so important in making Esperanza's story both accurate and fun — and I am so grateful to you for this. I also want to thank the two skating vetters and veterans, Sarah S. Brannen and Tim Koleto, for their technical expertise. Any mistakes in the book are my own. I should also note that United States Figure Skating is actually excellent at getting family visas for the Olympics — I just made Mamá's case a dramatic exception.

My gratitude goes to everyone at Scholastic for their support of this book — from acquisitions, to copyediting and production, to the Book Clubs and Book Fairs. Thank you to my wonderful agent, Miriam Altshuler, of course, and especially to Cheryl Klein, my tireless editor. Cheryl, I can't imagine another editor who would take on an ice skating novel with as much glee — it's so much fun to work with you. Lastly, thanks to Daniel Matus for being a fantastic model for Danny — no wonder Esperanza falls for him.

This book was edited by Cheryl Klein and designed by Kristina Iulo.
The production was supervised by Elizabeth Starr Baer. The text was set in
Georgia, designed by Matthew Carter and Tom Rickner in 1996, with
display type designed by Rian Hughes in 1992. This book was printed and
bound by R. R. Donnelley in Crawfordsville, Indiana. The manufacturing
was supervised by Angelique Brown.